A PLACE HALFWAY

SYNSK: BOOK 3

K.C. Finn

Clean Teen Publishing

A Place Halfway
Copyright © 2014 by: K.C. Finn

Clean Teen Publishing
PO Box 561326
The Colony, TX 75056

www.cleanteenpublishing.com

Cover design by: Marya Heiman
Typography by: Courtney Nuckels

ISBN: 978-1-63422-031-6

For more information about our content disclosure,
please utilize the QR code above with your
smart phone or visit us at
www.cleanteenpublishing.com.

CHAPTER ONE

A Wandering Mind

"Baby, don't you know I love you so? Can't you feel it when we touch...?"

Hanne's fingertip gently tapped my elbow, but I was already into the next line of the song before I noticed her, the words escaping in a whisper that lacked any kind of melody.

"I will never ever let you go. I love you oh so much..."

After that, she gave me a proper shove and I rocked on my wooden chair, the bandy legs of the old furniture giving an almighty creak. Miss Cartwright opened her pale eyes and fixed them on me, her whole face so tense that if she cracked a smile, it would've shattered. I looked away, a gulp in my throat blocking any excuse I could make to the furious teacher. Hanne was glaring at me too, her skinny arms crossed over her chest. With only the three of us in the wide, dark classroom, their accusing stares made my insides squirm a little.

"You were doing it again," Hanne huffed.

I let out a sigh, feeling my bottom lip pout out on its own. "I can't help it," I said. "My mind wanders when we do this deep thinking thing."

"It's not good enough, Josephine," Miss Cartwright snapped, shaking her head so that her long, blonde hair fell

1

forward over her stiff collar. "How do you expect to hone your skills when your head's full of rubbish?"

"The Drifters aren't rubbish!" I protested immediately.

I almost wondered how she dared to say something like that, but then I remembered that our teacher was older than she looked. Thirty-two was getting on a bit; she probably didn't know a thing about chart music, let alone how much more important it was to me than anything that happened in her classroom. The dark wood panelling of the walls made me feel sleepy even though it was barely afternoon; it shut out the last glorious days of summer that were waiting for me outside.

"If it wasn't your birthday," Miss Cartwright began slowly, "I'd have heard you answering me back just now, young lady. As it is, I heard you apologise for your misconduct, didn't I?"

I hung my head, still pouting. "Yes, Miss," I answered. "Sorry, Miss."

"You're never going to catch up with the others your age at this rate, Josephine," she continued. "Hanne is two full years younger than you, and she can do this meditation standing on her head. Honestly, I-"

I was spared the rest of the lecture by the opening of a door behind us. I turned, my face filled with relief as a friendly, cheeky smile erupted from the face of the man in the doorframe. He tried his best to flatten his sandy, wayward hair, stepping into the classroom with a multitude of parcels and bags under one arm. Hanne leapt out of her chair immediately and waved, even though he was barely six feet from us.

"My little psychics doing all right, then?" he asked with a grin.

"Uncle Leighton!" Hanne exclaimed.

K.C. Finn

"Hello darlin'," Leighton replied, setting down his burdens. "How's my favourite niece?"

"She's your only niece," I interrupted. "That joke is *so* old, man."

He stuck his tongue out at me as he approached. "*You're* so old," he retorted. "Sixteen today. You're ancient."

"I know, I know." I feigned a sigh, throwing a hand up to my brow. "You'd better have presents. You're useless to me without presents."

Students of Peregrine Place were supposed to call him Mr Cavendish, but I had always called him Leighton, even when I was tiny. Hanne and I were a little different to the others, having spent our whole lives living in the grand manor house, watching it fill up and empty of students, year in, year out. Right now, the whole west wing contained only the four of us, our laughter echoing out of the classroom and down the empty hall as we continued to tease Leighton. Slowly, the mirth on his face fell away, leaving an awkward smirk as he met Miss Cartwright's steely gaze.

"Are you keeping these two in check then, Faye?" he asked, the sudden tension of the moment making me want to bury my head in my blouse.

"I *was*," she answered sharply, her mouth pulled in small like she'd sucked on a lemon. It was hard to imagine she was the same age as the man beside her when she acted like such an old woman all the time.

"Do you mind if I take them off your hands?" Leighton said. "Only Claudette's got the food almost ready and…"

Miss Cartwright held up a hand to silence him. "No problem."

3

A Place Halfway

I took that as a sign to gather my things, ushering Hanne to do the same so we could escape the growing cloud of adult awkwardness that threatened to engulf us. I looked at Leighton expectantly, ready to go, but all he did was give my shoulder a little push.

"Wait out there a second, girls," he said gently. "I'll be out now."

Hanne shut the door behind us as we made our way out into the west corridor, a wide hall where tall, thin windows let short shafts of light in to illuminate the old paintings and tapestries on the walls. I rubbed my shoe along the emerald carpet underfoot with impatience.

"That was tense," Hanne whispered.

"I thought they were back together at the start of summer?" I asked her.

She shook her head, ginger curls wobbling. "Something went wrong the other week. I heard Mum telling Dad."

"Relationship drama," I concluded, "That's totally not for me. I like uncomplicated boys."

"Who are rich," Hanne added.

"And handsome," I said.

"And sing like angels," she said, starting to giggle.

"And play the guitar," I completed. "It's vital that they play the guitar."

We had descended into dreamy chatter about Neil Sedaka by the time Leighton emerged again with all his parcels. Hanne helped him carry a few, and we set off down the long corridor that would take us back to the living quarters of the school manor. I could already predict that my mother was up to her neck in sugar and cherries as she attempted yet another

4

of her culinary challenges to make my birthday cake. I cringed inwardly at the thought of her last attempt earlier in the month: two cakes in the shape of a three and a nine for Mr Haugen, Hanne's dad. The numbers were completely butchered by the time she'd finished with her cream and icing sugar. It had tasted like plaster of Paris.

"Please tell me there's a cake in one of these boxes," I pleaded with Leighton.

"I'm not sure you deserve any, the state of your deep thinking," he answered, his eyes gleaming.

I smacked him in the arm like I was swatting a fly. "It's not even term-time," I whined. "Do you know Miss Cartwright's the only teacher who keeps us two working over the summer?"

Leighton sighed. "She is a perfectionist," he reasoned. His face was tanned from whatever distant shore he'd been travelling lately, bringing out the faint lines in his brow as his eyes glazed over with a wistful look.

"I don't mind," Hanne said brightly. "I forget how to do meditation if I don't practice it."

"Brainbox," I snapped.

She pulled a face at me over the boxes she was carrying, her freckles grouping to make her look like a disgruntled giraffe. I laughed at her until she was laughing too; Leighton shook his head at us both.

"Well, no more studying today anyway," he began with a nod. "It's time to enjoy yourself, Josie. We've got plenty of surprises in store."

I quirked a brow at him, and then quickened my pace to walk in front of them both a little. Surprises? I felt sure that for a young psychic, there was no such thing. As I walked, I let my thoughts drift from the here and now, leaving my feet to move automatically as my mind sought out somewhere new. I couldn't keep a clear picture whilst I was moving; the visions came to me like a television set flickering in and out of its signal. It was as though I was watching the screen in my mind, but I could also still see the dark corridor ahead of me now and then in-between. I knew what I was looking for, the familiar connection to my mother's mind coming as naturally to me as breathing.

I was right about the disastrous attempt at a cake; I found her washing a thick, sticky clump of icing from her hands as I looked down into the sink through her eyes. She was singing a song to herself in French that I only half understood and the sound of other voices behind her caught my attention. The thick, Norwegian accent of Mr Haugen rang out over the other mingled words; his deep tone sounded agitated. Mum looked over her shoulder at some remark he'd made, giving me a chance to see the rest of the small gathering. Mr Haugen's dark hair fell onto his brow as he crinkled it over the newspaper in his grip.

"They're still reporting on that incident at Carlisle Street," he mused. "It's the sixties for God's sake; I thought this sort of thing would be over with after the war."

I felt a pang of sadness in my mother's stomach. It sat like stone deep within her, suddenly cold and out of place among her previous mirth.

"It's 'orrible news," she said softly.

Kit Haugen, Hanne's mother, sat beside her husband on our worn, brown sofa. Across her knee sat a toddler with hair so brown it was almost black—a gift from his father's side—but eyes that were bright blue just like Leighton's. Nikolas Haugen was acting like his usual tearaway self as he grabbed at his mother's ginger-brown curls and tried to yank them clean off her head. Mrs Haugen just chuckled, bouncing Nik on her knee until he settled. She peered into the paper over her husband's shoulder. I only saw the change of expression in her sorrowful eyes for a moment before Mum turned back to her own sticky hands and scrubbed off the rest of the icing.

"You've got to put this paper away before Leigh gets back with the children, Henri," Mrs Haugen said with a shiver in her voice, "I don't want Hanne seeing it. It's too upsetting."

"Best to keep it from Josie too," Mr Haugen added.

My mother gave a solemn nod, her eyes fixed on the sink. She felt heavier as every moment passed, and I strained to understand the mix of emotions building inside her. The image of the soapy sink started to flicker violently, as though I was losing the link with her mind. For one rueful moment, I realised that Mrs Cartwright was right about my deep thinking skills, but I managed to force enough concentration back to my mother just in time to hear the end of her words.

"Anyway, we can't 'ave all this talk of death on Josie's birthday." She sighed. "I need your advice on this cake, Kit. I think I've done something wrong with the baking soda."

They started to talk cakes, but the scene was fading once more. Death? What did Carlisle Street have to do with death? I didn't like surprises or secrets, so knowing that something bad was being kept from me turned my insides into jelly. I blinked my way back to consciousness to find my feet still moving down the long corridor, but I was too late to stop myself from approaching the dark wooden pillar that was jutting out on my left.

"Ouch!" I winged the pillar, smashing my shoulder hard into its polished corner, and then stumbled back into the centre of the corridor. Two voices giggled from behind me, and I turned to give them both my best glare.

"What have I told you about using your powers whilst you're walking?" Leighton chuckled, shaking his head. "Nobody does that. It's crazy."

I slowed my pace to walk beside them once more. "Just because you can't do it without falling on your bum," I retorted, resisting the urge to rub the bruise I already knew was forming.

"Did you see anything good?" Hanne asked over the boxes stacked against her small frame.

"Only that your mum's stepped in to save the cake," I replied.

"Marginally edible dessert, here we come!" Leighton cried, picking up his stride.

Hanne and I followed him with matching grins, but I couldn't help returning to thoughts of the deep sadness I had just felt in my mother's body. As much as I wanted to celebrate turning sixteen, it struck me that sixteen ought to be an age where I was allowed to see what was going on in the local newspaper. Deaths of important people were announced all the time on the radio news, but there must have been something really upsetting about this one for it to kill Mum's cake-making groove.

"Oi," Hanne whispered. "You're not drifting off again, are you?"

We had reached the grand foyer of Peregrine Place, its huge ceiling gaping like the jaws of a great whale that had swallowed us all. We didn't even get to step outside into the August sun to reach home as Leighton led us down one of the old servants' passages merging into the shadows of the foyer's south side. It was a shortcut to the staff quarters where we lived, at the rear of the manor, but my head was turned back to the school's closed double doors as I passed them. There was a world outside those doors that I realised I knew very little about. Carlisle Street was as good a place as any to start trying to understand it.

"We've got some nosing around to do later," I murmured to Hanne, fixing my eyes on Leighton's back as he sauntered on ahead.

Hanne's face lit up with the prospect of a secret to uncover, but I found the troubling sensation of stone-cold worry sinking into my stomach as I headed towards my party.

CHAPTER TWO

Change Afoot

I gave Mum a passing wave when we arrived at our quarters, breezing down the corridor to get changed into something pretty. Mrs Haugen tried to call a warning out to me as I opened my bedroom door, but the moment it swung away to reveal my room, I knew what she'd tried to say. Nik was sleeping in my bed. The toddler had the face of a pale angel when he slumbered, but I knew better than to imagine for a second that he was as sweet as he seemed. Hanne and I always got lumbered with him when Mr and Mrs Haugen had business to attend to, and every last one of our adventures in babysitting had ended in disaster. I crept across the room on my tiptoes, sliding the doors of my wardrobe open with every effort not to wake the little monster curled up near the wall beneath my Everly Brothers pictures.

My dress of choice was a pink polka dot creation that Mr Haugen had intended to make for Hanne. The beautiful fabric had got caught in the sewing machine in the wrong place last May and ended up a few inches too big for her, so it suddenly became mine. I wasn't about to complain, since every other dress I'd ever owned had been a hand-me-down from someone else my mother knew or, in extremely awful cases, from Mum herself. As owners of Peregrine Place, the Haugens were pretty well off, but

Mum would never accept a penny more from them than what she earned for her basic salary as the school cook, so I spent every summer waiting for my birthday to get something new for a change.

I was all of the way out of my room before Nik woke up. In the last moments of my carefully planned sneaking out, the door gave a loud creak and the little terror started to scream like a banshee within seconds of the noise. I gritted my teeth and turned back to the bellowing baby with a glare.

"Listen you," I griped. "This is *my* big day. You're not getting away with your usual shenanigans, all right?"

Nik didn't take my threat well. He sat up and threw off the blankets, screaming all the louder with a face like thunder. The loud thump of footsteps caught my ear, and the tall form of Mr Haugen swept past me to scoop the boy up in his grip. Nik clung to his father's shoulder, trying to beat the side of his face with his tiny fist. Mr Haugen gave me a little shrug, rolling his dark eyes.

"They say the noisy ones grow up to be trouble," he mused.

"He's already trouble," I replied. Nik stuck his tongue out at me as though he understood my words.

Mr Haugen chuckled. "Your mother's got a job for you, by the way," he added.

Mum had a thing about doing things elegantly, so it became my job to answer the interior door to our guests, even though it was unlocked and they could clearly just have let themselves in. I thought I was going to have Hanne for company as I stood and waited for the Bickerstaffs to arrive, but Mrs Haugen pulled her away to help arrange the savoury party snacks on my mother's oak dining table, a tiny, circular structure around which a ridiculous number of chairs had been arranged. When I was looking forward to my birthday earlier in the day, I'd forgotten how much of a fiasco my extended family would make of it, which resulted in me wearing a teeth-gritted grimace when the knock finally came at the door.

The sight that greeted me was so unexpected that my frown fell away into a dopey, open-mouthed stare. I let the heavy door go and it swung on, smacking into the wall with a bang that made me jump and then giggle embarrassedly as I tried to cover up my own stupidity. All of these things happened in the space of just a few seconds, making me look like the biggest idiot in the world in front of the six-foot dreamboat who was raising his blonde brow at me.

"Hi Dai," I said, horrified by the squeak in my own voice, "I uh... I didn't expect you to be tagging along."

Dai Bickerstaff was a towering Adonis of perfection: a broad, muscular hunk of eighteen-year-old heaven. He almost never smiled—at least, never at me—but I always thought that tight-lipped look of his gave him a dose of mystery. No girl could resist him and I didn't understand why anyone would ever try to, but Dai had always been very selective about the kind of girl he would want to be seen with. They had to be at least sixteen, for a start. I gave him my best smile, hoping to wipe away the car crash of expressions on my face when I'd opened the door. His pale blues eyes looked me over with thought.

"Nice bruise, Jo," he said, sidling past me to stalk inside.

I felt like I'd swallowed an ice-cold penny that had landed squarely in my heart. The dress I had chosen had pink, spotty straps to show off my shoulders, one of which was now a different colour to the other. Before I could even look at the

K.C. Finn

purple bruise that had appeared from my earlier collision, a slender pair of arms wrapped themselves around my torso and I felt the sticky lipstick of a kiss on my cheek.

"Hullo, love!" Blod Bickerstaff stepped back to reveal her pristine face. She was getting on a bit, but her make-up was spot on for a blonde bombshell vibe. She reached out a warm hand and rubbed at my now-slimy cheekbone. "Oh, got you with my lippy, did I?" She chuckled.

"You'll never get if off. That Yardley stuff's like indelible ink," said a dry, male tone behind her. "We could have used it on the sides of submarines in the war."

Blod rolled her bright eyes and stepped past me too, leaving me to give an awkward nod to her husband. Doctor Steven Bickerstaff looked about as happy to see me as I was to see him, but he gave me a little smile and I appreciated his effort, however false it was, to be polite.

"Happy Birthday, Josie," he said, sweeping his silver-blonde hair back into its old-fashioned wave. "Ness is on her way with the present from us lot. Late as usual: it's the Price family style, don't you know?"

I was caught between the limping doctor and his wife as Blod rounded on him and stuck out a perfectly manicured finger. Her frivolity from a moment ago had vanished, leaving only menace in her gaze.

"If you're going to be like that, you can go home," she warned.

"All the way to Wales?" Bickerstaff replied, a tiny smirk in the corner of his lip.

"If you like," Blod answered, unrelentingly severe.

The tension was so thick that I could scarcely breathe; I

wanted the wood floor to cave in and let me drop clean out of their way. Bickerstaff looked about ready to take Blod up on her threat, but Dai's Welsh boom rang out from the living room.

"Dad!" he called. "Henri's got cigars yur. Can I have one?"

Blod and Bickerstaff's eyes widened within a heartbeat of each other. The doctor shouted "No!" and his wife followed it with a "Don't you dare!" as they swept past me, united once more. I stood at the door, looking out into the corridor that led to other staff accommodations and, eventually, the exit to Peregrine Place. For one wild moment, I thought about just taking off, but I slowly realised that I had nowhere else to go.

We were all settled at the table by the time Ness arrived, carrying a large, cardboard box that Leighton leapt up to assist her with. I turned in my chair to watch her as she entered our little beige room, her short, blonde hair cut into a Connie Francis flick. Her locks had so much volume that it made me touch my own thin, chestnut strands, tapering my fingers right down to the bruise on my shoulder where they ended. When Ness and Leighton had set down the box, I revelled in the sight of her yellow mini-dress as she straightened it out.

"Wow, high fashion, Ness!" Mrs Haugen said as she gave the young woman a wave.

"Good grief," Bickerstaff added, a hand hovering at his chin. "I can't believe Kit and Henri let you work here dressed like that."

Ness looked herself over, smiling regardless of the doctor's sour look. She waved a hand at him like he'd told a funny joke. "All the girls at A and E wear this kind of stuff for a party," she replied.

"I dig it," Dai boomed.

"You would," Blod said with a laugh.

"Ridiculous." Bickerstaff sighed.

"Oh?" Ness said, one hand on her hip, "And who are you, my father?"

Bickerstaff's lips moved, but no sound came from them. Mr Haugen suddenly choked on his cigar and his wife had to give him a hard slap on the back, bringing the table to a weird sort of silence for several painful moments. Ness crossed the small space between the box and the table and leant down beside my chair.

"Noswaith dda, birthday girl," she said with a grin. "You're going to love your pressie!"

Chatter began to resume, but very slowly, as though something was holding everyone back from fully enjoying themselves. I suddenly felt a push against my mind, like someone poking a finger at the side of my temple. A giggle echoed in my head, growing in volume, until it sounded as though it was a voice from a dream. I glanced at Hanne sitting next to me. Her eyes were downcast on her plate, completely unfocused, and a vacant smile played on her lips.

Thank goodness we only have to put up with this for an hour, she thought straight into my mind. *I can't wait to give you my gift.*

I took in a breath, looking down at my napkin as I let my mind connect to hers. *Presents may not be enough compensation for the state of this lot,* I answered.

Hanne giggled again. *Dai's a nice surprise though,* she mused.

He's not my gift from you, is he? I thought back.

You wish!

We burst into giggles as my eyes refocused. Leighton sat opposite me with a knowing look, but before he could say anything about Hanne and me, Mum arrived with my cake. Her fair features were coated in a thin sheen of wet make-up where it had mixed with the sweat of her efforts, so I gave her the best smile I could, despite the impending disaster of her culinary feat. The cake landed on the table with a rattling thump, as though it was made of cement. Mrs Haugen was the first person brave enough to make a comment.

"Well Claudette, that looks a fair treat."

"I 'ope it tastes as good as it looks," Mum replied.

"I'm sure it will," I said, staring at the glue-like icing that she'd used to stick crumbling parts of the sponge back together.

The presence of food was a good thing, largely because it meant that everyone started eating and stopped talking. The wall of fire and ice between the Bickerstaffs seemed to level out as they sat listening to Ness moaning about coping with training at Accident and Emergency in Ashford on the weekends and working here at Peregrine Place as our school nurse during term time. I eavesdropped on her woes as covertly as I could; it worried me to hear she might not be happy in case she quit and took her fashion sense with her to a new destination. She was the only real link I had to new styles, a living example of all the cool looks I saw on television and in the magazines, the one I could turn to for style advice.

"Don't worry, love," Blod said, putting a hand over her little sister's knuckles. "You know it's all going to be sorted by next week."

"Speaking of which," Bickerstaff added, clearing his

throat loudly until Mr Haugen looked down the table, finding his eyes. "Is it about time, Henri?"

Mr Haugen had a mouthful of my mother's cake that he was struggling to chew through. He gratefully swallowed it down with a glass of water and stood up, clapping his hands together until the table fell silent. He smiled warmly, ruffling Nik's hair where he sat in his high chair for a moment before he started to speak.

"Before we let Josie get to her presents, I have one or two announcements to make," Mr Haugen started. "First, we sadly have to say goodbye to Ness, who has been our wonderful school nurse here for the last two years. She's moving on to bigger and better things at Ashford Accident and Emergency, and we wish her good luck."

Everyone charged their glasses, but I found Ness's eyes across the table. She chewed one side of her mouth in with an apology and I smiled, but in truth, I was gutted to see her go. Ashford was a fairly long way away, too far to travel for a flying visit, especially since Mum didn't have a car.

"So that leaves us missing a physician," Mr Haugen continued, starting to grin. "Steven has very kindly offered to take up the post until we find a suitable replacement for Ness."

Doctor Bickerstaff gave a little nod, clearly uncomfortable with all eyes being on him, but he didn't have to wait long before the attention was drawn away. Dai suddenly slammed down his glass, his lips pulled thin and pale by fury.

"Does that mean you're moving in yur at Peregrine?" he demanded.

"Both of us," Blod replied with a nod.

"I knew it!" the young man said, rising to his feet and

slamming his napkin down on his plate, "You don't trust me one bit, do you? You've taken this job to spy on me when I start university in London!"

His pale blue eyes were locked on those of his father, the two men engaged in a silent battle of resolve before Dai stormed off in the trademark style of his mother. I couldn't say that I was happy about Bickerstaff becoming our new school doc, but I did suddenly realise that having him and his wife under our roof would mean more frequent visits from the gorgeous Dai, assuming he ever calmed down about their betrayal. He was stunning when he was angry, marching away with his broad shoulders and strong, stiff back. The Bickerstaffs went chasing out of the flat after their son, leaving Ness to round the table, rubbing her hands together with glee.

"I know you're going to miss me," my fashion guru said with a kind smile. "I'm only going to be down the motorway though. Perhaps you can pop down and see me at Christmas?" I nodded fervently at the suggestion. "Also, you wouldn't be getting your fabulous present if I was sticking around," Ness added with a wink.

I rose, heading to the huge cardboard box on the sofa with eager fingertips. Ripping away the top layers, I peered in with curiosity, but all I could see for the moment was the wooden lid of something very large and square. Growing more impatient, I pulled down the entire front side of the box, standing back in amazement as I recognised the shape for what it was. I had seen it so many times in Ness's room, coveting this great contraption with jealous eyes for months on end. And now it was mine.

"What a lovely record player!" Mrs Haugen exclaimed from the tableside.

A tap on my shoulder made me turn in my amazement. Hanne shoved something square into my hands and I took it, staring down for a long moment before I could focus on what I was holding. The word **CUPID** started back at me.

"The new Sam Cooke single!" I cried, beaming at my friend. "Oh Han, I love it! It's going to be the first thing I play!"

"We'd better get it set up for you then," Mum said. She was matching my grin as she and Leighton started lifting the machine out of the box. Leighton cocked his head to one side as he nodded in the direction of the parcels he had carried earlier.

"I brought you some of my singles that I'm bored of," he explained. "They're from the last couple of years' charts; I'm willing to bet you'll find something you like."

I didn't doubt it for a moment; Leighton was about as cool with music as anyone in their thirties could be. Hanne and I dived for the boxes, unearthing treasure after treasure from the likes of Sedaka, Presley, Checker, and Berry. The cement cake, arguments, and upheavals aside, this birthday of mine had finally turned into one worth celebrating. It wasn't until hours later when I was sinking into bed, my legs aching from so much dancing, that I realised I had forgotten to look for Mr Haugen's newspaper. The brief thought of the mysterious death on Carlisle Street made me shiver but I forced it away, resolving to find a new way of investigating by the light of morning.

CHAPTER THREE

Halfway

I was already lying awake when I heard Mum slowly opening the door to my bedroom. She peered around the doorframe with sleepy, narrow eyes, offering me a smile that quickly turned into a yawn. Her hair was a mass of unbrushed ringlets, shining bronze in the sunlight creeping through the gap in my curtains.

"I didn't know if you'd be up so early," she said with a sleepy kind of gentleness.

"Just woke," I answered, feigning a stretch.

In truth, I had been up since the sun first crept into my room, formulating a good excuse to get down to Carlisle Street. Half-remembered dreams had disturbed me all night long, my visions switching from happy birthdays to strange scenes of dark, damp pavements and shadowed families with their heads in their hands. Nothing was clear enough for details, but my curiosity had made me all too alert.

"I thought I might go out on my bike with Hanne today," I said, hauling myself into a sitting position.

Mum came to perch beside me on my bed, pushing my wayward hair down flat with a gentle hand. "Didn't you tell me you were too ladylike for bicycles now?" she said with a knowing smile.

"There's a record shop in the village," I continued, delivering my carefully planned lines. "The Bickerstaffs gave me a bit of money in my birthday card. I thought I could buy another single or two for my new player."

I gave my mother my most hopeful smile. She stroked a hand down my cheek, her own smile fading a little. Her chin sank low as her hands returned to her lap, playing with a frayed edge on her nightdress.

"I wish I could afford to give you a little bit more to shop with," she sighed.

I wished she could too, but I never would have said so. With no husband to help foot the bills, Mum did her best to make our lives nice. Generous gifts from our friends, like the record player, were always a bonus though. I didn't want to talk about money, because money often led Mum into mentioning my father and, after the first glimpse of anything to do with Dad, she always went quiet and avoided me for a while thereafter. I didn't know anything about him really; just that he must have been a psychic in order for me to have my gift. Mum frequently blamed herself for not picking a better man to be my father, but beyond that, she offered me no details of the man who had never once tried to contact me in sixteen years. If I thought about that fact for too long, something deep in my chest started to ache.

I reached out and put a hand over Mum's to stop her fidgeting. "Are you joking?" I said as jovially as I could. "Leighton's brought me nearly fifty of his cast-offs. They're amazing songs. It's just that there's no Pat Boone. I've really got to have Pat Boone if I'm going to start a proper collection."

Mum looked up over my head to the pictures all over

my wall, starting to smile again. "Do you 'ave that one about the clown that I like?" she asked.

The Everly Brothers sang to us all morning as I got ready for a day's escape from Peregrine Place.

I had to sit on the skirt of my pink dress to stop it flapping everywhere as I cycled down the lane in front of Hanne. She had shorter legs than me and often yelled out that I was going too fast for her to keep up, so when I spotted a lay-by in the road up ahead, I pulled in and stuck one foot out to steady the bike and wait for her. The winding lanes between the grounds of Peregrine Place and the local village were usually abandoned and covered in green fields, so I was surprised to find that the lay-by was actually the opening of a yard for a brand-new building.

There were still a few piles of bricks and a builder's truck in the yard with two hefty blokes shoving a sign up above the door. The huge emblem read: **HALFWAY TO PARADISE** in bright red letters with the words **MUSIC, DANCING, AND MILKSHAKES** written underneath. I set down my bike and walked closer to the building to see more. Poster-boards on the outside walls showed various kinds of drinks and ice creams up for sale and through the window, I spotted shiny, new tables and chairs stacked as though they were almost ready to be set in place. I heard Hanne's panting behind me and the mechanical thump of her bike as she threw it to the ground.

"What's this place?" she asked, half-breathless.

"Looks like a new music club," I surmised, still studying the menus.

Hanne bent and started stretching her sore legs, frowning up at me. "For grown-ups?"

"I don't think so," I replied, "There's no alcohol on the drinks board."

With the club's banner set, the builders climbed down and lifted their ladders away. Once they'd retreated to their truck, Hanne and I stepped forward for a closer look at the main entrance and all my hopes were suddenly confirmed. A list of rules on the left side of the door explained how teenagers should behave if they wanted to be happy patrons at the new venue. I was even more excited by another sign to the right.

Help Wanted.

"It says they have a Saturday job for a teenager," I told Hanne, my eyes travelling greedily over the sign all at once. "Cleaning tables, sweeping, general chores. I could do that easily."

A job meant money for all the things I wanted to buy. I couldn't think of a better place to wipe tables than in the middle of a real milkshake bar with live music going on, the kind I'd only ever seen in American films at the cinema. I turned to Hanne, my face flushed with excitement, but she was squinting up at the building with a sceptical pull to her lips. When she saw my eager features, her expression didn't change for a moment.

"I'm not sure," she mused. "You don't know what kind of place this is yet. What if it's rowdy?"

I was about to argue my case when the screech of an engine behind us caught my ear. We both turned to see the builders driving away in their truck, swerving to avoid a boy who had emerged into the lay-by. He carried a huge guitar on his back in a thick, black case, its straps coming to rest over his navy-blue shirt, which was open at the top to show the edge of his bright white vest beneath it. He had jet-black hair so perfectly smoothed back that he looked like he'd stepped out of a Brylcreem advert, with thick, black brows that arched over bright turquoise eyes. The boy looked up as he approached the doorway, a sudden smile quirking his lips.

"Excuse me, ladies," he said, an East London accent sharpening his vowels.

We shuffled out of the way quickly for him and his huge guitar to pass. Hanne craned her head to see him enter the club, watching every movement he made until the door swung shut in our faces, blocking him from view. Her cheeks were glowing with two rosy red circles.

"Well," she said, half-mumbling, "I suppose it wouldn't hurt to step inside for a minute… if you want to make some enquiries."

"You're right," I replied, hiding my knowing smile. "He might be after my new job. Come on."

Hanne hung a few steps behind me as we entered the bar. It was spacious inside with a stage half-decorated in the far right corner and a perimeter of polished floorboards that suggested the edge of a dance floor. An overweight man with short, thick arms was balancing on a stool to screw a light bulb into one of the lamps above that area, whilst the dark-haired boy stood beneath him, a pleading look in his eyes.

"What are you kid? Twelve?" the large man groused.

"I'm fifteen," the boy replied pleadingly. "Just give me a chance, Mr Frost. I write my own songs and everything."

"Listen kiddo," the man called Frost said with a sigh. "I've got older guys already booked for the coming month, professional types. You bring your friends and come enjoy the atmosphere for now. If a free spot in the schedule comes up, I'll let you try out."

Frost finished with the bulb and stumbled down off the stool. The boy with the guitar looked like he was going to protest, but the older man gave a wave of his wide palms.

"Don't ask me again, kid, being in reserve is the best you're going to get right now."

"You promise you'll let me try out when the time comes?" the boy asked.

"Only if you get out and stop bothering me right now," Frost replied.

The boy didn't say another word. Adjusting his guitar on his back, he turned away from the stage and started heading towards us at the door. He flashed me a half-smile and nodded at Hanne as he exited, looking fairly disappointed with himself. Hanne's eyes trailed him once more.

"I wish he'd let him sing," she breathed.

"You don't even know what he sounds like." I giggled. "He might be awful."

"I don't care," she answered. "He was fine. Wasn't he fine?"

I nodded a little. The dark-haired boy was sweet, but he was no Dai Bickerstaff to me.

"We don't open 'til next Saturday girls," Frost said with a grumble. "Sorry to disappoint you, but tell your friends, all right?"

I cleared my throat, smoothing down my hair as I stepped forward. "Actually, Sir, I came about the Saturday job," I replied.

Frost approached us and leaned on the bar, looking me over with a critical eye. He had mousy hair that was greying at the roots and a thick moustache over the thoughtful curve in his lip. Beady, black eyes surveyed me carefully.

"Are you sixteen?" he asked. "You've got to be sixteen."

"Just turned," I said with a nod and a huge, promising smile.

"Hmm," he mumbled. "You know it's not a party working at Halfway. You'll have to do hard chores. It's not easy."

"I know, Sir," I answered. "I'm a hard-working girl."

Hanne coughed loudly, spluttering so hard that I was sure that she was trying not to laugh. I resisted the urge to turn and glare at her, hoping Mr Frost hadn't noticed her outburst. Frost folded his arms, his eyes still trained on me as I watched the gears of thought turn behind them.

"And your mother would be happy with you working here?" he continued. "We stay open 'til nine on Saturday nights."

"Of course," I said.

Hanne's coughing fell silent. It was one thing to lie about my work ethic, but we both knew I had no way of knowing how Mum would react to me finding a weekend job. On the one hand, I thought she might be thrilled that I could make my own money and buy the things she couldn't give me, but on the other, I hadn't even discussed the idea of working with her, let alone in a music club. I had spent most of my life secluded in the halls and grounds of Peregrine Place, but now it felt like fate had handed me a chance to spend a little time in the real world for once.

"And I live at the boarding school up the lane, so I'll never be late," I added. "Plus, I'm really good at washing up glasses, and I can clean floors, and-"

"All right, all right," Frost said, those chubby hands rising again. "I'll give you a try. I could do with a girl in the team. I've got too many boys here, and they get silly. You look like you could quiet them down a bit."

The old man laughed and I laughed with him, though

I wasn't entirely sure what he meant by his joke. He swerved behind the bar and pulled out a pad of paper, dropping it in front of me and retrieving a pen from his shirt pocket. I smiled nervously as he offered it to me.

"Write your name and your details down for me, kid," Frost began. "I'll call your Mum up tonight and give her the particulars. The name's Harry Frost, by the way."

"Josie Fontaine," I said with a nod.

Frost gathered up a box with more light bulbs and paced away, leaving me to frantically scribble my name, address, and number onto the page.

"Can you believe this?" I whispered to Hanne excitedly. "I'm getting a job! We've got to get back up to Peregrine right away."

"What about the record shop?" Hanne asked with a pout.

"Are you mad?" I replied. "It's going to take me all afternoon to convince Mum that this is a good idea before Frost rings her."

"But *is it* a good idea?" she retorted, glancing at the grumpy figure of Frost again.

"Of course it is," I answered. "Next time we get into the village, I'll be able to buy all the records I want. Plus, your dream boy is going to be hanging around, trying to get an audition here." I poked her over her heart with the back end of the pen. "Maybe I'll be able to introduce you two?"

Hanne couldn't help the grin that slid onto her freckled face.

"Thanks, Mr Frost," I shouted across the dance floor, giving the old man a thumbs-up.

"See you on Saturday, kid!" he replied. He was up on his

stool again, attacking a new light fixture. "Noah!" he shouted suddenly in the direction of the bar. "Get your brother out here and show him how to set my tables up right."

"Come on," Hanne said, taking my elbow quickly. "Or he might ask you to start helping right now."

We left Halfway and raced back to our bikes, blasting at full speed towards Peregrine Place. I spent every moment of the journey back thinking up good reasons why I should be allowed to take the job and praying that Mum was still feeling guilty enough about our finances to let me have it.

CHAPTER FOUR

Tommy Asher

There were three conditions under which I was allowed to take the job at Halfway. One: Mum could pop down and spy on me whenever she liked and I wasn't to speak a word of complaint. Two: I had to be sensible and hardworking at Halfway at all times. Three: under no circumstances was my schoolwork to suffer.

My mother didn't know how badly it was suffering already, so I supposed I'd have to make more of an effort with Miss Cartwright to avoid her reporting my terrible progress to Mum in the near future, thereby ruining my life before it had even started to get interesting. But other than that, I was getting a job. Mum had written down everything I needed to know from her chat with Mr Frost, and I spent the remaining days of summer studying all the details of my new position to get ready for Saturday, September the 9th.

Before that milestone, however, I had the first week of term to contend with. Peregrine Place was at its best on the first day of school, when around fifty kids between the ages of eleven and seventeen gathered in its wide, grand foyer, waiting to be told where to go and what to do. A fair chunk of the older ones had usually spent some time with us before, but most of the young additions came to the school after being 'discovered' by the government; young psychics with the potential to work for Queen and country were in high demand.

I didn't have any ambition to work for the State, which was just as well with my current skill level. Hanne and I stood at the back of the uncertain crowd, scanning our schedules, which we had pinched from the headmistress's office before joining the gathering. Once we had looked at our own week's times and classes, we made a switch and studied them all over again. What I saw there made me frown.

"You're in my meditation class," I said to Hanne, pointing at a box on her card.

She took it from me and studied the details underneath, raising her head to me with a look of sympathy that I really didn't want to see. "No, you're in my meditation class," she answered. "I've moved up one level and you've moved down."

I squirmed inside, embarrassed that my academic progression had not only come to a halt, but had now started going backwards too. At this rate, I was going to know less by the end of the year than I'd known at the beginning. The rest of my classes were fairly standard: Geography with Mr Cavendish senior, Leighton's father; English and Maths with Mrs Haugen; Needlework and Drill with Mr Haugen; History and Science with Mr Roth. And every single class involving my psychic skills was led by Miss Cartwright. There were a couple of other teachers who also handled psychic training, but I felt sure my schedule was a deliberate arrangement on her part. I could already see Miss Cartwright's wide blue eyes expanding in surprise at my total lack of progress every time I left one of her lessons. I scrunched my schedule up and shoved it into my pocket, turning my attention to the growing crowd instead.

Above us all, three pairs of legs began to descend the stairs. A hush overcame the mumbling crowd as they looked up respectfully, the three figures coming into better view. Hanne and I just exchanged a grin. Her parents always dressed up in their absolute best for the first day of term. Mrs Haugen wore an elegant beige skirt and jacket, coming down the stairs with one hand on the banister and the other clinging to her walking stick. Mr Haugen was by her side in a fine navy suit, guiding her at the elbow, offering his other hand to the older woman to his left. She was Mrs Cavendish, Hanne's grandmother, and our headmistress for as long as I could remember.

"Good morning, young people," Mrs Cavendish said, silver lines of age scattered across her pale, soft features. "It is a delight to see so many new faces this year at Peregrine Place. I am your headmistress, Mrs Gail Cavendish, and these are your school directors, Mr and Mrs Haugen. Mrs Haugen and I are psychics, just like you, and Mr Haugen is a fine example of the kind of diligent field agent that you'll be expected to work with in the future, should you choose to use your skills to defend our great nation."

Mrs Cavendish paused there, wearing a proud smile as she locked eyes with each and every student in the mix. "This morning you may leave your bags and parcels in the reception room just there," she said, one willowy arm pointing outwards. "They will be delivered to your quarters, which you'll become acquainted with after lunch. For now, you may collect a schedule from me and make your way to your first class of the morning. I look forward to meeting you all as individuals as the term progresses."

Mr Haugen produced a stack of schedules from his jacket

pocket, but Hanne and I were already prepared. I walked with heavy, stomping steps as we headed up the long corridor of the west wing, a throng of confused and excited students gradually starting to follow us. The half-open door to Miss Cartwright's classroom loomed before me like the gaping jaws of a beast waiting to swallow me whole. When I entered the dark wood-panelled space, my teacher stood with her arms folded, sharp eyes assessing every student that entered after me. I knew the drill well enough for day one in Miss Cartwright's class; I might almost have been able to enjoy the way she intimidated them all, had I not already known that I was on her bad side.

Hanne and I sat down first at the front of the class, and other boys and girls milled in around us. My dread increased with each new face as I realised that every single one of them had to be younger than me, until one blue-eyed visage made me blink a few times to be sure I'd seen it right. His slicked-back hair and small smile were unmistakeable; it was only the lack of a huge guitar case on his back that gave me pause.

It's the boy from Halfway! Hanne suddenly shouted into my mind. Oh my goodness. Do I look all right? Is my collar too frilly?

I grabbed hold of Hanne's shoulder to shake her from her psychic state, leaning in close. "Just turn and smile at him, dippy," I told her.

Hanne did as she was told. The boy completely missed her eager smile as he craned his neck around, studying the almost-full room for a seat.

"Excuse me," Hanne said gently. "This one in the middle's free."

She was pointing to the seat on my other side. The blue-

32

eyed boy looked at her, slowly registering what she had said, and then his eyes fell on me. He started to smile.

"Oh right, of course," he said. "Sorry. Thanks, I mean."

"When you've quite finished mumbling, young man," Miss Cartwright said in her clipped tone.

A few people giggled as the boy sank into the seat beside me. He was smaller with the guitar absent from his back, and he seemed much less sure of himself here than when he'd been trying to convince Frost to let him play at Halfway. I reasoned that he must have recently come to the village ready to start school here and spotted the club on the side of the lane just like us. Miss Cartwright cleared her throat, commanding utter silence from the assembled kids.

"Answer me when I call your name," she instructed. "Let's make sure we have no dunces who have come to the wrong room."

The boy looked down at his desk skittishly.

"Thomas Asher," Miss Cartwright said.

The boy suddenly looked up again, eyes widening. "Oh, um. Yes, Miss," he replied, "I mean, here, Miss."

Miss Cartwright gave him her best glare, but said nothing more on the matter. She began to move across the room as she called out names, studying every face in the rows before her.

It's Tommy actually, a voice suddenly said in my head. *Only my nanna calls me Thomas.*

I took a deep breath, pushing my mind towards his. *Did I give you permission to speak in my head?* I asked him.

Although I was tuning out of the room to speak with him, I could still see the outline of his face as he smiled at me; I was caught somewhere partway between reality and full psychic concentration.

Sorry, Tommy answered, but I certainly wasn't going to whisper out loud with her staring at me. Scary woman, that one.

I tried my best not to giggle. You have no idea, I answered. She's been teaching me for six years.

Not cool, Tommy replied.

A book suddenly slammed down on my desk. I leapt in my seat, my old, wooden chair rattling as I looked up into the thunderous face of my teacher. "Josephine Fontaine," she said, her teeth gritted. "Are we in such a state of distraction that we can't answer our own name on the register nowadays?"

I gave Tommy a withering glare, watching him bite his lip to hold back a laugh.

"Sorry, Miss," I answered. "But you do know I'm here. I mean, it's not as though we're strangers." I regretted adding the bit after the apology immediately.

"Oh no, we know each other very well," she answered primly. "I suspect you're going to be repeating this class until we're both white-haired and wrinkled."

She picked up her book and opened it again, turning her back on me. "Hanne Haugen," she said sharply.

"Here, Miss," Hanne's bright voice replied.

Haugen? Tommy thought. *Is she related to the bloke who gave our schedules out?*

I didn't want to be distracted again, but if Tommy was taking an interest in Hanne, I couldn't let her down by not encouraging him.

Mr Haugen's her father, I answered, slipping halfway out of my consciousness again. *Her whole family works in this place.*

ENOUGH!

Another voice entered my head, this one so loud it made

me cover my ears in a feeble attempt to block it. I looked up to the front of the class, watching as Miss Cartwright's blank gaze returned to one of consciousness. She clasped her hands tightly in front of her, surveying us all.

"Out of the fifteen students in this room, eight of you have already decided to engage in psychic conversations with one another," she began, her tone crisp and wry. "I can hear every word you're saying and, frankly, it's tedious. The next person to speak, out loud or otherwise, will be sent away to write me a profuse apology for the headache I'm getting."

"You can hear us?" asked a voice from the back of a room. It belonged to another boy of fourteen or so, about Hanne's age, who was clearly new enough not to fear Miss Cartwright's punishments yet. "But that's mind-reading! Nobody can do that!"

"*I* can," Miss Cartwright replied, not bothering to hide her pride. "And so might you, if you can keep your mouth shut long enough to learn something in this room. And *yes*, I do know about the chewy sweet you've already stuck to the underside of my desk. The guilt is written all over your mind, young man."

I always tried not to think about the fact that Miss Cartwright could read my thoughts. In the years that I'd been learning at Peregrine Place, I'd only ever seen two students graduate the school with the same abilities. We weren't all built for it, and I was certain my chances were slimmer than most of having such a grand skill. With the class uncomfortably subdued by the extreme skills of their new teacher, we fell into the usual practice of hearing about the theory of meditation and deep thinking. I tried to listen hard, conscious that my progress in this area was something that could take my new job away in a heartbeat, but it was just too boring for anything to stay.

A Place Halfway

I was staring at the board and watching Miss Cartwright chalk up some key words, but part of my mind seemed to detach from the immediate scene, as though I was slipping into a daydream. I knew it was more than just my imagination by the sudden feeling of anger that flooded my chest, which I knew was not my own. I felt like I was watching two television sets at once, the one in the classroom where I should have been present and listening, and the far more interesting one that called my consciousness away.

I was looking at the bar at Halfway, now beautifully polished and shimmering, but then my vision flickered down to my hands, which were masculine, wide, and chubby. In one of them, I held an empty bottle labelled 'Bell's Fine Whiskey'. When I spoke in this new body, the gruff tone and the tickle of a bushy moustache told me exactly whose head I had wandered towards.

"Noah! Why is this in our bin? There's no alcohol on these premises! I'll lose my business licence!"

Frost was livid. He spun on the spot, making me a little dizzy as he turned to face the boy he was addressing. The sight of him took me aback for a moment; his skin was dark like coffee with cream. He was a tall, skinny thing with wide eyes and a small nose that made him look a little bit like a startled barn owl. He seemed as shocked as I felt as he looked straight into Frost's eyes.

"It was lying on a box out the back, Mr Frost," he explained, something foreign in his accent that I couldn't quite trace, "I just brought it in to throw it out. I'm sorry, I-"

The other scene in my mind started moving. Miss Cartwright was giving out books. I forced myself back into the

36

present moment, grateful that both visions had stayed open so that I wasn't caught off-guard. The textbook's title glared up at me ominously: **Techniques of the Synsk**. I had received the same book that I had studied from all of last year, penned by Miss Cartwright herself. The image of Noah's face stayed in my mind. He was a coloured person. I listened to their music all the time on the radio—I adored the deep tones of Chuck Berry and the Drifters—but I had never actually seen a non-white person in the flesh. Now it looked like I would be working with one. I wasn't certain how I felt about that.

A scrap of paper rubbed against my knee. I took it from my left side, giving Hanne a disbelieving glance. She never passed notes in class, goody-goody that she was.

He's so dreamy. I think I'm in love.

I smiled to myself, slipping the note into my pocket. It was nice to see my best friend taking an interest in a life outside her studies for a change. I chanced a look at Tommy, expecting to see him reading, but instead, he was scrawling something into the back pages of his notebook. When he saw me looking, he flashed me a shy grin, lifting up the corner of the page so I could see his words.

Do you have a boyfriend, Josephine?

From that moment, I knew that a whole new mass of complications were about to invade my once-quiet life.

CHAPTER FIVE

The Bolton Brothers

For the first time in my life, the first week of school did not fly by in a blur of new topics, new pressures, and new textbooks. Monday to Friday dragged at an agonising pace as I eagerly awaited the grand opening of Halfway and my first official day of earning my own money. Aside from returning to classes and finding out what boring topics I'd be stuck with all year, I also had to avoid Tommy Asher at all costs in case he said something flirtatious to me in front of Hanne. This was especially difficult when I was with Hanne, because every time she saw the dark-haired figure coming down the halls, she begged me to loiter in case he stopped and started to chat. I was running out of excuses fast, and I didn't plan on playing the cat-and-mouse game all year either. Something would have to be done.

Friday's evening meal finally came around, and Hanne and I took our usual spot in the dining hall: at the end of a long table right next to the kitchen door. I dreaded casserole night because of the giant dumplings that sat like stones in the watery gravy. Stabbing at one absent-mindedly with my fork, I was surprised to find it falling apart perfectly, the soft, spongy insides letting out of a waft of steam. I looked up at Hanne as she brought a morsel to her mouth, rushing to do the same. We chewed thoughtfully.

"No offence to your mum," Hanne began cautiously, "but this is surprisingly nice."

Mum's dinners weren't anywhere near as bad as her baking, but they didn't usually have me wolfing down the stuff until I was wiping every drop of gravy up from the bottom of the dish. Hanne and I were doing just that when the kitchen doors opened, but instead of my mother, it was Blod Bickerstaff who offered us a smile. It was strange to see such a made-up face attached to a cooking apron; her fine jewellery was tucked inside long, white sleeves that had been splashed with something red and sticky. She approached us and crouched beside our table, tapping one long-fingered nail against the side of my dish.

"All right for you, girls?" she asked merrily, "I'm helping your mum in the kitchen, I am."

"It was nice," I said calmly, not wanting to overdo the enthusiasm in case it hurt Mum's feelings.

"Was it just a one-off with you helping, Auntie Blod?" Hanne asked. "These dumplings were *ever* so good."

I nearly choked into my cup of cordial with the sweetness in Hanne's tone. Auntie Blod indeed. She was clearly angling for second-helpings. I had never, for example, heard her call Bickerstaff 'Uncle Steven', and I didn't suspect I ever would.

"Oh, aren't you lovely," Blod said, patting Hanne's head. "Well, I think it'll be more than once a week. The flat yur isn't very big to clean and Dai's off to London to start uni on Monday, so I reckon I'll be a bit bored if I don't start pitching in around the school."

"You couldn't help Doctor Bickerstaff in the medical room?" I asked her.

Blod pulled a face that lifted her years. "It's not a wise woman who gets in the way of a man when he's got work to do," she half-whispered. "Remember that, Josie love. It might come in handy now you're out in the world a bit more."

She wished me good luck for tomorrow and excused herself, returning to the kitchens to prepare dessert. Hanne leaned forward immediately, her wide eyes suddenly serious and pleading.

"You will remember what you promised about Tommy, won't you?" she urged me.

"Yes," I sighed, for what felt like the thousandth time. "If he comes in, I'll be sure to tell him that you'll tutor him in maths if he likes. But I don't think it's going to come across quite the way you want it to."

"I don't care," Hanne replied. "Even if he thinks I'm big-headed for offering, at least then he'll come and shout at me and we'll have had some sort of conversation."

Despite the year's age difference, Tommy Asher was in Hanne's maths room and, in her considered opinion, he probably wasn't even clever enough for that level of sums. He hadn't said a word to her in the class that they shared, but he was all too keen to speak to the both of us any chance he got in Miss Cartwright's lessons. Hanne was a clever girl, but I recognised the signs of being too blinded by a crush to see the reality of what was actually going on. Dai Bickerstaff had been my weak point in that area for all too long.

"Do you think Tommy will come in whilst you're working tomorrow?" Hanne asked eagerly.

"I hope so," I replied, and this time the answer was honest. He and I needed a little chat.

Halfway was due to open for milkshakes and music from two o'clock onwards, so I was called in at midday to start sweeping out the floor and lining up the glasses to have ready for when the drinks staff came in to serve. At first, it was just Mr Frost and me straightening the place out, but soon I heard the rumble of an engine pulling up behind the club. Some moments later, the back door to Halfway must have opened, for an argument echoed through the kitchen as two sets of footsteps drew nearer.

"I'm never letting you drive that car again," said a voice I recognised.

"So I winged a lamppost," another voice replied. This one, also male, was sharper and lower than the first. "I did it once, Noah. Once."

"You're no Stirling Moss, mate," Noah answered with a sigh. "And I'm seventeen and you're sixteen, so I figure I still get to say what's what around here."

The two young men entered the bar area just as I finished lining up the glasses. The first face I looked into was the one I had seen in my half-vision some days ago, the wide-eyed, soft features of Noah looked back at me, startled. He was even taller in person now that I wasn't looking at him from Frost's height.

"Oh, um, hello," I murmured, trying to smile without looking too nervous. "I'm Josie."

"I'm Noah," the boy replied, matching my smile with shiny white teeth. "And this is my brother, Jacob."

"It's Jake," the brother snapped immediately.

Jake was shorter than Noah by about six inches, but he

was still a full head taller than I was. His skin was the colour of half-burnt toast and his eyes shone a pale shade of golden brown from beneath a heavy, frowning brow. Every muscle in his face was tight with irritation as he glared first at his brother and then at me.

"Nice to meet you, Josie."

Everything about Jake was aggressive. He didn't say 'Nice to meet you' in the way that I heard most people say it; he sounded like Doctor Bickerstaff did when you could tell the last thing he wanted was to be talking to someone he clearly thought was an idiot. Jake stuck out his hand as though I was going to shake it, but he kept on looking between his pale palm and my startled expression, his eyes gleaming like he thought I wouldn't dare touch him.

"A pleasure, Jacob," I said, grabbing his hand hard and shaking it for all I was worth.

Jake snatched his hand away as Noah laughed, but before anything more could come of the interaction, Frost approached us and put his hand on Noah's shoulder.

"Nice to see you kids getting along," he said, beaming. "So Josie, these are the Bolton brothers. Noah's my odd job man, and Jacob washes dishes in the back kitchen. So you're going to be my pretty face to do chores in the main club when guests are here."

Jake looked like he was chewing the inside of his mouth. I could practically feel the anger radiating from him before he suddenly turned on his heel.

"I'd better get the sinks ready," he mumbled, vanishing through the door.

As he went, there came a rap at the front door and I saw two pale, spotty faces looking in that I didn't know. Frost's moustache did a little dance on his lip.

"Aha! That's the band for today," he exclaimed proudly. "Josie, help Noah carry some snacks in from the storeroom. There's a good girl."

With that, he was off and I was left standing with Noah, whose eyes were on the now-closed door to the kitchen. His dark lip was pink in the one spot where he was biting it, those wide eyes consumed by worry. When he caught me looking at him, we both started a little, but then he swept one hand in the direction of the storeroom and offered a shaky smile.

"You can carry the scratchings; they're lightest," he offered.

"Thanks," I mumbled, following him out to the room.

Box loads of food sat staring at us from shelves that went all the way up to the ceiling in the small space. Noah barely had to stretch to reach the topmost ones. He was placid and cheerful as he brought the boxes down, and I felt my heart relaxing a little as I firmly decided which of the Bolton brothers I was happier about working with.

"So, can I ask about your accent?" I said, stacking up a few light boxes, ready to take them through. "I can't place where you're from."

"Oh we're English, Jake and me," Noah said, hefting a huge stack and leading me back towards the bar. "But my dad's got this deep Florida accent. He never shook it. I guess we pick up a twang here and there."

"He's American?" I asked, excited by the idea that I was befriending someone so linked to the culture I saw in magazines all the time.

"He was," Noah answered. "I mean, he came over as a G.I. in the war. And, well, he met my mom and he never left."

A Place Halfway

"How romantic," I said with a smile.

Noah dumped his boxes behind the bar, looking away sharply. There was a long, awkward moment where he didn't move, he just stared down at the floor with his back to me. I felt a prickle of nerves all over my body.

"Sorry," I mumbled. "That was nosy of me."

Noah turned, smiling sadly. "It's not that," he answered. "It's nice of you to ask, actually. Most of the people who work here don't even talk to me and Jake." Noah picked at his nail, not meeting my eye. "I mean, Frost's an old boot, but he's good to us."

I could fully understand why nobody would want to talk to Jake Bolton; the chap was hostile from the word go. But Noah was quiet and ever smiling, so there could only be one reason that other people didn't care enough to speak to him. His skin shone like coffee with cream as I watched him return to the storeroom for another box. I didn't want to admit that that might be the reason for the neglect he perceived, but when the drinks servers and the band for the afternoon were in place, I discovered that Noah wasn't wrong about them. Everyone welcomed me and asked me all sorts of things about myself, but every time Noah passed them by, it was like he didn't exist.

When the customers started to pile in for the grand opening, he was relegated to the back room to continue his chores, leaving me alone to make sure the main room didn't get into a state. The band was a poor imitation of the Everly Brothers, but they were good enough to make me grin as I wound around tables, picking up empty packets and glasses. I avoided it for as long as I could, but eventually the tray of empty glasses on the bar had piled up far too high.

"Hey, new girl!" someone shouted over the music. "Take

44

those out to be washed, would you?"

I could hear the water running in the sinks when I arrived in the little back-kitchen, but when I set down the heavy tray of empty shake glasses, Jake was nowhere to be seen. For a moment, I was relieved, ready to shoot back out of the cramped space before I had to speak to him, but then a silhouette at the back door caught my eye. It raised a bottle to its lips, the golden liquid inside glowing as it absorbed the bright sun in the backyard. I caught the start of the label's markings and was able to fill in the rest.

Bell's Fine Whiskey.

Jake took the gulp with a hard swallow, his lips pursed and his eyes screwed up like he hated the taste. He shook his head like a wet, shaggy dog before replacing the cap of the bottle and stashing it behind a dustbin. For a moment, I wished desperately that I had those deep thinking skills Miss Cartwright was always banging on about. The bitterness in his features made me want to step right into his head and ransack his thoughts. Whilst I was having that thought, I made the mistake of loitering too long.

"What're you looking at?" Jake demanded, storming forwards as he caught my gaze.

He was tall and angry and I stumbled back at first, like a cat that sensed it was about to get a kicking, but when I retreated, I caught sight of my reflection in the big, silver fridge where Frost stored all the milk. I looked like a scared, little girl. That wasn't supposed to be the point of getting a job in the big, wide world. Though I was still shaking inside, I folded my arms and leaned back against the sink counter.

"There's no alcohol on these premises," I said as calmly as I could manage. "Mr Frost could lose his business license if he finds out you're doing that."

I thanked my lucky stars for the random vision in Miss Cartwright's class. For the first time, I saw a crack in Jake's furious armour. His face faltered, one corner of his mouth twitching as a momentary flash of panic crossed his shining eyes. It was easier to believe that he was my age when that wave of insecurity crashed over his dark looks. He looked how I'd looked the first time Mum found me planting a kiss on Elvis Presley's lips on the poster on my wall.

"How about this…" I continued, wanting to escape before Jake had the chance to get angry again. "You try being a little bit nicer to me, and I'll consider not telling Mr Frost that you're a good-for-nothing drunk, all right?"

Jake picked up a dishrag, screwing it up so hard in his fist that I could see the veins in his knuckles standing out like spaghetti strands.

"Don't pretend you know anything about me, Fontaine," he griped. "I'm not a drunk. I just needed a drink."

I didn't understand the difference, but I backed away slowly, still facing him in the cramped, little space. "Just think about what I said," I replied.

Jake turned his back on me, but I was sure that he nodded just once. I rushed from the kitchen and swept past the bar, ready to bury myself in work again. A pair of huge, blue eyes and a sweep of Brylcreem-tamed hair stood in my way. I crashed headfirst into Tommy Asher and he caught me at the forearms, peering into my face with a curious smile.

"Watch where you're going, beautiful." He chuckled.

I had prepared so many things that I was going to say to Tommy. I meant to tell him that I didn't want him calling me beautiful. I meant to pass on Hanne's message and try to make the idea of tutoring sound like an appealing one to him. Most of all, I meant to make it clear that he was just another boy to me. Jake had made all those carefully planned thoughts fall out of my head.

"Thanks, Tommy," I stammered, holding onto him whilst I got my balance again. When I saw his grin, I swiftly let him go, but it was too late.

"Do you take a break anytime?" he asked. "Because this music's not too bad and there is a dance floor, so-"

"Can't," I said quickly, fumbling my words. "Um, sorry. I'm working, you know?"

He nodded, moving like he was going to leave. I didn't want to encourage him, but I couldn't let Hanne down.

"Tomorrow," I added. He raised a dark brow at me. "Come by my place at Peregrine tomorrow after tea, okay? Staff quarters, flat four."

"Staff quarters?" he asked.

I suddenly noticed Frost glaring at me from across the room. A sea of dirty tables full of empty glasses surrounded me. "My mum's the cook," I said hurriedly. I raced into the pack of tables nearest me, grabbing glasses and wiping up split milk for all I was worth.

"I look forward to it!" Tommy shouted over the din.

I tried not to think about the impending disaster I had just arranged.

CHAPTER SIX

Tangled

Hanne and I were all too often recruited for the tedious task of babysitting little Nik. Hanne had to love him because he was her baby brother, but I felt no qualms whatsoever in stating that I loathed the little brat. Mrs Cavendish often called a staff meeting on a Sunday night, leaving Hanne and me to suffer through a couple of hours with a screaming, ranting toddler as he ran riot through my flat and broke everything he could get his pudgy little hands on. For this reason, I had firmly closed my bedroom door to keep my precious new record player out of Nik's sights.

"Why do we never babysit him in your parents' apartment?" I asked Hanne as I struggled to hold the infant back from attacking the television set.

"Too much top-secret government stuff," Hanne answered with a shrug.

"Are you serious?" I replied, "What am I, a lethal spy or something?"

"I'm joking," she said, slapping my arm. "Nik's got too many toys and things at ours. Mum says he'll settle to sleep better if there's less for him to play with."

"Leggome!" Nik shouted, kicking me hard in the shin.

I winced. "Yes, well, that theory's working out a fair treat," I remarked.

A sharp knock at the door startled us both. Hanne looked at me, her hands flying to the sides of her face. "Is that Tommy? Oh my goodness, you answer it, Josie, I can't. Okay, what do I say? What are you going to tell him? What-?"

I let go of Nik with one hand to cover Hanne's mouth with it. The toddler struggled free of my remaining grip and ran to the door, knocking on it from the inside. The outside knock came again in reply.

"Just relax," I told Hanne. "We'll have a laugh. It'll be fun."

I didn't believe a word of what I was saying, but I was going to try my best to make this little visit work in my best friend's favour. Nik knocked back on the door again, giggling, and the reply was one deafening bang against the outside that made him leap back in fright.

"Stop mucking around and let me in!" demanded a booming Welsh tone through the wood.

I rushed to the door and opened it, my heart in my throat. Dai Bickerstaff looked livid as he stood with his muscular arms crossed over his chest. I felt everything that Hanne had felt a moment before when she thought the visitor was Tommy; I was terrified to speak in case something stupid or utterly non-verbal escaped my lips.

"Are my parents yur?" Dai asked.

"What? Um, no," I stuttered. "They're in a meeting. It's usually about, er, another, er, another hour before they're done."

"Typical," the dreamboat answered with a huff. "I'm supposed to be packing to go down London tomorrow, and Mam hasn't even ironed my best shirt. I'm going to look like a

49

beggar going in there. I'm supposed to be a law student!"

I couldn't remember a time when Dai had said that many words to me in one go. The sight of his lips moving so much inspired a brilliant idea. "I could iron it for you," I offered.

Dai smiled. It was a wonderful sight, the way his bright blue eyes narrowed and his perfect cheekbones lifted. He leaned on the doorframe, flexing one hand against it as he ran the other through his glorious, blonde hair.

"Couldn't do a couple of other bits too, could you?" he asked, his voice deeper and smoother than before.

"Anything," I said without a moment's pause. Hanne giggled somewhere in the living room.

Dai vanished for a moment down the dark corridor, and Nik tried to follow him out of the apartment. I grabbed the toddler by the waist, and he looked up at me with bright, pleading eyes.

"No way, José," I said firmly, turning him around and pushing him back towards the space where Hanne was inevitably eavesdropping on me.

Dai returned a moment later with a stack of crinkled clothes in his arms. When he handed them to me, I felt the warmth of his forearms brushing over mine. I tried to smile at him over the clothes, but the pile was just a little too high for him to see me.

"I'll nip back and get them later, right?" Dai asked.

"No problem!" I answered, pushing the door shut again with my foot.

Nik was running circles around Hanne in the kitchen as she fetched him a drink. When I reached her to grab the iron and the board, she was giving me a knowing little grin that I didn't like the look of.

"Well, it's better than offering to tutor him and making him feel stupid," I snapped before she could get a word in.

"If you'd rather be his slave, then that's not my business," Hanne answered.

"You'll see," I answered, a warmth building in my chest. "He'll remember this. He'll owe me a favour."

Our iron was a cream-and-black beast from Morphy Richards. It was almost ten years old, and it had the tendency to spit water from its point if you held it the wrong way. I had never been much good at doing shirts, but the thought of Dai's face lit with gratitude helped me focus on making a good job of it. He'd brought me ten shirts and a jacket in all, and I was about halfway through them when the knocking at the door resumed.

"Unreal," Hanne said with a huff. "He can't think you've finished already."

Nik refused to get down from her lap, so Hanne had to take him with her to the door, stomping all the way. She looked like she was about to give Dai a huge piece of her mind, but when she swung the door open with a bang, her whole freckled face turned crimson in seconds.

"Oh," she stammered. "Hi, Tommy."

Tommy stepped in gingerly, his face brightening a little when he saw me across the room. Nik threw a chubby fist out that almost glanced his chin.

"No!" the toddler cried.

"Sorry," Hanne said, her voice trembling. "This is my brother Nik. He's a pain."

"So I see," Tommy replied.

He leaned towards Nik and pressed on the tip of his

51

nose lightly with one finger. Nik scowled for a moment, but then he started trying to lean out of Hanne's grip like he wanted Tommy to do it again. When Hanne set him down, the toddler immediately followed Tommy as he crossed the room to where I stood with the iron. The spluttery old thing chose that moment to shoot a wild spasm of hot water out and Tommy leapt back against the wall with half a grin, his dark brows rising in surprise.

"Whoa, nothing in this flat seems to like me." He chuckled nervously.

I chanced a glance at Hanne with her wide, doting eyes and small smile. If only he knew.

"Have a seat," I offered. "The settee won't swallow you, so long as you sit on the good side."

Tommy crept along to the old, brown sofa with a quizzical look. Hanne sat down in the middle of it and pointed him to the part that wouldn't have him sinking down almost to the floor.

"I didn't know you had chores, Josie," he said, sitting forward with his hands firmly gripping his kneecaps.

"Oh, she doesn't," Hanne piped in, that playful sting in her voice again. "These are a favour for Dai. He's her dreamboat. But he's going away tomorrow."

"Oh," Tommy said. "Right."

There was a drop in his tone and for once, I was grateful to Hanne for giving away too much information. If Tommy knew I fancied a boy like Dai, then maybe he'd stop flirting with me and start looking in Hanne's direction. If, of course, they weren't both sitting tensely beside one another and deliberately not making eye contact.

"I've only got this jacket left to do," I explained, trying to fill the silence. "You two keep Nik away from the iron."

"Can do," Tommy answered as Nik attempted to climb up onto his lap. "I think he's found someone new to mess with."

"Watch out for the fists," Hanne said in a small voice. "He packs a bit of a wallop. I've got bruises all over me."

It wasn't the greatest conversation starter I'd ever heard. I set Dai's brown jacket down, ready to start on the sleeves, but I paused to look up at the awkward pair opposite me.

"Tell Hanne what it was like at Halfway yesterday," I said to Tommy. "You saw a lot more of the band than I did."

He began a stumbling explanation of the duo that had sung like the Everly Brothers, but the more Tommy spoke, the more the story became a rant about how he was a lot better than them and about how Mr Frost ought to give him a chance to perform. Hanne listened intently even though Tommy hardly ever met her eye, nodding with fierce agreement every time he talked about how supposedly brilliant he was with his guitar.

When I got to the front lapels of the jacket, I paused, taken aback by the sight of a yellow piece of card poking out of Dai's top pocket. I couldn't run the iron over it without risking it being ruined, so I set the old machine down and slipped the card out, turning it over in my hands. It was a formal invitation, handwritten in bold, black letters that leapt off the page. I knew I shouldn't have read it, but the print was too clear and my brain started taking it in before I even had a chance to put it down.

"What's that, Josie?" Hanne asked.

"We cordially invite you to attend the social introduction of the Society of the London Light," I read aloud. "The gathering will be held at Finsbury Square on Wednesday, 13th of September, 1961. No additional guests permitted."

"Wow," Hanne said. "Dai's getting invited to places be-

fore he's even started university."

I finished ironing the jacket and hung it over a dining chair, placing the yellow card back in the pocket. "What do you think the London Light is?" I asked.

"Probably a posh club for the rich and successful types," Tommy suggested.

"Dai's not rich and successful," I answered.

"But he will be soon, if he's rubbing shoulders with people like them," Hanne replied.

I crossed the room and took the last spot on the sofa next to Hanne, sinking deep into the fabric where the springs were broken. Nik, who had eventually made it onto Tommy's lap, crawled across Hanne like she was nothing more than a bridge and landed on me. He sat facing me and clapped his hands together in front of my nose.

"Singsong," he said.

"No," I answered firmly. "No singsong for you. You broke my radio last time. No way am I letting you get near my new turntable."

"You've got a player?" Tommy asked, awestruck. "Nice."

"It's really neat," Hanne added, looking at me as pleadingly as her little brother was.

"Singsong," Nik said again.

I squirmed in my sunken seat, my loyalties torn between my friend and my precious record player. The perfect solution hit me, and I smiled.

"I'll let Hanne show it to you," I told Tommy with an encouraging nod. "I'll have to stay here and hold onto Nik, so he doesn't try to destroy it. You two go."

Hanne leapt up immediately. Tommy was a little slower

to follow, but he sidled along behind her in the direction of the corridor. They were almost out of sight when there was a knock at the door again. Hanne leapt back a few paces, she and Tommy peering back into the room as I got up to answer it, holding Nik on my hip. Dai was already smiling at me as I hefted the door open once again.

"All done," I said proudly. "You'll have to come in and get them though. I've got Nik."

"Ta Jo," he said in his luscious, deep tone. "Nice of you to do it, like."

As Dai reached his neatly folded pile of clothes, his sharp blue eyes shot to the sight of Tommy Asher. Every bit of his smile fell away, and his usual stiff-lipped look returned. He straightened up and approached Tommy, but then looked back at me over his muscular shoulder.

"Does your mum know you've got a boy in yur?" he demanded.

"You're a boy," Tommy retorted. He was trying, and failing, to make himself as tall as the blonde Adonis staring him down.

"I'm a man, mate," Dai growled in reply. "Big difference. Slink your hook, right? You shouldn't be in this part of the manor."

Tommy looked as though he was putting every morsel of his energy into not letting his bottom lip wobble. "Yeah well, I was about to go anyway," he lied. "See you in meditation in the morning, girls."

Dai picked up his clothes and waited, eyeing Tommy until he was out of the door. The tall Welshman gave me a little nod, eyes gleaming like steel, and then he too was gone. When I shut the door, Hanne stomped back across the room, looking totally crushed. Even Nik was solemn for a moment, looking at the closed door like he expected Tommy to return at any moment. Hanne and I slumped back onto the sofa together.

"He's just being protective of us," I tried.

"Of you," Hanne replied immediately. "It was you he asked if you had permission to have a boy in."

For her sake, I didn't celebrate that fact with an outward smile, though a little flock of butterflies did sprout their wings in my tummy. "That was only the first attempt with Tommy anyway," I offered. "You've got all year."

Hanne nodded, but her frown didn't fade. Instead, she shuffled, arching her back as she suddenly leaned forwards. She curved her body around and fished down the back of the sofa with one small hand.

"What on earth am I sitting on?" she grumbled, pulling out a crumpled newspaper from the gap between the seat and the cushions.

We straightened the paper out together, its black-and-white pages staring back with fairly fresh ink. The date at the top of the page caught my eye. My birthday. I took the paper quickly from Hanne's hands and started turning the pages.

"What are you looking for?" Hanne demanded, her head at my shoulder as she tried to look too.

"Carlisle Street!" I exclaimed. "This is your dad's paper from the other week. With everything going on, I'd totally forgotten."

"The death!" Hanne added as she remembered all I'd told her. "Let me help you look."

Considering it was a death, the report hadn't even made the front half of the paper. It took us a while to find the article that mentioned Carlisle Street, a small strip to the side of a page with the headline: **Tragic Death in Small Kent Village**. I felt the hard, cold sensation of sadness and fear building as I began to read it.

The tragic death of a coloured man in Green Village, Kent, continues to baffle police. The gentleman's body was found in the morning hours of August 20th on Carlisle Street, the village's central thoroughfare. He suffered several wounds and injuries that were consistent with those of a mugging, but none were so serious that the gentlemen ought to have lost his life. The family of the coloured man has declined to comment on the situation and will not release his identity to public knowledge unless the police fail to gain information on the incident through other means. Anyone who may have been present in the area at the time of this tragedy is urged to come forward and telephone Kent Police on the number below.

"How awful," Hanne said, "And he got mugged in our village, too."

That must have been the reason that our parents hadn't wanted us to see the paper; it was awful to think that the people who had hurt this poor man were out there somewhere, maybe even looking for more victims. The strangeness of his sudden death disturbed me even more.

"Don't worry," I said, folding up the paper. "He was mugged very late at night, I bet. We don't go out in the dark down that way."

"But you might," Hanne answered. "When it starts getting dark down at Halfway. You might not be safe coming back alone."

I shushed Hanne and put on the television, assuring her that she was being silly. As I sat watching John Wayne strut

about on the screen, however, the reality of her words were all too
quick to sink in.

CHAPTER SEVEN

V.W

I was already starting to notice the sunset getting earlier by the time I went to Halfway for my next shift. I fancied the sky would be a shade of watery blue ink by the time I was finished that night. For now, I found myself cycling through a biting wind, cloudy skies gathering overhead as I let my bike freewheel into the backyard of the music club. The Bolton brothers were just getting out of their car as I arrived. It was a little Volkswagen Beetle in a shade that reminded me of peppermint toothpaste, but its headlight was damaged on one side and the front bumper was about ready to fall off.

Noah gave me a wave as he somehow managed to pull his tall frame out of the tiny car. I waved back until I saw Jake alight, glaring at me like I was a plate of Brussel sprouts at Christmas. I walked ahead of the brothers quickly and slipped through the kitchen into the main room, surprised to find Mr Frost in the process of laying up a big table with a crisp, white cloth. He ushered me over quickly, all hand gestures and very few words as I helped him finish smoothing the cloth down. The portly man moved like a creature possessed as he arranged two chairs at either side of the table.

"Big important meeting before we open today," Frost

explained. "Got a very important person coming in. Fetch some water and glasses for the table, kid."

As I turned to fetch a water jug, I got a nod from Noah at the kitchen door. I gathered two glasses and laid them on the table and, a moment later, Noah returned with a jug full of water to put in the table's centre. Frost stepped back, hands on hips, surveying the scene. He nodded, his moustache wiggling thoughtfully on his lip.

"It'll have to do," he surmised.

"What's the meeting for, Sir?" Noah asked.

Frost tapped one pudgy finger on the side of his wide nose. "Aha," he chuckled. "You'll find out later with any luck. I'm hoping to make a very big announcement when the club's packed full this afternoon."

There came a knock at the door. Frost flicked at us with hands, beady eyes suddenly widening. "Out, out, out," he demanded. "All you of stay in the kitchen and shut the door until I say so."

Noah and I stumbled to the kitchen, both trying to look backwards for any signs of the mysterious visitor who was about to enter the club. We didn't catch so much as a glimpse of him before we had to shut the door behind us. Jake was washing out the sinks with a thick rag, staring into the faucet where a jet of water streamed straight down into the drain.

"Did you hear all that?" Noah asked him. "Sounds like Frost's preparing something big."

Jake shrugged. Even though he was staring at the water, I had a strange, prickly feeling on the back of my neck where I stood in his peripheral vision.

"Can we help you prepare the kitchen or something, Jake?"

I asked, trying my best friendly tone. "Only Frost said we have to stay out here until-"

"Everything's done," Jake snapped back, lunging out to switch off the taps. He dried his hands on his brown trousers and stormed past me, keeping his head low. "I'm going out the back."

Frost had told us to stay put, but I wasn't going to be the one to argue that point. Jake strode out into the yard, letting the door swing back into place behind him. It was open just a crack as it had been on the day I caught him drinking, but now he wasn't standing in the same spot as before. I couldn't see him at all. Noah craned his head as if he too was looking, but then he shook it with a sigh.

"So Josie," he said, turning his back on the doorway. "I heard you're a student at the manor house up the lane from here."

"Peregrine Place," I replied with a nod. "Well, my mum's the cook there, so technically, it's my home too."

"I can't imagine living at school all year round," Noah replied with a grin. "I got out and started working the moment I could. Jake did too; he just finished this summer. He was going to start work with my dad but…" Noah bit his lip for a moment, and then smiled crookedly. "That didn't work out. So I got him a job here. I used to work for Frost when he owned the ice-cream parlour in Tonbridge."

Noah paused, eyeing me with those wide, glassy orbs of his. "I'm talking too much, right?" he asked.

"No," I said immediately. "It's interesting. I was just…" My eyes wandered to the gap in the door again. "Jake's pretty tightly wound, isn't he?"

"He wasn't always," Noah answered, his smile fading.

He didn't offer any more information than that, so

61

I busied myself with drying some of the glasses that were on the sink-top. I wanted to ask Noah about the whiskey bottle; I wondered if he knew about Jake's drinking and whether he would want to help his brother out if he did. A strange feeling was holding me back from broaching the subject. The gap in the door bothered me, even though all I could see was an empty yard beyond it. As I dried another glass, I let part of my mind detach and wander out, looking for Jake.

My suspicions were confirmed the moment I saw the world through his eyes. He was standing just to the side of the door, peering in enough to see some of the kitchen cupboards. I focused a little harder on him, letting more of my mind flow towards his until I could feel the tension in his body, the way he was waiting and craning his ears to hear what more his brother and I might say about him. In my other vision, I could still see the polished shake glass I was holding in my hands.

"I just wonder how he's going to keep this job with an attitude like that," I mused aloud.

I felt Jake's fist tighten as though it were my own.

"It's not permanent," Noah said somewhere behind me. "At least, I hope it's not. He's... We're... Actually, it's best if I don't talk about it."

In that moment, a wild surge of mental energy took me over. The sight of the glass in my hand was gone and I was totally consumed by Jake, feeling the tightness of his muscles and the heat of anger welling in his chest. The anger wasn't the only thing that gripped me, for beyond it there was a feeling like none I'd ever experienced. A deep emptiness sat cold and heavy in his body, sending chills through us both like the kind you'd get from walking through a graveyard alone at night. He was full to the brim with anger, fear, and despair, so much of it that I could hardly tell one from the other. I didn't understand how one person could feel so much inside them and not just want to scream all the time. I wanted to scream, and I had only had the feeling for seconds.

Panic rose within me as I tried to get out, realising this was the deepest mental connection I had ever been able to make. Miss Cartwright would have been proud, except for the fact that I didn't seem to be able to pull my mind back from Jake's all-consuming presence. I need to focus on receding back to my body, but the body I was in was so pained and confused that new feelings were hitting me all the time, making it hard to tell where Jake's fear ended and my panic began. Terrible thoughts ran through my head, like what would happen if I were trapped with Jake forever, never able to return my mind to the body it belonged in. Why hadn't anyone ever warned me how dangerous deep thinking could be?

Jake was running into the kitchen, a sudden rush of new urgency making his nerves quake. I saw the horrifying sight of myself standing at the sink, my pale eyes open but glazed over like no-one was at home. Noah was clutching my hand where a stream of crimson blood had gathered in my palm. When I saw myself through Jake's eyes, a moment of clarity appeared and I latched onto it, thinking of my body and the pain my hand must have been in from whatever had caused the bleed. The moment I thought it, my palm began to ache and I focused on that, feeling myself float away from Jake's intense emotions as I returned to sensing my own.

"Josie!" Noah cried. "Josie, are you all right?"

"I guess I must have been in shock," I said, surprised to

find my voice breathy and weak.

"Don't just stand there, you idiot," Jake snapped at his brother. "Get her some ice and a cloth to stem the bleeding."

"Right," Noah said, crashing into things left, right, and centre as he followed Jake's commands.

I closed my fist tight, looking down at the broken remains of a glass on the floor as I realised what I must have done when my mind shot over to Jake's completely. The cut was deep but very small. When Noah inspected it, he found no glass shards left in the wound. I held ice cubes until the pain was numbed away and, eventually, the bleeding stopped. When I gingerly opened my hand to see the crusty, little dent in my palm, Jake peered in too, a dark brow raised.

"Too small to need stitches," he said, his voice much quieter than I had ever heard it. "Keep your hand as still as you can to let it heal."

I looked up into his golden eyes, remembering the terrible mess of emotions he had raging inside him, yet here he was, trying to be helpful to me. "You're really good at first aid," I said with a smile.

"I only started learning a couple of weeks ago," he answered. Jake didn't smile back, his expression turning bitter again as he made to walk away.

"Well, thanks," I added quickly.

He nodded, and then headed back outside.

None of us initially saw the man who had met with Mr Frost in the front room, but when I came out into the club later to start cleaning tables, there was a stranger sitting in a booth near the stage. The first thing I noticed about him were his shiny black shoes, so perfectly polished that they were reflecting the faint glow of the light bulbs above the dance floor. He was sharp suited and thin, wearing a flashy, burgundy jacket, a thick, silver watch, and a collection of expensive-looking rings on both hands. The stranger's head was half-turned to the jukebox in the corner, his fingers tapping on the table along to the beat of Johnny B Goode.

To my surprise, the man at the table was starting to sing along to every word of the song. His voice hit every beat and every lyric, but he was terribly out of tune with a deep, throaty rasp that suggested he smoked far too much. I was impressed by the way he knew every word, especially since his dark hair was starting to turn grey at the temples, not usually a sign of someone who was hip to the charts. I tried not to look at him as I went about my business, my feet shifting along to Chuck Berry's melody and the twang of his guitar. The tables I need to shine up were getting closer to where the stranger sat and Mr Frost was nowhere to be seen, so I slowed my pace and re-shined a few that were farther away.

The music stopped abruptly; the jukebox had come to the end of its rotation. My back was turned to the stranger as I heard him get up, those polished shoes clicking on the dance floor. When I turned, I saw his face properly for the first time. He had a triangular jaw and thin eyes, his lips parted in a smile that showed a collection of bright teeth that were uncommonly long. He was the kind of fellow my mother would have called slick. He held out a hand to me, silver rings shining on every knuckle.

"You must be Josie," he rasped in a deep tone. His accent

was northern, but I couldn't place it completely. "Sorry I didn't come over sooner, but I think it's sacrilege to talk over Chuck Berry."

I agreed totally, but all I said was, "Nice to meet you, Sir."

I took his hand and he shook mine very gently, his smile twisting to one side of his mouth like he was amused by something.

"Vince Walsh," he said, tapping his lapel. "But I go by V.W. You know, like those nippy little German cars?"

"There's one parked out the back," I said brightly. "It belongs to the Bolton brothers."

"The kitchen boys," V.W. replied with a nod. "Yeah, old Frosty told me about them. It's nice to see kids working in a kids' venue. Keeps the place hip."

He spoke like the announcers on the radio did when they told you about the week's hits. He was clearly wealthy and important. He knew every word to Johnny B Goode. And he had called Mr Frost *Frosty*. I couldn't help but be impressed.

Our introduction was short-lived as kids began to pile in at the stroke of two o'clock. Mr Frost appeared and took V.W. away towards the stage, pointing out various things to him and introducing him to the two-man band that was setting up to play something for the kids to dance to. I collected glasses and cleared up spills, swirling around the room and watching the men's conversation with interest. Frost had said there was going to be a big announcement, and I wasn't going to miss it.

It was a little later when the moment came, after the singers had performed a few songs and Halfway was crawling with lively teens. Mr Frost took up one of the microphones and a few kids sniggered, joking to each other that he was about to break into a rousing chorus of Volare. Instead, he cleared his throat and asked for silence.

"Now youngsters," he began, pride swelling in his voice. "Here at Halfway, we've been given a very special opportunity, and we've been visited here today by a very special guest from Manchester. Kids, this is Mr Vince Walsh."

Some polite applause followed, but most of the teens looked impatient as the slim, well-dressed figure approached the mic. V.W. gave them all one of his sharp-toothed grins.

"All right, I know you want to get back to grooving," he crooned in his throaty tone, "so let me say this fast. I know plenty of you kids out there have got talent. You can sing, you can dance, and you can play instruments." V.W. pointed out into the crowd. "Well, I want to see it. We're going to hold a massive talent contest, right here at Halfway, to find the best new act in Kent. And that act's going to come back to Manchester with me and get signed to a record label. How does that sound to you?"

The teens reacted with much louder applause than before. When V.W. dismounted the stage, the band resumed playing, but now every table that I passed was consumed by conversation of what the talent show would have to offer and who would be brave enough to audition. I could already think of one guitar-toting boy I knew who needed to be in on this information as soon as possible. When I returned to the bar, I found V.W. handing out stacks of flyers to a crowd of excited kids. He caught my eye over their heads and flashed me another grin.

"Here kiddo," he said. "Give some out at that school of yours."

I took the small clump of leaflets from him, quirking a brow. "You know about my school?" I asked.

V.W. winked one of his narrow eyes. "I know everything Josie. Remember that."

CHAPTER EIGHT

Practice Makes Perfect

Mum always got up early on a Sunday to set out breakfast in the hall for the students, but she and I usually had our own private breakfast later in the morning in the flat. I was just pouring some orange juice into a jug on the table when she returned from the kitchens, letting down her curling hair and flapping her hands at her pink, flushed face. She smiled at me, but there was something forced about it. Her eyes were glistening a little. I helped her get her apron off, and she practically fell into her seat.

"What do you 'ave for me, sweet'eart?" she asked.

"I made scrambled eggs," I replied, lifting the covers off the two plates in front of us. "And some toast."

"Perfect," Mum sighed. "You're going to be a better cook than me someday."

I just smiled in reply. Mum started to eat, pouring herself a steaming cup of tea from our little, yellow teapot. I pushed a few wobbly pieces of egg around on my plate for a moment, my thoughts swirling in and out of focus. There were things I wanted to tell her, like about Jake and his whiskey bottle and the fact that I'd finally seen the paper and knew what happened a few weeks ago at Carlisle Street. She looked so relaxed now after walking in in such a huff; I couldn't bring myself to say anything that might make her worry.

"I met these brothers at work," I began, "and they said their dad came over from America during the war."

Mum nodded, swallowing a bite of toast. "The G.I.s," she explained. "Lots of soldiers came 'ere to train before they joined England in the war. Many people came to England in that time, to fight and to 'ide from the Nazis. Like Mr 'augen."

"And like you," I interrupted.

"And like me," she continued with a nod, "All the way from Guernsey in a tiny, little boat. I thought I would die before I saw the English shore. But I made it 'ere. I went up to the North where there was work in the factories. And then-"

I knew the rest well enough, though the details were never fully revealed. "Then you met my dad," I said. A silence fell upon us and we both had a mouthful of food, chewing for a long moment. "I bet you regret that," I added quietly.

"Of course not!" Mum exclaimed, reaching for my hand across the table. "Josie, your father was a very bad man, no mistake. But if it were not for 'im, I would not be 'ere right now with my beautiful daughter and the best scrambled eggs in the world."

I glowed at her words, but a sudden remembrance hit me as I rose from the table. "Oh, there was something else at work," I said, rushing to my coat to get out the stack of flyers about the music show. I handed one to Mum. "Do you think you could leave these on the tables when you lay up for lunch?"

As I resumed my breakfast, I watched Mum's bright eyes perusing the leaflet.

"Hmm," she answered. "I can ask Blod to do it. It will keep 'er out of my kitchen for a few minutes at least."

My mother was too polite to ever show it outside of

our flat, but Blod Bickerstaff helping out in the kitchen wasn't turning out to be the most amicable of arrangements. Mum was growing more and more tired of her routine being interrupted as the days went by.

"Hey," I said with a giggle, "V.W. is looking for volunteers to judge the auditions. It says so at the bottom there. Maybe you could send Blod down to be a talent judge?"

"I'm sure she would suit it better than boiling cabbage and roasting chickens with me," Mum replied, staring to grin. "Who is this V.W.?"

"A music producer," I answered brightly. "He knows every word to Johnny B Goode."

A fair brow rose on my mother's face. "Is 'e young or old, this man?" she asked.

"Oh Mum!" I said, realising what her look meant. "He's ancient! He could be my dad! I just meant he's cool for an old fogey, that's all. I want to tell Tommy Asher about the contest. He thinks he's the next Bobby Darin; now he's got a chance to prove it."

"Why don't you just use your powers to send 'im the news?" Mum pressed.

It was a good question, but since the horrific event of being trapped in Jake Bolton's messed-up head, I was even less inclined to practice my deep thinking than ever before.

"I'm tired from work," I lied, rubbing the side of my head. "I need a non-psychic day today to get ready for class tomorrow."

"That's my good girl," Mum answered, beaming. "Learning to balance 'er life."

A little squirm of guilt made my tummy rumble. I needed to find a solution to my lack of progress in class, and

quickly. Hanne was too finicky a teacher. Miss Cartwright was a nightmare of an option. I reasoned to myself that maybe Tommy Asher was the answer to more than one problem that day.

I was too embarrassed to ask Tommy to help me with my deep thinking. I didn't think I would be, at first, but then every time I tried to open my mouth to ask him for help, we just ended up talking about his upcoming audition for the talent show. It was Thursday when I found myself sitting in Mr Roth's history class, bemoaning my own total lack of courage. Mr Roth was a silver-haired gent with a thin moustache and twitchy features. He spent most of his time telling us stories from the war rather than teaching us from the textbooks, which was good or bad depending on the story he chose. Today's tale was a really boring one about his basic training in Wiltshire, so I was drawing a scribbly picture in the back of my notebook when a sudden voice interrupted my daydreams.

Look up at the door.

I did as I was told. Tommy was peering in at me through the glass window. He waved and grinned, but then suddenly set his face to a serious, urgent look.

Go along with this, okay?

I didn't have time to reply before he was knocking at the door. Mr Roth walked to it slowly and let him in, one hand on his hip.

"What's this now?" he asked.

"Sorry, Sir," Tommy said with a nod of his head, "but I need Josie Fontaine, Sir. Her mother needs her to go down to the kitchens. It's a very urgent family matter, Sir."

The pleading in Tommy's tone set Mr Roth's twitches off. He nodded fervently and looked at me, making a shaky sweeping motion with his hand. "Go on then, Josie. Out you go," he urged. "We'll catch you up next time."

"Thank you, Sir," I said, hurrying to grab my bag and follow Tommy down the hall.

We walked down the long hall with Tommy a half-step in front of me. Instead of leading me downstairs towards the kitchens, we veered off to the very rear of the building where few of the classrooms were in use. When I was sure that we had passed out of reach of anyone who might see us, I slapped Tommy's shoulder and gave him a good glare.

"Urgent family matter?" I asked. "I haven't got any blinking family! You wait until Roth realises that; I'm going to be in for the chop!"

"This is important," Tommy hissed. "I need your advice."

He opened the door to a spare classroom. It was a dusty space with very few tables and chairs, but in its centre, Tommy had set up his guitar. It was a beautiful shade of bright yellow with a square black panel over the top right corner. The word **FENDER** curled behind the strings at its head.

"You like my Tele?" he asked proudly. "It was my leaving present from my parents, for getting in at Peregrine."

"It's amazing," I answered in earnest. "But isn't someone going to come looking for you up here?"

Tommy shook his head, a mischievous glint in his gaze. "I'm supposed to be in drill with Mr Haugen. I pretended to hurt my foot having a kick-around. He sent me to Doctor Bickerstaff, but I didn't go. No-one's any the wiser."

"You hope," I replied with a laugh. "Does this mean you've picked a song?"

Tommy closed the classroom door and stepped over to his guitar, pulling its strap across his slim shoulders.

"If you think it's a good one," he said. "I trust you, Josie. You know about music."

I liked the little swell of pride that hugged my heart when he said that. After I gave him my blessing, Tommy plucked a few notes, fiddling with a box on the ground that the guitar was attached to. From my side, it was just a little suitcase with a radio speaker sticking out of the front. He made sure the volume was quiet enough not to attract the whole school to our bunking off from class, then gave me a grin, sucking in a deep breath before he started to play.

When Tommy had first said he was a good performer, I thought he would just be all right. In all honesty, I didn't even think he would be as good as the boys who played for Mr Frost at the club, I suppose purely because Tommy was only fifteen. But now he was smashing out Buddy Holly's 'Peggy Sue', his fingers flying so fast over the strings that I had to stop watching them and focus on his face. He kept his eyes fixed on a spot past me, concentrating hard on the song as he mixed high notes and deep ones in a perfect blend. He had everything he needed to win V.W.'s show, and I found myself dancing uncontrollably to his beat.

"Wow," I said when the song was over. "You're not going to need to be a mind reader to get what you want out of people!"

"You think it's a good song?" Tommy asked.

"The best song," I answered. "The perfect song to knock them out of their chairs. You're going to win; I just know it."

Tommy shut off his amplifier and set down his guitar, reaching out to squeeze my hand for a moment. His look was so full of gratitude, his little, white teeth gleaming and his eyes shining at me.

"You're the best, Josie," he crooned.

I saw the warning signs of flirtation again and stepped back, clutching my hands together. I couldn't hide how excited I was by his talent, but a certain freckled face popped into my mind.

"You know who would love to hear this?" I told him. "Hanne. She's crazy for Buddy. She cried for weeks when that plane went down. You'd make her so happy if you played it for her, Tommy."

His look evaporated, a paleness setting into his jaw as he shook his head, lips tight. "Oh no," he mumbled. "I wouldn't play it for Hanne. I mean, I couldn't."

My hands came to rest on my hips in a style I knew my mother would be proud of. "Right," I said. "We're having this out now. What have you got against Hanne?"

Tommy looked up, his brow crinkled. "What do you mean?"

"I mean," I continued, "that when she and I are together, you talk to us both happy as Larry. Then you never say a word to her when we're apart, like in that maths class you share. It's just rude to do that, Tommy, so I'm wondering if you have some sort of problem with her."

Tommy's mouth flew open time and again as my accusations kept coming. He put his hand to his chest and waited, his head bobbing as he tried to find a spot in my rant to interrupt me. I didn't let him until I stopped to take a deliberate and judgemental exhale.

"Her mother teaches that class!" Tommy retorted. "You think I just go chatting girls up when their mothers are breathing down my neck?"

"Would you have, if Mrs Haugen wasn't there?" I pressed.

Tommy bit his lip, trying not to grin. "Well sure," he said. "She's as cute as anything."

It was my turn to be confused and outraged. "So you *do* like her?" I asked.

"Look," Tommy said, sweeping his palms out flat, "as soon as you told me about her that first day, I knew I had no chance. Have you *seen* her dad? He's built like John Wayne. And he's a spy *and* a solider. No way was I going to risk a limb flirting with a teacher's daughter, no matter how pretty she is."

"So you thought you'd try me instead?" I demanded.

"You seemed more available," Tommy replied, "until I met Dai Big-head-staff, that is."

I smacked his arm hard, and he winced at me. All this time that Hanne had been moaning about him giving her the silent treatment, and now I'd found out that he was doing it because he liked her. I decided there and then that the only kind of boys I understood were the ones who sung about their feelings on the radio. A thought struck me, and I started to grin.

"You know what?" I said suddenly. "I've decided I don't like that song anymore."

"What?" Tommy said. "What's wrong with it?"

"Well, all the best new boys are writing their own stuff," I replied. "Paul Anka wrote himself a hit when he was younger than you. He was singing it all over the world at sixteen."

"So?" Tommy replied, affronted.

K.C. Finn

"So you should write a song," I said with a wry smile. "A song for a certain girl we both know."

"Oh Josie," he said, shaking his head. "It's too risky. If she didn't like it, I'd be embarrassed my whole life."

I knew that Hanne would love Tommy forever if he wrote her a tune, even if it was no more musically amazing than the alphabet song. I had a feeling Tommy's talent would stretch to making it far more impressive too.

"Paul Anka never got to be with Diana," I reasoned, "but that song did make him an international superstar."

The prospect of that put the gleam back in Tommy's gaze. I clapped him on the shoulder.

"If you're a real artist, you have to write about what's real," I said. "And you never know, Hanne might just fall for your dulcet tones too."

Tommy's pink cheeks flushed even brighter. "You really think they're dulcet?" he said with a chuckle.

"Smooth as honey," I replied.

CHAPTER NINE

Attitude

"Have you seen this clown?" Tommy shouted suddenly. "I hope he's not auditioning. If he is, I'm going to win so easily."

He had appeared at the bar where I was stacking sticky, milky glasses, his sudden outburst almost making me drop the whole tray. Since the announcement that Halfway had its very own talent scout on the premises, the music club had been doubly packed every shift I'd worked in the run-up to the big audition night. Tommy's face was shining with the wetness of humidity as he pointed to the young man on the stage, who was swivelling his hips to both whoops and jeers from the crowd.

"I mean," Tommy continued, "they said he won the Butlin's Elvis Presley lookalike contest. Do you believe that?"

"Josie!"

One of the bar staff was calling me, but the space was so crowded with kids getting drinks and snacks that I couldn't see which. Tommy was still hanging on me for an answer.

"Poor imitation," I said quickly, "and he won't audition. Frosty's not letting any established artists sing for V.W."

"Frosty!" Tommy repeated with a giggle. "Good one."

"JOSIE!"

The source of the shouting had finally appeared in the

form of a flustered young woman covered in milk. She bounded up to me so fast that I had to be careful of the drips flying in every direction.

"We're down to one glass. Get back there and fetch some!" she demanded.

"Going right now," I said through gritted teeth.

I picked up my tray and backed carefully into the kitchen. The sinks were full of half-washed glasses, but the space was completely empty and the back door open once again. After the tense, sticky humidity of the crowd, it was a welcome relief to feel the chilly breeze of an October night creeping into the small room. I grumped over to the sink and started to wash glasses, livid that Jake had such a cool, noiseless temperature to work in whilst I was doomed to weave my way through sweaty, dancing teens all night, wiping up their numerous spillages.

"Hey, that's my job."

I had almost finished three full trays of sparklingly clean glasses by the time Jake appeared. I could see him in the corner of my eye where he loitered at the door.

"It won't be for much longer if you're never here to do it," I replied. "And I'm the one getting all the abuse out front because the shake glasses aren't done."

"So get out of the way and I'll do them," Jake answered. I could hear his back teeth gritted through every word.

I threw him a tea towel over my shoulder. "Dry those."

"I said get out."

I felt him move closer, the tiny hairs on my arms standing up. As I finished the last glass, I turned to face him, placing it on the tray without looking into his eyes. The smell of what I thought was paint fumes came from his breath, but after a moment, I realised what it must have been. I wondered how little was left in his bottle of Bell's that was hidden out in the yard.

"I'm helping you catch up here," I said, drying a glass and still not looking at him. "If we finish it together, it'll be quicker."

Jake raised a hand suddenly, and I flinched. For one horrible moment, I felt like he was going to grab me to get me out of his path. Instead, he picked up a glass and wrapped the tea towel around it, twisting it in his grip. He was much better at drying them than me; I stared at his dark hands as we stood close together, trying to copy his efficient moves. A few moments passed, and my nerves calmed enough to look up at him properly. Jake's golden eyes were miles away, lost to thought as he did his job on automatic.

"How's your hand?" he said suddenly.

"Oh," I said, glancing briefly at the now-healed dent in my palm. "It's good. I used lots of ice like you said. Good tip, that."

Jake nodded awkwardly.

"I never said thank you," I added.

He turned away to find another glass. "Why do you keeping doing that?" he asked.

I looked at his broad back, following the creases in his navy-blue shirt as my brain tried to work out what he was implying. I came up with nothing.

"I don't know what you mean," I answered.

"You're covering for me with Frost," he began, his vowels dropping in that half-American way, "and you could have sold me out to the bar servers for not doing my job here. Why are you such a goody-goody?"

I half-laughed, half-scoffed at the prospect. I was the girl who drifted off and sang song lyrics aloud in lessons. I was the

K.C. Finn

girl who bunked off class to encourage Tommy to write his song for Hanne. I was the girl about to fail the only skill that had ever made me feel remotely important.

"You don't know me that well," I answered.

Jake turned. I had been expecting his usual scowl, but now his face was a picture of sadness. His coffee-coloured skin was tight on his jaw as his eyes flicked around, never really meeting with mine.

"Look," I said sternly, "we're both sixteen. We both work here. I just assumed we were going to be friends, but if you don't want me to be nice to you then, believe me, I'll turn it off. We can be totally robotic with each other."

His black eyebrows curved down, lips pouting. "Why would you want to be my friend?" he asked.

I picked up one of the trays of finished glasses. "Honestly, I'm starting to wonder that myself now," I replied.

He was hurt by that. I actually saw the wince in his look for one brief moment before he covered it with a grimace. I felt a little bad inside, but I held up my resolve.

"Get one of those trays," I added sharply.

Jake's bright eyes widened. "Why?" he demanded.

"You think I'm going to carry three of these back and forth to the bar?" I asked. "Help me."

He shook his head all too quickly. "No way," he replied. "Frost would kill me."

I paused in the doorway that led back to the humdrum of the club. Cocking my head to one side, I took in Jake's raised shoulders and the bright whites I could now see surrounding his golden pupils.

"Are you scared of going out there?" I questioned.

81

Jake's lip curled into a scowl. "If every face out there was black, wouldn't you be?" he answered.

I didn't like his question. I turned and took the first tray out, only to be berated by the bar staff for taking so long. Tommy tried to catch my eye again but I avoided him, racing back into the cool kitchen for the second tray. Jake was waiting right by the door with it for me.

"I don't expect you to understand it," he said.

I took the tray and left again without speaking. I didn't understand it. Would I really feel so different if everyone in here was a different colour to me? I had never thought about anything like that before. It was Jake's attitude that drove me up the wall; the darkness of his skin had never been part of the problem. Unless the two were related in a way I hadn't considered. When I came back for the final tray, he was waiting again, his eyes downcast. I felt awful now that he had suddenly been so helpful and calm.

"How about we start over?" I said as he handed me the last tray. "I'll play the role of 'girl willing to forgive you' and you–"

"I get it," Jake replied. "I'll play 'boy trying really hard not to be a jerk'."

It was the first time I'd ever seen Jake Bolton smile. He didn't smile at me; he was still mostly looking at the ground, but he gave a little nod and the whole shape of his face changed as he flashed bright white teeth just like Noah's. A shout from the other side of the door caught my ear.

"Right then," I replied before I dashed back into the madness.

The place was such a mess after so big a crowd that Frost threw them all out at ten to nine to give us a chance to speed up the cleaning process. I took a mop and bucket over to the stage where a whole table's worth of milkshakes had avalanched, and Noah appeared with thick gloves to pick up the shards of glass amid the mess. I had started to notice that all of Jake's clothes were dark-coloured; he was like an angry shadow swooping down on unsuspecting dust mites with his broom as he circled us. A grim reaper of cleanliness. I was smiling at my own joke when he looked up and caught my eye. He smiled back.

A sudden loud voice boomed across the space. The deep accent made my insides flutter. "All right there, Jo?"

"What are you doing here?" I asked, turning as Dai crossed the floor.

He looked superb in a pale green shirt, his bright eyes shining and his blonde hair slicked back. I suddenly thought how much of a mess I must have looked after so many hours serving in a den of humidity and spilt milk, rushing to smooth down my long hair. Dai didn't seem to notice; he approached and took me by the elbow.

"Leave them do that a minute, eh?" he asked.

We both looked at Noah and Jake. I was surprised to see them suddenly so silent, looking down at the floor like it was terribly interesting to them. Jake's fingers were whitening where he kept a firm grip on his broom.

"Oh," I said. "Don't you want to meet-?"

"Come on," Dai said, leading me away and putting down my broom for me. "My mam's yur. We're going to give you a lift home."

I was starting to walk with him, but I looked back at the

Bolton brothers as they carried on working. "I'm supposed to clean up," I said.

"Nah," Dai replied loudly. "They can manage without you. Come sit with me a minute, love."

He had never called me love before. I'd heard him say it to girls over the years, just a casual thing he added to the end of some sentences, but never to mine. I let him lead me to the other side of the club, near to the door that led to Frost's office.

"Mam's in there talking to that bloke about being a talent judge," Dai explained, "and then we'll give you a lift back up to Peregrine. We've already got your bike on the back of the car."

"Thanks," I said, shifting my weight from foot to foot. "Um, so how's uni? You're back for the weekend?"

"Just for tonight," Dai answered. "I've got to show my face, see? Or Dad'll stop my spending money."

"I bet there are all sorts of things to spend it on in London," I said, grinning as I imagined the freedom of the life he now had.

Dai nodded and tapped his nose. "That's for me to know," he replied.

I giggled far too loudly, a little embarrassed with myself. I heard a clatter and looked back to the dance floor. Jake had dropped his broom. I frowned at him, curious as to why he was still sweeping the same spot as before. He was usually super-fast and over here by now. Before I could meet his eye, the door near us opened. Blod Bickerstaff looked fabulous in a two-piece suit made of silver fabric, her blonde hair curled to perfection. A long arm in a shiny blue suit was hooked around her shoulders, a huge, silver watch dangling from its wrist.

"I think you're going to make a perfect addition to the panel, Mrs B," V.W. said in that schmoozing rasp of his. "You'll bring a bit of class to the table."

"Oh, well, thank you, Vince," Blod replied with a little laugh. "I like to think I know good music when I hear it."

"Come on, Mam. I'm starving," Dai urged.

Blod looked at him, her red lips falling into a rounded 'o' shape. She slapped his arm.

"Don't be so rude!" she chided. "This is V.W.; he's a very important chap, and I don't need you embarrassing me." She turned to V.W. with an apologetic look, putting a hand on his lapel. "This is my son Dai. Don't mind him."

"Good to meet you, young man," V.W. crooned.

He slipped his arm off Blod's shoulders and stepped up, offering his hand to Dai. When they shook, the record mogul gave him that sharp-toothed smile, studying him like a magpie would study something shiny on a windowsill. His narrow eyes fell to me before the shake was even over.

"You all know each other, do you?" V.W. inquired. I just nodded brightly.

"My husband's a physician up at the boarding school," Blod explained. "He's waiting in the car, actually. We ought to go or I'll never hear the end of it."

"I'll walk you out," V.W. offered.

He and Blod went first and Dai stepped up, holding the door open for me. A little flutter began in my stomach again at the sight of his smile. I was halfway through the door when I suddenly remembered something, craning my head back into the room.

"Bye, Noah! Bye, Jake!" I called.

Dai rested his fingertips on the small of my back, pushing me out through the door before I could even hear if they had replied. "You don't have to be so nice to them, you know," Dai muttered against my ear.

Was he jealous? Was I completely mad to even hope that he was jealous? I didn't have time to press him and find out. V.W. stayed in the shadowy doorway of the club, kissing Blod's hand before he let her go. As we walked off, he lit up a cigarette and, by the time we had reached Doctor Bickerstaff's shiny, white car, V.W. was little more than a shadow with a bright orange dot glowing in the middle of his head. Dai held open the door behind the driver's side for me and I clambered in, looking at the doctor in the rearview mirror. His blue eyes were narrowed on the figure in the doorway, deep in thought.

"What's the matter, love?" Blod asked, tapping him on the shoulder.

Bickerstaff shook from his thoughts, glancing at her and then back at the shadowy fellow under Halfway's dark awning. He ran a hand through his silver-blonde hair.

"It's nothing," he said.

It didn't sound like nothing, the way the words came from his lips and his eyes returned to V.W.'s form once more. He started the car, and we were all enveloped by silence most of the way home.

CHAPTER TEN

The Audition

Hanne leant Tommy her bike so the three of us could get to Halfway early on the day of his audition. He gave her the most bashful thank you I had ever seen as he took the bike, but Hanne seemed to miss the flush in his cheek as he rode off ahead of us, his guitar wobbling precariously in the case on his back. Hanne stepped onto the back of my bike and put her hands on my shoulders to keep steady.

"Are you sure he likes me?" she asked as I started to pedal. "Because he never even smiled at me when he said thanks."

"Just you wait," I promised her. "Tommy Asher's going to fall head over heels for you; I know it."

"But *when*?" Hanne asked, squeezing me harder as I sped on down the lane.

I knew exactly when. Tommy had been scribbling away in every meditation class we shared, hiding his book from Miss Cartwright so fiercely that you would have thought he had international secrets laid out on the page. I had disappeared a few times from class to hear him play the melody, but so far, he hadn't let me hear a word of the actual lyrics he was writing in Hanne's honour. When he hummed the tune in his melodious tone, I knew it was going to be great, but I was determined not to spoil the surprise for my best friend. Tommy would win both a place in V.W.'s show and one in Hanne's heart this afternoon, if everything went according to plan.

When we parked up the bikes and entered Halfway, Noah was pushing tables back to make room for the big auditions. I rushed to help him, gathering up loose chairs from around the tables as he shoved them into the far corners of the huge room.

"Thanks, Josie," he said brightly. "Can you line up some chairs next to the stage? Frost wants all the acts in an orderly line over there before they go on."

"Is he expecting a lot?" Tommy asked.

Noah looked up, his wide eyes falling warily on Tommy, who was oblivious and friendly as ever. I gave Noah a pat on the shoulder before I set to work with the chairs.

"This is Tommy and Hanne from my school," I explained. "Tommy's auditioning today." I flashed my friends my best smile. "Say hello to Noah Bolton, you two."

"Nice to meet you."

They had all spoken in unison, the three of them looking at one another and breaking into matching, awkward grins. Tommy set down his guitar and moved to help Noah with a table he was handling. I saw the older boy give him a truly grateful smile.

"I heard Frost say there's people coming up from London to try out for V.W.," Noah said.

"This guy must be something special," Tommy supposed.

"He's a bit odd though," Noah added.

I had returned to where the boys stood to get more chairs, but I paused and put my hands on my hips. "Why?" I demanded.

Noah looked a little cowed. "It's probably nothing," he

said, shaking his head.

I poked him playfully in the shoulder. "Come on," I urged. "What have you heard about him?"

"It's not what I heard," Noah answered. "It's what I saw."

"Well, we're all interested now," Tommy said with a chuckle. "You can't leave us hanging, mate."

The word 'mate' stirred something in the dark boy, and he raised his head. Noah looked between the three of us and perched himself on the table. When Hanne and Tommy leaned in towards his serious look, he seemed to start enjoying the attention. Noah raised his hands, ready to tell us his tale.

"It was so freaky," he began. "V.W. asked me to take him a coffee this morning, right? I knocked on the office door, but there was no answer, so I thought I'd leave the coffee inside in case he'd gone out for a smoke."

"And then what?" Hanne pressed.

"V.W. was in there," Noah replied, "but he didn't even see me. His eyes were wide open but... I don't know. It was like they were totally empty. He was miles away in this daydream. I spoke to him, and he didn't even hear me apologising. Talk about far out."

Two voices shot into my head, one after the other.

Are you thinking what I'm thinking? Tommy asked.

That's too freaky to be a coincidence, Hanne added. *Perhaps he knows about Peregrine Place.*

I turned to get more chairs, shaking their voices away from my thoughts. "He might have been meditating," I suggested out loud.

"Or drunk," Noah chuckled back.

"Yeah," Tommy said warily. "That must have been it."

"Oh shush," Noah said suddenly, raising a hand. The sound of tyres rumbled outside. "That'll be him back from the high street."

He was right. For moments later, the shiny shoes of V.W. clicked in through the front door. A cigarette hung from his lips as he stood and surveyed the huge, empty space and the line of chairs leading to the stage. His narrow eyes swept the room sharply, but when they met mine, he bowed his greying head a little. Flicking the cigarette up behind his ear, V.W. swept across the room to where we were gathered.

"Good job so far, kid," he said with a nod to Noah. "Now all we need is a couple of tables in front of the stage for me and the other two judges."

"Yes, Sir," Noah replied, moving off to get to it.

I moved to help him, but V.W. put a slim, steady hand on my shoulder.

"You haven't introduced me to your friends, Josie," he crooned.

When I glanced at them, I found that I didn't really want to. Tommy was staring up at the record mogul like he was made of solid gold, whilst Hanne was giving him a suspicious, nasty look based, I supposed, on what Noah had just divulged. I reluctantly exchanged names for everyone, and V.W. shook their hands briefly. He was smooth and charming as always, but Hanne's narrow-eyed glare never faltered. V.W. pointed at Tommy's guitar case behind him.

"You got a Strat or a Tele in there?" he asked.

"Oh, a Tele," Tommy said. "I'm here to audition today, Sir."

"I'd guessed that much, kiddo," V.W. replied with a laugh. "Tell you what. How about you go and sit in my office for a while?

Cool your jets right? I'll call you when we're ready to start."

Tommy picked up his guitar, and I noticed how badly his hands were quivering.

"That'd be brilliant," he mumbled. "Thank you."

"Hey," V.W. said, arms wide, "any friend of Josie's is a friend of mine."

He gave Tommy a sharp wink and pointed the way to 'his' office. I was pretty certain it was Frost's office, but maybe the old man had given it up gladly for the likes of V.W. to operate from it.

"You feel free to fix yourself a shake while you wait, cutie," he added to Hanne.

She folded her arms. "I'm fine, thank you."

The tension was clear in her tone, and it was starting to rile me. I really hoped she wasn't going to try anything daft, like poking around in V.W.'s mind. Even if he was psychic like us, I was sure he wasn't going to appreciate the intrusion.

"Is this good for you, Mr Walsh?" Noah asked.

V.W. and I turned together to see the judge's table. Three chairs sat behind three connected tables with a fine white tablecloth over the top.

"Noah Bolton does it again," the mogul said. Noah beamed with pride. "Now go fetch some snacks for the kids while they wait in line, I'm expecting them soon."

"Hey, Noah," I added quickly. He had started moving, but he suddenly jerked to a stop again. "Take Hanne with you. She's good at carrying boxes, and she's not doing anything."

Her mouth fell open. "Neither are you!" she demanded.

"Actually," V.W. said, suddenly putting a hand on my shoulder, "I do need a little word with Josie, so it might be for the best if you helped out Mr Bolton here for a bit."

Hanne gave me her classic 'what are you playing at' glare before she went. I had gotten to know V.W. a little over the last few weeks. If there was a subtle way to discover whether he shared my gift or not, then I thought I'd be more likely to pull it off than Hanne would. V.W. ushered me to the judge's table where we sat down together, silent for a moment.

"So," I said, swinging my legs. "What did you need to tell me?"

"Oh nothing," V.W. chuckled, retrieving his smoke and lighting it up. "It just sounded like you needed a break from your friends."

"I did," I confessed. "Tommy's been stressed all week about this. I don't know what for; he's going to knock you all out when you hear his voice."

V.W.'s sharp jaw broke into a grin. "You sweet on him?" he asked.

"No way," I said immediately, grinning too, "but Hanne is. So that's more drama right there."

"Well, don't worry about Tommy," V.W. replied. "He's got the right face for the business. If he sings and plays even half as good as that, he's a shoe-in for a place in the main contest. I'd put money on it."

My opportunity had reared its head. "Betting man, are you, Mr Walsh?" I said brightly.

He pointed a finger at me. "You've got a tricky look about you," V.W. rasped amid his smoke. "Why'd you ask?"

"I just like to play guessing games," I lied casually, "because I always win."

"Not today," the mogul said immediately. "You name it, I'll guess it better."

It was hard to tell if his confidence was born from pride or actual ability, so I thought hard about what we could guess at that would give me some proper proof. Tommy's nerves were so bad that he would surely be rehearsing a little in the office not far away.

"Bet you can't guess the colour of Tommy's guitar," I challenged.

"Hmm," V.W. said.

He sat forward and let his cigarette drop low in one hand, leaning on the other for a moment. I tried not to let on that I was studying his eyes, but they were so dark and narrow that it was hard to tell whether he was glazed out or not. He tapped one finger on the end of his sharp nose for a few moments.

"Fender Telecaster in yellow with a black panel over the top right corner," he concluded.

"Have you seen it before?" I demanded.

"I'm right, aren't I?" he chuckled.

"That's too specific," I added quickly. "You can't just guess perfect details like that out of the blue."

"Well, I guess I'm cheating then," V.W. said, but he didn't look as though he was serious about that part. "Unless, of course, you can think of a better explanation?"

I could, but I didn't want to say it. Something had made me lean back in my chair, away from V.W.'s dark looks and his sharp-toothed grin. He looked, in that moment, like a shark ready to snap. His stare was unblinking as he continued to meet my gaze, waiting for my reply, like he was goading me to say the thing that we both already knew. Had he rumbled me before I'd even started this little game with him? Was Hanne right that he might already know about Peregrine Place and what the school was really for?

You're psychic, like me.

I felt myself thinking it. A second later, V.W. winked.

There was no time for him to speak. Knocking began at the door and he rose, gliding over to open it to a sudden stream of people. Most of them were youngsters, somewhere between fifteen and twenty-five, plenty of them carrying guitars and wearing smart jackets and bright-coloured ties. It made me worry that Tommy ought to have dressed up. Amid the throng that V.W. was directing, I saw a bright blonde hairdo making her way towards him.

"That's it, kids; contestants have a seat there," V.W. was saying over the din. "Friends can loiter at the back, and snacks are coming. There she is—my bombshell! How are you today, my dear?"

Blod Bickerstaff took V.W.'s hand as he led her out of the pack of eager teens. "You'll have to excuse me, Vince," she said, clearly flustered. "I was doing my bit setting up for lunch at the manor. I feel just awful leaving poor Claudette in the lurch."

I had never seen V.W. stunned before, but there was a moment where he just grinned and mumbled a little, his smile all too fixed on his angular face. He scratched at his jaw briefly. "Your husband's not coming to see the fun?" he asked.

"Oh no," Blod said with wide eyes. "Steven hates the new music. We went to Butlin's a couple of years back and they were playing it through the tannoy, see? He pulled the wires out! I thought they were going to have him for criminal damages!"

V.W. gave a huge, raspy laugh. "Everyone's a criminal these days," he said, guiding Blod to her seat.

Noah and Hanne had returned with the snacks, but it was

time for Noah to get on with clearing the backyard. He seemed all too happy to leave the main room, and it made me remember what Jake had said about being a different colour to everyone else. Every kid auditioning was white-skinned. It made me wonder where people like Sam Cooke and Chubby Checker had come from; perhaps only America had coloured singers in its bars. As I scanned the kids, a group of older boys caught my attention, particularly one tall, blonde figure in the bunch. I leaned down beside Blod at her chair.

"Is that Dai?" I asked.

"Oh yes, love," she answered. "He's not singing, mind you. His friends are part of a four piece. See them there in the blue jackets?"

I nodded. Beyond Dai sat a line of harsh-looking boys in thin-lapel jackets. They were stern and serious in their expressions as they eyed the stage and everyone else around them. Dai was grinning and replying to them jovially, but their dark glares never faltered. They made my spine quiver, and I looked away from them to find V.W. approaching.

"I'll go get your mate," he said with a smile, "Do you think he'd be better to get it over with first?"

"Definitely," I added, cringing at the thought of Tommy waiting in line with the twenty-odd acts that were gathered by the wall.

Mr Frost arrived and took his seat as V.W.'s other judge. I took some snacks around to the people present, quickly bypassing Dai's lot and rounding back to the bar where Hanne was waiting. She was biting at her nail and watching the direction from which Tommy and V.W. would emerge soon.

"Noah's nice," Hanne mused. "I didn't know coloured

people were so nice."

"Of course they are," I said, rolling my eyes. "They're not bloody aliens."

"I've never met one before," Hanne said with a defensive shrug.

Tommy emerged, his Tele slung over his shoulders like he was already a star. V.W. took him up to the stage and rubbed his shoulders for a moment in the style of a boxing coach before a big fight. He whispered something in Tommy's ear, and the boy's face turned serious and resilient. Tommy plugged in his guitar as V.W. clapped his hands together.

"Let's get going then," he called to everyone. "Please welcome Tommy Asher."

Hanne and I started a cheer that caught on. I noticed that Dai and his friends didn't join in. Tommy took up his stance to play as the cheering died down, looking out over the crowd. He found my eyes, and I gave him a huge thumbs-up. His gaze flicked to Hanne for a minute, and then he bit his lip, looking up at the ceiling. I waited excitedly as he began to strum his introduction.

"Buddy Holly!" Hanne squealed as soon as Tommy started to sing. "Oh, I love this one!"

Buddy Holly? What had happened to the song he'd been working on for days on end for Hanne? Tommy looked out into the crowd and at the judges, smiling and beaming as he smashed out the notes and sang for all he was worth. V.W. and Blod were both clapping along in delight. I glared at him over the fracas, and he was actively trying not to meet my eye whilst he got through the song. Hanne poked me in the crook of my elbow.

"What's that face for?" she said accusingly. "You're

supposed to be supporting him!"

I thought I had been, until now. When Tommy descended the stage, there was rapturous applause. Nobody could deny how superb his performance had been; V.W. got up to shake his hand at the end, and the next kid in line looked four times as intimidated as he had before. Only Dai's friends were still irritatingly cool where they lounged in their ugly jackets.

"Wow!" V.W. roared. "This is going to be one heck of a show already!"

Tommy was still grinning until he made it to us at the bar. Hanne was full of congratulations for him, but I folded my arms and looked out to the stage, ready to watch the act that had to follow him.

I'm sorry, came Tommy's quiet voice in my mind. *I bottled it. There are too many people here.*

I ignored him completely and cheered for the nervous singer coming next.

CHAPTER ELEVEN

The Weight of the World

How difficult would it really be for Tommy to just tell Hanne that he liked her? I tried suggesting that he could sing his song for her any time in private at the manor, but he wouldn't hear anything about it, so I eventually gave up. Hanne didn't like that I was ignoring him when we went to class with Miss Cartwright. It made Tommy moody and less likely to chat with her. I didn't care. He didn't deserve to chat with her if he wasn't going to be honest about his feelings.

Miss Cartwright was in her usual acidic mood when we started our studies for the day. She had us reading from her prized textbook and discussing the finer points of what she called 'deep listening', the skill of interpreting subtle noises inside the minds of others to decipher their thoughts. Most of the class were fascinated by the idea, but I had heard it all last year. I knew that I was never going to be adept enough to do that kind of thing; I couldn't even stand to stay in someone else's head for a moment, let alone keep calm enough to hear the madness going on in their brains.

"You're supposed to be making notes," Hanne told me.

"Stuff the notes," I grumbled, leaning on one hand.

Hanne took my book away and started making them

for me; all the while, I could see her glancing over my shoulder. Tommy was working with the boy to his right, so she could only be watching the back of his useless, Brylcreem-coated head. He had passed his audition with flying colours, but he was still a scaredy-cat to me. Everything had taken a definite slump in the wrong direction since audition day, and every moment that I spent in class was only making me yearn for the weekend.

"What do you think about the theory of inner voice?" Hanne asked, obviously trying to get me to participate.

"I think it's preferable to your outer one right now," I snapped back.

She put her head down and started writing again. I tapped my fingers on the table, a Chuck Berry song starting to float through my head. A hand covered in silver rings flashed through my mind. I still needed to talk to V.W. again. I was certain now that he'd meant exactly what I suspected he was inferring—that he was psychic and, perhaps, he knew that I was too. He had reached out to me, but we'd been interrupted by the auditionees piling in, so now I didn't know how I would get back to the topic when I saw him again on Saturday. I wondered if he might be a more useful source of advice than the neurotic bunch who surrounded me at Peregrine Place.

"Neurotic indeed?" asked a voice behind me. "That's a new word for you, Josephine."

I let my head fall forward onto the desk with a groan. "You know," I said, my lips almost touching the varnished wood, "I think it's a disgusting invasion of privacy that you just wander through our thoughts like that, *Miss*."

Miss Cartwright rounded the table, crouching down beside where my head was half-hidden. "Believe me," she said sternly, "I really don't enjoy the vast majority of what I hear. If I could turn it off, I would, but your reluctance today is very, very loud in my head."

I hated everything about the way she spoke to me. It was starting to feel like everyone around me was determined to confuse and complicate my life. The stress of the moment was far too much; all I wanted was some peace. I sat up straight, sucking back the frustrated tears that were threatening to leak from my eyes.

"Well," I said sharply, "I think I know how to fix your problem." I got up and walked straight out of the room.

Though I could tell in my other lessons that people were spreading the word of me being so cheeky to the ironclad Miss Cartwright, my storm-off during meditation class didn't seem to have got back to Mum. I made it all the way to Saturday lunchtime without her finding out and was more than happy to cycle down in the autumn rain and reach Halfway. I parked my bike beside the Bolton brothers' car and hid under the awning at the kitchen door for a moment, trying to fix my hair after it had been exposed to the breeze and the drizzle.

The sink taps were running already in the kitchen, but as I stood there, preening, I heard another sound. Someone was singing in the kitchen. I pressed my ear up to the little gap in the back door. It hardly took me any time to recognise the song; it was a recent hit from early summer that I played at home on repeat. 'Cupid'. And the boy singing it was a dead ringer for Sam Cooke. He hit every note in a smooth, deep melody, keeping perfect time with the song, even though he had no music to accompany him. I stood there in the damp atmosphere, totally transfixed by the sound of him, all the way to the end of the song.

I let the door creak open and stepped slowly inside. Jake was elbow-deep in soapsuds, his lips parting like he was about to start another song, when he suddenly saw me coming in. Hesitation flashed quickly over his golden eyes.

"Oh it's you," he muttered. "There's a clean towel behind me if you want to dry off."

"Thanks, Jake," I said. The last thing I needed was any more tension, so when I was next to him with the towel I added, "Nice singing."

He dropped his head, staring intently at the soapsuds. "Right," he replied flatly.

"No, I mean it," I pressed. "You were… brilliant. You sound like Sam Cooke."

Jake nodded slowly. I could only see the side of his face, but he didn't look like he was scowling any more. "I like Cooke all right," he answered, "but Berry and Presley are the best. They've got more rhythm."

"I know," I replied, suddenly feeling brighter. "Did you hear 'I Feel So Bad' on the radio this week? I want to buy it with my wages."

"It's a double single," Jake answered. "The other track's a country ballad. Weird mixture if you ask me."

"Not as weird as Ken Dodd," I said with a laugh. "He's higher in the charts than Craig Douglas. How does something like that even happen?"

Jake laughed. It was a deep laugh, deep as the notes he'd pulled when he thought nobody could hear him. He swivelled and took the towel from me. I watched him pushing the bright white suds off his coffee-coloured hands. It made me think of all the pale-faced kids who'd been trying to audition for V.W. the week before.

"You know what you should do?" I began. "You should audition for V.W.'s show. You'd float all the way to the finals with a tone like that."

His smile fell away. "Don't be silly," he said, that spiteful edge creeping back into his voice. "I can't go doing things like that."

"Why not?" I pressed.

Jake stared at me for a moment and I could see the anger bubbling in him, reminding me of the mess he was inside.

"I wonder what you see sometimes when you look at me," he griped. "Take a long look, Josie. You see anything here that might put V.W. off the idea of having me on his stage?" He pointed viciously at his own face. "I'm not even allowed in the main room when there are people here."

I shook my head immediately. "A talent's a talent," I insisted. "V.W.'s not going to care about your skin."

Jake's bright eyes narrowed cruelly. "You really look up to that guy, don't you?" he asked. "He's a sneak, Josie. He's a fake and a creeper, I'm sure of it."

"You're just saying that to make excuses not to audition," I bit back, not wanting to hear anything that I'd just heard.

"He won't want me on that stage," Jake insisted.

"But Sam Cooke and Chuck Berry-"

"Are making it in the States," he interrupted. "And they're still getting booed off and shot at by a bunch of white people who don't see their talent the way you and I do. This world is not

102

how you think it is."

Jake turned back to the sink, his head dipping low.

"V.W. likes Noah," I countered bitterly. "Maybe if you were nicer to people, it wouldn't matter to them what colour you are."

He gripped the metal edge of the sink hard. "You don't know anything about it, Josie," he snarled. "You're just a stupid kid."

The one place I thought I could go to and unwind had let me down. I stormed from the kitchen and refused to go back in there all night, leaving it to the bar staff to exchange the dirty glasses that I collected with Jake. V.W. was nowhere to be found on my shift, ruining my plans to find out about his potential powers. There was only Frost barking orders at me as I rushed to clean up spilt milk and, to my horror, vomit, on the dance floor. I exhausted myself rushing back and forth for hours, not even stopping for a break as my bad mood boiled over.

Frost sent me home a little early. I was fuming as I forced the door of my home to swing open with a bang. I kicked off my shoes in the doorway, letting them hit the wall with two loud thumps, and dropped my bag on the floor as I turned to slam the interior door shut again. My whole body felt heavy and empty against it from so much anger and so many un-cried tears. I spun, ready to collapse onto the old, broken sofa and smash my fist into a few pillows to get rid of this horrible feeling inside me.

That was when I saw Mum sitting at the kitchen table. She was facing the front door, looking oddly rested and strangely still. She watched me with patient eyes, her arms folded in front of her on the dark, round table. Her hands were resting on top of a book. I approached the table, cowed into silence by her strangeness, looking down at the book's title. **Techniques of the Synsk, by Faye Cartwright.** I felt a sudden dryness in my throat. Mum raised a slim finger.

"Don't say a word," she began. "Just sit."

I did as I was told, all my rage from the fight with Jake and my horrible shift abating, only to leave a fearful emptiness in the bottom of my stomach.

"I 'ad a little talk with Miss Cartwright today," Mum said. "She told me all about your little outburst with 'er this week and 'ow your skills in the meditation are fading. You're not working 'ard enough, Josephine."

"It's not that!" I protested immediately.

I didn't know how to explain it to her, the way that deep thinking gripped me so totally, how it felt like I would never get back into my own body if I visited someone else's mind. Mum wasn't psychic; she wouldn't be able to picture the way the double screen happened in my head when my powers left me halfway between the place I was in and the one I was trying to get to. I wanted to describe it for her, but I was so upset that all the words in my head were a jumble. Mum was already riled by my tone, her face growing harsher as her mouth fell open at my outburst.

"You're right!" she shouted back. "It's not *just* that. It's that you're more interested in records and pop charts than your studies. It's that you'd rather disappear from 'istory class to spend time with boys-"

My mouth fell open.

"Oh *oui*," Mum said, the pitch of her voice getting higher. "I just discovered that one today! And you know what else, Josie? It's that you'd rather be out there in the world at that job of yours than 'ere, with your own kind of people."

104

"My *kind* of people?" I asked. "What are you on about?"

"You 'ave a gift, Josie," Mum pleaded. She reached out and took both my hands across the table. "You 'ave a special, supernatural ability, one that could 'elp so many people. Your focus should be 'ere at Peregrine, where you can learn to serve your country."

I wriggled my fingers free of her grasp, dropping my hands into my lap. Three lectures in two days. Three lectures from people who thought they had a right to tell me how to behave and what the world expected from me. I felt my skin prickling with heat all over as I sat with my teeth gritted tightly together. A long silence fell upon us, but Mum was resolute, waiting for my answer with a sternness in her gaze that I detested.

"What if I don't want to serve my country?" I asked, quiet but spiteful. "What if my path is different?"

"You weren't given this power to just throw it away!" Mum retorted.

"No," I bit back, rising from my chair, "I got it because *you* made a mistake with some dodgy bloke sixteen years ago!"

I had crossed a line. I knew it as soon as the words flew from my lips but, once they were spoken, there was nothing I could do. I watched Mum's face contort with shock, hanging in that awful state of surprise for a few seconds before her expression returned to anger. She rose too, looking down at me, her eyes glistening.

"If that's 'ow you feel," she said. She tried for a nonchalant shrug, but she was already shaking like she was going to cry. "No matter. One month, Josephine. You 'ave one month to improve before I make you quit that job. You work, you babysit, and you study, study, study. Nothing else. One month and then we'll see."

A Place Halfway

Her voice was shaking too by the end of her words. She walked away and I stood, dumbfounded, until I heard her bedroom door close with a click. I wanted to run after her instantly, to tell her how sorry I was for what I'd said about her and my father. But what was the point? She had told me exactly what I'd have to do to make up for the mess I'd been slowly sliding into since the start of term. I should have known that it was coming, but it didn't stop from me being devastated now that the moment was here.

CHAPTER TWELVE

Things That Go Bump in the Night

V.W. pitched a brilliant money-making idea to Frost that month. The Saturday before Halloween, Halfway was going to be transformed into a spooky-style party venue, for which all the teens would pay their ticket money on the door to get in. At first, Mum was livid at the prospect of me going to a party (whether I happened to be working there or not), but when Frost offered me a lift home and double pay to stay late, my mother thawed out slowly on the idea. I tried to steer clear of begging or pleading so as not to wind her up, going with the tried and tested line: "Whatever you say, that's what I'll do."

It was the best way with Mum, and things had been like that for me since the day that Miss Cartwright delivered her textbook to my flat. The moment I finished lessons I had to go to Mum in the kitchens, book in hand, and study all the way until dinner was ready. Even though she was swamped by her cooking duties, Mum took special care to keep passing by to make sure I was actually turning pages. It wasn't a case of me not reading the textbook, but more a case of me not making sense of anything that was written it in.

There are two states of conscious being. The first state is the usual consciousness, in which one's mind is solely focused

on one's own existence. For the Synsk, the second state of consciousness is that of entering the mind of another and experiencing, to varying degrees, the intensity of that person's actions, emotions, and sometimes even their thoughts.

I broke from the book often when Miss Cartwright wrote about mind reading, because every time I thought about it, the image of Jake Bolton popped into my head. I hated his intrusion in my mind; the sight of his angry expression, the shape that his dark lips made when he called me stupid. If I ever did get the power to read thoughts, I sincerely wanted to read his. I wanted to know what he thought this world was about and what had happened to make him so confident that he knew *everything* and that *I* was an ignorant little kid. Sometimes I got so wound up in those thoughts that the textbook's hard edges curled under my fingertips.

I had another problem with the two states of consciousness. I had never read the textbook from cover to cover before and, the more I read, the less I found about the halfway state that my mind seemed to go to. Nowhere did Miss Cartwright describe a situation in which a psychic could be both in the current moment and in the mind of someone else, yet whenever I let my mind slip away, that duality seemed to be my normal state. In the book, the two states of consciousness were an all or nothing kind of thing. Even without her scathing presence beside me, I could hear Miss Cartwright's voice telling me that I didn't fit in with the rest of the students at Peregrine Place.

"'ow are you doing with that?"

I looked up into Mum's flustered face. She was peering at me over a pan of mushy peas, the green goo bubbling in thick lumps.

"Better," I lied with a smile. "For example," I added, "I just learned that a psychic can only connect to the minds of the living, never the dead."

Mum returned my smile approvingly.

"Is it all right for Hanne to come over later?" I added quickly.

She paused in stirring the peas, giving me a suspicious glare.

"It's not for fun," I assured her. "Mr Frost wants me to wear a costume when I work at the party tomorrow, but I don't have one. Hanne's bringing some things for me to try on."

Hanne was going with Alice in Wonderland, her costume of choice. To my memory, she had never worn anything scary for a Halloween shindig in her entire life. In fact, all of her costumes for parties were plucked straight from whimsical children's books. The thought of her second wardrobe in the spare room gave me a short, sad moment. I had never had the money spare to have even one costume, let alone a father who was still so adept at tailoring as to make me anything I wanted at the drop of a hat. It made me wonder if my own father would have made things for me, if he'd been around. Would he have whittled toys out of wood for me to play with? I shook the thought off. He was probably a cash man, the kind who would have thrown a few coins at me with a grin.

"What are you smiling at?" Hanne asked. Her bright eyes lit up. "Is it a boy? Is it Dai? It's Dai, isn't it?"

"Shush," I said, shaking my head at her. "I'm just relieved to have a break from H.M.P. Cartwright."

"You've been paroled for one night only," Hanne giggled back. "Try these on."

She handed me a pair of furry triangles on a black headband. I turned them right side up, discovering what they actually were.

"Cat ears?" I questioned. "Why do you even *have* cat ears?"

"Do you not remember doing Dick Whittington on stage when we were tiny?" she asked.

"I've put those sorts of memories far behind me," I assured her.

It had been a long time since Peregrine Place had put on a school play. I could still remember early attempts to present the school as a normal place, like the time when Leighton had sung like a strangled cat in the choir service and the roof had started to leak, as though God himself was asking Leigh to cease. Over the years, the school had receded from public view in order to hide its secrets better. Since the news came over the radio that America was doubling its troops in Vietnam, Peregrine Place hadn't had a single visitor who wasn't in the know about the ways of psychics. I put on my cat ears, my lips pouting out in thought.

"Do you ever wonder what you're going to do when you get out of this place?" I asked.

Hanne shrugged. "I'll go into field work like Mum and Uncle Leigh," she said, "or maybe teach here."

I could well believe that Hanne would be happy to be confined to Peregrine Place her whole life; it was the perfect combination of studying and structure that she adored. All I could think of was how annoying it would be to still be rooted to this place after I'd finished my education, especially if Mum stayed on as the cook. Perhaps if I didn't squander my wages, I could save us up enough to start over somewhere new in a couple of years' time.

"Well, all my costumes are too small for you," Hanne huffed. "You might need to buy one."

I shook my head, pointing at the ears still fixed to it.

"Oh Josie," Hanne said with an eye roll. "You can't just do ears. Didn't Frost say a proper costume? He'll brain you."

"I've just thought of something," I said.

After a quick scuffle in the wardrobe, I approached Hanne with a black dress draped over my arm. It had a lace petticoat creeping out under its hem and a thick ribbon at the back that sort of dangled down like a cat's tail. The dress was a hand-me-down from Mum, but it was shiny and looked as though it had never been worn. I suspected that, in her younger days, Mum had probably only ever worn it for funerals. Hanne gave it a critical glare.

"You can draw some whiskers and a nose on me with an eyebrow pencil," I reasoned, "and then I'll still be able to wipe tables without some clunky costume getting in the way."

"That's a plan then," Hanne replied flatly.

She set down some of the accessories she was messing with, suddenly resting her face in her hands like a cherub. A serene smile washed over her features. "What do you think Tommy's going to wear?" she asked.

Tommy Asher still wasn't my favourite conversation piece, but I'd slowly been thawing out over his total lack of guts at the audition. He had insisted recently that he was still working on the song for Hanne, but that it was not yet ready. Choosing to believe him was easier than keeping yet another grudge going. I had enough on my plate, between Miss Cartwright and Jake

Bolton, to keep me griping to the end of the year as it was.

"Whatever he wears, you're going to think it's the best thing ever," I concluded.

"I know," Hanne squealed in delight. "Romance is great, isn't it?"

I said nothing, struggling to find a reply that wouldn't deflate her rosy grin.

Halloween at Halfway, as V.W. had proudly named it, was an overwhelming success. Every kid that was fourteen or older had come down from Peregrine Place, and all the teens from the local grammar school seemed to be gathering around the dance floor in packs. There were plenty of older people too, of university age. As the night wore on, the age balance of the venue was steadily shifting in their direction. I wore my half-cat creation, but I was sweating so much in the humid space that my whiskers had washed clean off my face by eight o'clock.

It was all hands on deck in the music bar, but we were all far too busy to even notice each other, let alone break into conversation. Jake and I were civil and silent as we hurriedly exchanged glasses in the kitchen, kids were shovelling ice cream down their throats faster than Noah could refill it in the back fridge, and V.W. was circulating the room, getting people to commit to attending the first big heat of his talent show. Tommy's real competition would begin in just a couple of weeks' time. The chance for all his musical dreams to come true was waiting so nearby that it made me a little jealous.

He had dressed as Elvis Presley for the occasion, which

reassured me that he and Hanne were definitely compatible, since neither of them had a clue what a proper Halloween costume should have been like. I had seen enough Universal Horror to inspire a lifetime's worth of proper looks, but most people in the crowded music club had simply come dressed to impress. The university boys were all wearing suits. I saw a pack of them enter the venue as I was collecting glasses, thrilled to see a familiar blonde figure leading them in.

Dai wouldn't have seen me if I'd tried to wave, the place was far too crowded, so I let myself watch him for a moment as he scoped out the bar. Behind him were his companions, the pasty, surly foursome I had seen trying to sing for V.W. on audition day. The mogul hadn't been very polite in his commentary of their alleged talents and I'd had to stifle a laugh when he referred to them as the Unrighteous Brothers. One of the group, a tall boy with dark hair pressed flat against his head, put his hands on Dai's shoulders and said something close to his ear. Dai nodded fiercely, pushing his way to the front of the bar to get them some drinks.

I decided it would be a good time to change some glasses over with Jake. If I timed it right, I could bring out a fresh tray whilst the bar staff were serving Dai and I'd be able to at least get a glimpse of his handsome face close up. When I entered the kitchen, I found it deserted, the back door ajar like it always was. Night was closing in with an inky blue glow outside. I couldn't see Jake, but I knew where he'd be and what he'd be doing. A sigh escaped me as I washed a few glasses, my heart sinking as I pondered what was so great about sipping whiskey on your breaks.

"Something wrong, kitten?"

A Place Halfway

I spun at the voice, shocked by the stranger standing close behind me. It was the flat-haired guy who had spoken to Dai moments before. He must have followed me into the kitchen only seconds ago, which meant he'd made a beeline for me in order to get there so fast. That fact did not escape me as I looked at his smug smile, which crept unevenly up the right side of his face. He was even paler close up, with beady eyes and a long thin, nose.

"You're not supposed to be back here," I said, trying to hide the quiver in my voice, "it's staff only."

"But you won't tell on me, will you?" he mock pleaded. "You're a friend of Dai Bickerstaff, right? He talks sometimes about how sweet you are. I can see now that he was right."

I didn't have time to process the idea that Dai could have said anything like that about me, because the flat-haired crawler was advancing. I leant on the sink, debating whether to reach for a glass or not. I didn't even know what I would use it for if the boy came any closer.

"Who are you then?" I asked.

"Gil Croft," he answered, flicking a speck of dust from his lapel. "I'm one of the new presidents of the London Light."

The yellow invitation I had found in Dai's pocket returned to my memory. "That's some posh club, right?" I asked Gil, stalling for time and hoping someone else was going to need to use the kitchen soon.

He nodded, smoothing his hair down even flatter against his forehead. "Very exclusive," he agreed. "We only accept the best."

That was clearly what he thought of himself. I could feel goose pimples rising on my bare arms in the cold atmosphere of the kitchen, but my palms were clammy as I fumbled against the sink edge. Gil took a wide step in the narrow space, standing over me directly in the way of both the back door and the door that led back to the throng of Halfway. No way out. I felt a tightness in my stomach and my heart beat loudly in my ears as he gave me that awful lopsided smile again.

"It must be hard for you," Gil crooned in a sickly-sweet tone. "Being such a pretty girl and having to work instead of party."

He reached out and let his pale fingers trail down through my hair. By the time they reached my shoulder, I had all but leapt away from him, shaking my head forcefully as fear continued to build.

"Don't do that," I said. I couldn't believe how weak I sounded.

"Relax," Gil replied. "It's a just a bit of fun."

Even though he was skinny, up close, he was taller than I was and I couldn't help noticing how strong his hands looked as they approached my arm. He took hold of me at the elbow and I struggled away from his grip, but I was right about his strength. He held me fast and shook his head.

"This isn't fun for me," I insisted, eyes flashing everywhere at once, looking for something large that I could grab to hit him with. There was nothing useful in my reach.

"It will be, once you get going," he said.

There was a darkness in his eyes as he yanked me closer. I tried to get away but he locked his arms around my shoulders and tried to kiss me, his foul lips half-open right in front of my eyes. I squealed like a child, tears brimming in my eyes.

"No please," I sobbed. "I don't want to. I don't-"

A Place Halfway

And then Gil Croft was gone. It took me a moment to work out what was happening; the flurry of movement was so swift that my eyes could scarcely keep track. Gil flew backwards through the air like he was being pulled on an elastic band, then there was another figure who rounded him and dropped him to the ground with a sound punch to the gut. I saw Gil's eyes bulge at the impact before he crumpled. The dark brown fist that had thumped him cracked its knuckles.

"She said no, you pasty creeper," Jake snarled.

"What do you know about it?" Gil wheezed on the floor. "You dirty, black-"

Jake kicked him hard and Gil flipped onto his back, his long arms flailing at his sides to try and deflect the attack. I saw the fire in Jake's golden eyes, a little foam rising on his dark lip as he lined up another attack. I rushed forward as Jake started kicking Gil repeatedly in his exposed side, grabbing him by the shoulders to pull him back. My whole body was shaking as I tugged at his strong chest, throwing my arms around him.

"It's okay," I yelled. "Jake, it's okay. You've stopped him. Let him go. Let him go."

As I worked to restrain Jake, Gil scrambled away, clutching his side and muttering something venomous that neither of us could hear. When he was gone, there was just Jake and me, with my arms wrapped around his heavy, panting chest and the feel of my heartbeat smashing against his back. I let him go slowly and he took as few steps away from me, staring at the door to the club with his fists clenched.

"If that happens again, you call me straight away," he said, not looking back at me even for a moment. "Do you hear me, Josie?"

"I do," I breathed, tears starting to fall. "Thank you."

"Don't," Jake answered, his voice as harsh as it had been the first day we met. "It's no big thing. It's what anyone would have done. Get back in there, where it's crowded and safe."

I didn't understand what he thought was unsafe about the kitchen now that it was just us standing there. I watched his fists; thick veins on his knuckles rippled and shifted as he moved his tense fingers, like he was digging his fingernails into his palms. A few deep breaths later, I sucked up my tears, returning to the busy club to find that Dai and his friends had left. I was suddenly overwhelmed with gratitude that Mr Frost was going to give me a lift home.

CHAPTER THIRTEEN

Opportunity Knocks

I didn't tell anyone what had happened with Gil and Jake, not even Hanne. I thought it might frighten her to know that creepers like Gil were out in our local area. In truth, it had frightened me more than I would willingly admit, and I found myself glad that I was in my mother's constant company each night as I continued to study from Miss Cartwright's book. The book had some passages on techniques of psychic disablement and distraction that I suddenly became very interested in, but they all required high levels of deep thinking that I knew I just couldn't do. Even my extra gifts couldn't defend me from the likes of Gil Croft.

I was relieved to see Halfway so peaceful and quiet when I arrived at work the following Saturday. It seemed as though the sun had made a special appearance to lift the shadows of my day, despite there being a crisp November breeze in the air. Frost sent me straight to Noah for the usual snack unload, and we traipsed back and forth from the stockroom with boxes galore. As we worked, the strains of a familiar melody travelled to my ears from the kitchen. I struggled to hear them properly, but the low tones and punchy rhythm sounded like an Elvis track. Only I knew full well it wasn't Elvis that was singing.

"Hound Dog," Noah said with a faint smile. "Dad's favourite song. He always says, 'That son of mine is gonna be a star someday'." I liked his impression of his father's Deep-South American timbre.

"He must be in a good mood," I said, still struggling to pick up Jake's notes through the wall.

"I wouldn't bet on it," Noah replied. He set down a few boxes, his smile fading once more. It should have been a funny remark, but there was something off in his demeanour today that stopped me from laughing at the comment.

"Are you all right?" I asked.

"Yep," he said immediately, starting off for more boxes.

I could hardly keep up with his long-legged strides as I raced to follow him. He didn't sound all right in the least. I wondered if there was some universal law that meant that both Bolton brothers couldn't be happy at the same time, but the musing quickly passed as I returned to the main room. The sound of clicking footsteps caught my ears. As I was dropping off the last of the snack boxes, V.W. emerged from Frost's office, running an impatient hand through his wave of dark, greying hair. He didn't look cool and collected like he normally was. The mogul crossed to a far table and sat down alone, poring over a sheet of paper in his other hand.

"I'm going to start sweeping," Noah said, all tone absent from his voice. He was gone before I could even respond.

"Damn it," V.W. murmured.

He had put the paper flat on the table, now leaning on both his hands and staring at the page like it was going to do something magical for him at any given moment. I took a bottle of pop from the bar, wrenched it open, and crossed the floor to where he sat. We were alone for the first time since he'd made those hints about guessing things too accurately. If I could fix whatever problem was vexing him, then maybe I could start reopening that conversation and figure out what he'd meant by the words he'd said.

"Can I help?" I said brightly.

"Not unless you can sing or dance, kiddo," V.W. said. He eyed the bottle and took it from me. "Pity Frost doesn't keep anything stronger around here."

"What's the problem?" I asked, peering at the page on the table.

It looked like a time schedule. I saw the name Tommy Asher written near the top of the paper. V.W. took a deep swig of the drink. I heard him swallow loudly, noticing for the first time that he had some sort of mark at the base of his neck. It looked like the end of a written word, probably a tattoo, but it was disappearing down the edge of his high-collared shirt. He tapped a beringed finger at the page where a name had been crossed out.

"This girl from Orpington dropped out," he said in his smoky rasp. "She was bloody good too, voice like Patsy Cline. So now I'm short a singer and the schedule's off."

A brilliant thought struck me. I held out my hand, palm up. V.W. looked at it, then up at my face. His sharp features looked softer than usual that day.

"Come on," I urged.

He took my hand. I led him swiftly up to the bar, turning back to put one finger to my lips. V.W. nodded, grinning as he gripped my fingers. I felt his silver watch banging against my thumb. We crept along to the kitchen door, where Jake's faint

120

notes could still be heard. I let go of V.W.'s hand and tiptoed forward, pressing both palms flat against the door and pushing it open ever so slightly. The gap widened silently, releasing the full volume of Jake's lyrics into the main room.

He had moved on to a Bobby Darin number, though his natural voice was lower and smoother than the original. I could hear him sloshing dishwater at the same time as he sang. I turned back to see V.W.'s reaction. His narrow eyes were closed as he listened, his mouth breaking into that familiar, sharp-toothed grin. His head bounced along to the beat and, when he opened his eyes again, he nodded at me gleefully. V.W. signalled a big thumbs-up, then passed me by and took hold of the half-open door.

"Well," he said loudly, entering the kitchen, "with pipes like that, you're mixing with the wrong kind of plumbing, kid."

I followed V.W. hastily into the kitchen. Jake froze, his hands dripping in mid-air. Three languid drips fell from his soapy fingers before he found the courage to turn around. He looked surprised to see me standing there too, glancing between V.W. and me, but never really settling his gaze on either one of us.

"He's really good, isn't he?" I said, looking up at the record mogul.

"Good?" V.W. asked. "He's golden. This is the next Chuck Berry right here, Josie. I could do a lot with a voice like that in my show."

"Oh," Jake said, looking flustered. His gaze fell to the floor. "Oh no, Mr Walsh, I couldn't do that. It wouldn't be right, someone like me out on that stage."

"Are you joking?" V.W. urged. "Aside from Tommy Asher, I've got a bunch of spotty, crooning kiddies trying to be Sinatra.

You, my friend, are exactly what this contest needs."

Jake flinched when the mogul said 'friend', but I could see the soft glint of hope building in his eyes. I remembered his earlier fears as I watched him rub his fingers together, trying to dry them.

"You could try it once," I offered. "Do the first heat. If you don't like it, then you can stop. There's no harm in that, is there?"

V.W. put his arm across my shoulders. "Listen to this girl, kid. She could be good for you."

It was hard to tell because of the dark hue in his face, but I could have sworn Jake was starting to blush. He didn't quite make it to a full smile, but his bright teeth were showing a little as he spoke again.

"I don't play a guitar or anything," he mumbled.

V.W. shook his head. "No need. I've got a backing band coming in for people who need them. They'll play any hit you want, son."

Jake let out a slow breath. "I guess I could try it then."

"That's my boy," V.W. said, reaching out and slapping Jake jovially on the back of his shoulder. I heard the thump against his solid muscles, a strange quiver running through me as a flash of a memory hit my mind. What it had been like to hold his broad chest was lingering somewhere in a shadowy corner of my thoughts. I tried to shake it away, clapping for Jake and smiling at V.W. instead. The mogul ruffled my hair with a smile.

"You're a genius, Lady Fontaine," he crooned.

When V.W. left the kitchen, I chose to stay, beaming at Jake. He was looking around like he didn't quite know what to do with himself.

"See," I said with a nod, "I told you he'd want you for the

show. Talent is talent."

"My dad always wanted me to be a singer," Jake said quietly. "Josie, I... I don't know how to say..."

"Thanks?" I asked.

Jake nodded.

"Don't worry," I replied. "You did more than enough to earn a favour last weekend. Your secret's out, Jake Bolton: I know that you can be a nice guy now, when you want to be."

He cracked a tiny grin. "Don't spread the word, all right?" he asked. "I have an attitude to maintain."

I chuckled, shaking my head as I turned to leave.

"Hey Josie," Jake said quickly.

I stopped, looking back at him. "What?"

"It's just," Jake began. He looked as nervous as when V.W. had been speaking to him. "Do you know they're having that big bonfire and fireworks thing in the village tomorrow night?"

"Oh," I replied. "Um, no actually. That sounds cool."

"It is," Jake said with a nod. "Well, I'm going to be there. So I thought that if you were there, we could... both be there." He shook his head, presumably more at himself than at me. "My mom makes the best snacks for these things," he added with haste.

I felt my lip curl, Miss Cartwright's textbook floating around in my imagination. "I don't know if I'm allowed to go," I said with a sigh. "Mum's making me study a lot because I'm failing my-" I caught my breath just in time to stop myself saying 'meditation class'. "Well, I'm failing a really important subject."

"Oh," Jake said. I couldn't tell whether he believed me or not. He moved back to the sink, turning his face away.

"If I can be there," I said, trying to sound more hopeful,

"then I'll look out for you. I'll have to ask tonight. Where are the fireworks going to be?"

"Carlisle Street," Jake replied.

I felt myself take in a sharp breath. "Isn't that the street where they found that poor man dead the other week?" I asked.

Jake's shoulders tightened, his head hanging low. "That's the one."

I had expected to be babysitting Nik on Guy Fawkes's Night because it was a Sunday, which usually meant the staff meeting was on. I was surprised when Mum told me that I would have the night free. She told me late on Saturday evening as we sat together in front of the television, though I was still half-trying to read my textbook. Mum put her arm around my shoulders and pulled me close. I fell into the dip where the springs were broken under the seat, giggling as I flailed, trying to get upright again.

"I've dropped my book now," I cried. "Stupid sofa. How much does it cost to get one of these things fixed? Maybe I could give you some of my wages. I've got a packet saved up, you know."

"I don't want your money, sweet'eart," Mum said softly. "Oh, leave the book where it is. You've done enough studying for one night."

"Wow," I mused. "No studying and no babysitting. Perhaps I can wipe the dust off my record player for a little while then?"

"A little while," Mum repeated, "and not too loud."

I was on my feet when the telephone rang. Picking up the noisy unit, I carried it over to Mum, resting it carefully on the arm of the sofa as she picked up the receiver. I started to walk to my room as her conversation began.

"Oh Kit, it's you... What? No, I didn't know they 'ad fireworks down there."

I froze, looking back over my shoulder towards the sofa. Mum was nodding as if Kit could actually see her, listening carefully.

"Well, it sounds very nice. One moment."

She held the phone away from her ear, beckoning me closer. "Kit and 'enri are taking their children to the bonfire night party in the village tomorrow," she explained. "Do we want to go with them?"

I felt like someone had lit a catherine wheel inside me. I nodded eagerly. Mum put the phone to her ear again.

"We'll come down with you, yes. It's on the street, it is? That sounds fantastic. I 'ope it doesn't rain, though."

Carlisle Street was the widest street in the village, but even that was crammed full of people when we arrived. Mr Haugen had parked his car a little way away, suspecting crowds, and we found ourselves walking towards a huge pack that were lit orange by the bonfire's glow. The smell of roasted nuts and sweet candyfloss wafted through the air. The brown-brick buildings here were packed together tightly, framing the long street as people sat on their porches to take in the sights and the night air. I sometimes wondered what it would be like to live in a proper house, one with a front door that actually led to the outside world. It was fun to see normal people doing normal things for a change.

I realised that, despite the crowds, it was going to be

fairly easy to spot Jake. In the early frost, every face I passed was pale as snow and wrapped up in hats and scarves against the breeze. His coffee-hued skin and bright eyes would surely stand out a mile in this pack. I thought about the crowded scene at Halfway and how he hadn't wanted to look different amongst them. I began to be concerned that he might have changed his mind about coming to the party that night. My head was craning around every corner as we ambled through the crowd in a clump, but everywhere I looked, there were only pale faces.

"Who are you spying for?" Hanne asked, tugging my arm.

"Do you know someone here, Josie?" Mrs Haugen asked.

I glanced across at her. She was walking with a walking stick over the cobbles, but her youthful face beamed up at the bonfire as she held her daughter's hand. Mr Haugen was ahead of her with baby Nik, who was crawling all over his chest as the former soldier tried to make a safe passage for his wife to get through the people. I gave her a little nod.

"Someone from work," I replied.

"We can 'elp you look," Mum added. "What do they look like?"

The first word that came to mind was not one that Mum and the Haugens were ready to hear, although it would certainly have been the easiest way to spot Jake.

"Well," I began, my stomach starting to squirm, "he's got very short, dark hair, and he's, um, he's quite tall."

"*Oh*," Mrs Haugen said. She looked at my mother conspiratorially. "And is he handsome?" she added with a chuckle.

Yes. Jake was handsome. I hadn't consciously thought about it, but when Mrs Haugen put that teasing look on her face, the thought of Jake's sharp jaw and the feel of his broad chest shot into my head again. Those bright gold eyes were in my memory, the way they glowed in those rare moments when he smiled.

"He's just a friend," I said aloud.

Mum and Mrs Haugen gave each other the look again.

Who are you talking about? Hanne's voice suddenly erupted into my head. *Tommy's not here, is he?*

She stumbled suddenly from having her eyes closed. Mrs Haugen helped her up, apparently oblivious that she'd been using her powers. "Be careful where you're going, dear," her mother warned.

"It's not Tommy," I whispered to Hanne. I couldn't bring myself to add more.

"Per'aps you should go look for 'im, cherie," Mum said.

I stared back at her, wondering who she was and what had happened to my real parent. She shrugged as though she understood my expression.

"It's not fun for you to be dragging along with the old fogies," she continued. "Go, find your friend. But come back now and then, so I know you're all right."

"What about me?" Hanne asked.

"You're too young to go wandering off."

It was the first time Mr Haugen had spoken properly all night. He didn't seem to be enjoying himself, but perhaps that was understandable with Nik trying to make a jungle gym out of his head and shoulders. He had stopped in a clearing right near to the pyre, which was an impressive eight foot or so off the ground. Its heat stung my eyes, making them water as I adjusted. Mum was giving me a free pass to find Jake and, as much as I loved Hanne, I had the chance to do it alone.

A Place Halfway

The pyre was in the centre of the long street, right outside the record shop I had been meaning to visit for quite some time. I had enough wages to buy every track I could have wanted now, but the shop was closed for the night. As I glanced past it and up the side street attached to it, a rare sight caught my eye. So that was where the coloured people were gathered. A mix of dark and pale faces were to be seen some way off down that street, which led onto the bonfire. They could see everything that was going on, but they were separated from it a little.

"I think I know where he'll be," I said to Mum over the crackling flames.

She nodded with a gleam in her eye. I set off through the crowd again, solo this time, and shocked by the size of the nervous lump in my throat.

CHAPTER FOURTEEN

The Boy and the Bonfire

I spotted Noah first because of his height. He towered above a small woman who had a makeshift stove out on the street. Her hair was dark and curly, a stark contrast to her bright white skin, and she stirred a pot that was brimming with steam. Noah was looking into the pot and rubbing his hands. As I approached, I was fairly glad that Jake wasn't there right away. I could hardly believe the way my nerves were acting out, or the fact that I was feeling this way at all at the prospect of seeing him. The woman looked up at Noah and I saw that they both had the same wide, bird-like eyes, a shimmering shade of brown. Jake's eyes must have come from his father's side instead.

"Hi Noah," I called, waving a little.

His lanky frame turned as he sought me out. "Josie?" he said. He sounded surprised. "What brings you down from the grand manor?"

I chuckled at him, mocking a curtsey. "Jake said he'd be here," I explained.

I realised instantly that that was something I ought to have kept to myself. To my horror, Noah and his mother gave each other the exact same look that Mum and Mrs Haugen had exchanged.

"Did he now?" Mrs Bolton said, beaming. "I will never understand that youngest boy of mine."

She had a London accent, but she spoke slowly and with an easy kind of grace. I approached the merry lady and nodded my head to her.

"It's a pleasure to meet you, Mrs Bolton," I said.

"So you're Josephine," she mused, her wide eyes glowing. "How would you like some chicken and rice? I can't have my neighbours out in the cold without food in their bellies."

I caught the scent of the bubbling pot and nodded immediately.

"Well, grab that bowl quick, dearie," Mrs Bolton added. "Noah, you call the others."

As I received a bowlful of the delicious-looking dish, Noah stepped a few paces away and hollered out to the street. He didn't call anyone in particular and, to my amazement, more than half the people gathered in the side street started to approach. There had to have been two-dozen people around us, dark-skinned and light, suddenly asking for bowls and thanking Emma, which must have Mrs Bolton's first name, for all her efforts. I stumbled back out of the way, marvelling at her generosity. She had that same look that my own mother wore when she'd got all the food out on time for lunch at Peregrine—a proud look filled with love.

"Psst," said a voice behind me. "Move, move. I'm going to get in and steal a share."

A shiver ran through me as a hand touched my waist and shifted me to the side. Jake crept past, keeping low to the ground. I saw the top of his dark hair as he rounded his mother's blind side, picked up a bowl and scooped it quickly into the pot when she was turned away. He wasn't as stealthy as he thought, for a second later, she caught him and clipped him across the ear before he could run. Jake guarded his bowl fervently and ran back to me, grinning.

"So," he panted, "you weren't shut-in studying after all."

"I'm as surprised as you are," I replied.

"You met my mom?" Jake asked.

I nodded eagerly. "She's great."

There was a silence. Jake straightened up fully and fished a chicken leg out of his bowl, eyeing me like he was wondering whether to chew it in front of me or not. He had been gleeful for a moment, but now he was fading back to his awkward, fidgety mood, the kind where he would usually have turned away from me. But now there was no sink to occupy himself with. I felt butterflies rising in my tummy that had recently only been reserved for Dai Bickerstaff. We were suddenly lost for words.

"Hey," Noah called. We both turned our heads. "Show Josie the view at Bennie's. The fireworks are on soon."

Jake nodded and swallowed hard. He turned back to me, chewing his lip for a moment.

"Bennie's Café has a flat roof," he explained. "We could go up there. It's a better view than back here." His face flashed with concern for a moment. "Oh, but you want to get back to your family, I bet."

"No," I said. I spoke far too quickly, berating myself for sounding so eager. "I, um… I just need to tell Mum where I'm going, then we can go. Where's Bennie's?"

Jake smiled a little. He pointed to a concrete building that I had walked past on my way down the street. He held our food as I ran back to Mum to let her know where I'd be. She seemed happy enough with the idea, though it had now become her turn to hold baby Nik, so she might have been too distracted to hear exactly what I'd said. I took her muffled answer as a yes and headed for the café.

The flat roof was accessible via a ladder at the building's side. I scurried up it first, eager to get to the top so I didn't feel like I was going to fall off. Jake followed swiftly and we stood atop the structure, looking down on the people not too far below. He pulled our small bowls of food from the pockets of his coat. For the first time, I noticed that his thick, black overcoat was far too big for him across the back and shoulders. I took my bowl, eyeing his clothes.

"My mum buys everything a size too big too," I said with a smile. "Oh Josie, you'll grow into it."

I did my best impression of her French accent on the long vowels. Jake quirked a brow.

"Your mom's what, Chinese?" he asked.

"French," I replied. "How didn't you get French from that accent?"

Jake shook his head. I fished a tiny, wooden fork from where it had been buried in the rice. It looked like the sort you would get at the fish and chip shop. It wasn't too good for eating rice, but I tried my best not to look messy. When I chanced another glance at Jake, he was finally devouring his chicken leg. We were in silence once more. I found myself thinking that we'd had more conversations that were arguments than civil ones, so now that the smoke had cleared between us, I didn't really know what to say to him.

"It was my father's coat," he said suddenly.

"Ah right," I replied, nodding. "Gave it to you, did he?"

Jake stopped eating and swallowed, setting down his

bowl on the floor of the roof. I watched his dark frame as he stepped forward, his silhouette lit up against the bright orange glow of the bonfire. The tips of its flames weren't far below where we stood.

"He left it to me," Jake explained.

Left. It took me a moment to understand him. I stepped up to where he was and let out a sigh. "It's okay," I said. "My dad left my mum too. He left before I was even born, actually. How rotten is that?"

Jake shook his head. He didn't look at me; he just kept staring out at the bonfire. "He's dead, Josie."

"What?" I asked. "No." For a moment, I thought about the few months I had known the Bolton brothers. "Noah talks about your dad a lot. He never said-"

"I know," Jake replied. "I can't figure him out. One minute, he's talking like Dad's still alive. The next, it's as though we never had a father at all. He won't talk about what really happened."

"What do you mean?" I pressed.

I wanted to know all sorts of things. When did this happen? And how? Was this the reason Jake kept those bottles of Bell's hidden when he came to work? It felt too rude, too prying to ask for more. I set down my food and waited beside him. Jake's golden eyes were orange now in the firelight. He surveyed the street and the scurrying crowds everywhere.

"Tragic death in small Kent village," Jake said.

The memory of the crumpled newspaper down the back of my sofa rushed into my head. What had it said about the man who died? He was mugged. And he was coloured.

"Oh Jake," I said, a tightness in my throat making me choke out the words.

It was so recent, only a couple of weeks before I'd first met him at Halfway.

"I just," Jake began, swallowing hard again, "I just didn't want you to think that I was a jerk to you for no good reason. You stuck up for me with V.W., and I... I thought about how I was behaving with you before that."

I shook my head, stepping forward to try to get a better look at his face. "I forgave all that the second you saved me from that crawler Gil Croft," I said.

Jake met my eyes. The psychic moment I had had with him came back to me then. All the anger and hurt and incredible, overwhelming emotions in his heart. That was grief for the loss of a parent. I had never felt it before and I hoped I wouldn't have to, at a young age like his. I wanted to cry for him, but I was afraid to let anything I was feeling show. I didn't want to make him feel any worse than he already did.

A sudden bang scared the life out of me, and I stumbled backwards. We were close to the edge of the roof and I shouted out suddenly, but my cry for help was cut off when two strong hands grabbed my forearms. Jake pulled me back towards him with a yank, but I couldn't get control of my feet and I fell into his chest. We clambered for a moment, arms and hands everywhere as he tried to get me steady, and I unwittingly went against his movements. My face was flushed pink by the time we were right again. Jake put his hands on my shoulders, surveying my face carefully as he kept me still.

"I probably should have told you the fireworks were starting," he said sheepishly.

Another series of bangs went off behind us. I flinched just a little, but then Jake let me go and I turned to watch them, my insides swirling in a mess of confusion. Bright golden bursts lit the sky like sunshine, followed by star-shaped blasts of red and green. Jake stepped closer to me, his upper arm brushing against my shoulder. The bangs and squeals of rockets filled the air, and he leaned in towards my ear so I could hear him speak.

"Dad hated fireworks," he told me. "He said they reminded him too much of the war."

I nodded, straining on my tiptoe to reach his ear to speak back. Wobbling a little, I held onto his shoulder for balance.

"Our school doctor's the same," I replied. "We asked him this morning if he was coming with us. You should have seen the fuss he made. But he's a grumpy old git at the best of times."

Jake laughed a little, and then he suddenly pointed upwards. "Wow, look at that blue one."

We both watched the huge burst of blue fire as its trail sank like the branches of a weeping willow tree. We were closer to the fireworks than anyone was, and some of the sparks were starting to land at the edge of the roof. Jake put an arm around the back of my shoulders and guided me backwards, away from the little leftover flames.

"You could come say hello to my mum later, if you want," I told him.

He let me go, his hand sinking away so fast that it left me shivering. "You know that's not a good idea," Jake replied.

I took his arm and made him face me, the familiar scent of an argument between us hanging amid the smoke in the air.

"And why not?" I asked. "I just met *your* mum."

"That's different," he insisted.

"Why?" I demanded, hands flying to my hips. "My mum's not… Well, she's not the type to boo you off the stage with a shotgun."

"You don't know that until you try a person," he bit back.

"How dare you?" I exclaimed. "You don't know even *know* my mum!"

"And it's better that way, believe me," Jake retorted.

He shifted away from me, putting a couple of feet of distance between us. He turned his back like he always did when he was getting angry, but this time, I wasn't having any of it. It wasn't fair for him to be so honest and protective one minute and then turn into a total git the next. I couldn't handle the simultaneous feelings of having butterflies in my tummy and suddenly wanting to throttle him out of pure rage.

"And what makes you think that?" I demanded, shouting over the explosions overhead. "All white people can't be trusted, is that it? Did you ever think *you* might be the one with the problem?"

Jake turned, and I was genuinely afraid of the livid look all over his face.

"It wasn't an accident," he snarled.

"What wasn't?" I retorted.

"My father's death."

All the words I might have said fell straight out of my head, my mind turning blank. I felt woozy suddenly, inhaling a gulp of bonfire smoke by mistake that churned my stomach up. Jake stepped closer to me, taking deep breaths and looking at the ground for a long moment. When he met my eye, it seemed as though he'd calmed himself a little.

"He wasn't mugged," Jake began. "Nobody took any money or his wallet or anything. Whoever did it, they beat him up for *fun*." The last word came from his lips like it was poison.

"Like that crawler thought he was going to have *fun* with you at Halfway. Don't thank me for that, Josie. I didn't just beat into him for your benefit."

He tried to walk away but I grabbed the sleeves of his coat, pulling him back. I shook my head, tears brimming in my eyes. His own gaze began to water over.

"Don't tell me half the story," I demanded. "The papers said his injuries weren't enough to kill him."

"He..." Jake started. His low voice was breaking. "He had a heart attack from the shock." Tears flowed freely from his golden eyes then. Jake rubbed them away furiously, his dark hands balling into fists. "And you want to know what the worst part is?" he asked, anger filling his tone once more. "Nobody helped him."

He pointed out to the masses below, who were cheering as a few scraggy Guy Fawkes dolls were being thrown onto the fire.

"If someone had got him a doctor, he might have been all right," Jake sobbed. "But this whole village just left him on the street to die. Don't tell me not one person walked by. It's a high street. He died around the corner from our house, and we didn't even know."

I burst into a wild sob, and Jake turned back. Covering my mouth, I tried not to show him my face as the explosion of emotions overcame me. I couldn't bear the idea that a man had died simply because of the colour of his skin. Would people really have just left him there when he was in need? I wouldn't have. How could anyone else have been that cruel? I felt Jake close his arms around me, and I sobbed against his father's coat.

"I'm sorry," Jake murmured against my ear. "I've ruined a good night for you. I'll understand if you want to go back to the silent treatment at work."

I wrapped my arms around his middle, and he took in a sudden, sharp breath.

"You're not getting rid of me just because I've seen you cry," I told him, my forehead against his chest. I pulled back, still holding him at the sides of his stomach. "You know what you're going to do?" I asked.

He looked at me nervously, eyes wide and jaw set as he waited.

"You're going to sing," I said. "'That son of mine is gonna be a star someday.'" I gave the line my best imitation of an American accent. Jake's brow furrowed.

"Dad used to-"

"I know," I replied. "Noah told me yesterday. So you have to sing in that contest. And you have to win. For your dad."

"Win?" Jake asked, his damp eyes creasing with disbelief. "Josie, they're not going to let someone like me-"

"Stop it," I said quickly. "Someone like you? Someone who had a dad, even if it was just for a short while, who believed in him and wanted him to shine? What good are you to his memory if you don't stop thinking in the opposite way?"

Jake smiled. He reached out a thumb and pushed a few leftover tears from my cheek. "Other people are not going to see this in the same way that you do," he assured me.

I felt drained and empty, but the butterflies were back. "You let me worry about that," I replied.

CHAPTER FIFTEEN

Baby Steps

The Haugens had gone out for dinner to celebrate Mr Cavendish's sixtieth birthday, but they had decided against taking baby Nik to the posh restaurant in Orpington. It was a weeknight and Mum was busy giving the kitchens a deep clean with Blod Bickerstaff who, for once, was a great help to her in the unpleasant task. That left me wrestling with a toddler as I tried to get him to sit still and watch some evening television. Nik loved television, but he always had a wild urge to run at the screen and kick it, so I couldn't even leave him there for a moment to do anything else. And I had plenty that I wanted to do.

The first key element to my plan was to get out of confinement with my mother and my textbook. This would involve a significant improvement in my psychic skills, and it had to be fast. I didn't want to try Jake's mind for my practice; the thought of his intensity was far too much to handle, and it felt wrong to spy on him somehow. If I connected with any of the other students at Peregrine, they would know about it, and I didn't particularly want to know what Mr Frost got up to during the week. That left me with very few possibilities as I plotted my bid for freedom.

I bounced Nik on my knee as we both watched the

screen. There was some sort of old gangster film on where short Americans wore big hats and carried violin cases filled with money or guns. I let my mind wander, wondering if I could find a stranger to connect with, when an image started forming in my mind. I had that two-screened, halfway state again. In one part of my vision, I could still see Nik wriggling on my lap and I could feel his little heel digging into my knee. In the other, I had the viewpoint of someone who was looking down into a sink filled with sloshy, soapy water.

When the vision looked up, he was standing in front of a bathroom mirror. I froze, almost dropping Nik as I realised who I was seeing. V.W. took a razor to the unfinished side of his sharp jaw, sliding the blade up with an audible scratch as it passed through a thin layer of shaving cream. He was watching his own cheek intently in the mirror as he moved with clear precision. I wondered what he was doing shaving at this time of night. I had always presumed that was a morning thing for men. V.W. paused suddenly, his eyes roving as if he was listening for something.

"Josie?" he said aloud.

Oh no, I thought immediately into his mind. *I'm so sorry.*

V.W. grinned. "I wondered when curiosity would get the better of you," he said.

He began to wash the remainder of the shaving cream from his face. It occurred to me that he wasn't at all bothered about me snooping around his mind.

You know about me? I asked.

"I know about Peregrine Place," he explained, rubbing his jaw with a towel. "So it wasn't hard to guess."

And you? I added. *Are you psychic too?*

"From the day I was born," V.W. replied proudly.

140

K.C. Finn

Nik made a leap for freedom but I caught him, turning him over to tickle his belly. The vision of V.W.'s flat stayed in my mind. The room was boxy and brown with a yellow ceiling and faded wallpaper. It looked even shabbier than our mix of second-hand stuff. I found it curious that he was living in such a tiny, awkward space when his clothes and his silver jewellery were so expensive.

How did you know it was me? I asked him.

"Let's just say I've got a few extra tricks up my sleeve," he rasped.

I felt him tap his nose twice. V.W. moved through his small room to a built-in kitchen where a kettle was just starting to whistle. He took it off the small stove and poured himself a mug of hot water, stirring in three heaped spoonfuls of coffee. I was glad I couldn't smell the strength of it, especially when he also retrieved a bottle of whiskey and dropped a measure of that into the mug too.

"You're a bit faint, you know," he told me. "You sound like a long-distance phone call."

Well, I said sheepishly, *I'm not very good at deep thinking.*

"You should be," he said, sounding genuinely surprised.

I furrowed my brow. *What makes you think that?*

V.W. paused for a long moment that made me wish I were good enough at meditation to listen for his thoughts. He suddenly shrugged, taking his coffee over to a battered, little armchair.

"Just a guess," he replied as he sank into the seat.

That's the first bad one you've made, I said.

He gave a little chuckle, and then sipped at his coffee with a faint slurp. "So this is practice, is it?" he asked. "You're fishing for minds?"

I laughed at the expression. Nik turned and glared at me like he wanted to know the joke. I bounced him again. *I suppose so,* I replied. *I wasn't really trying. I just sort of let my mind wander and… it led me to you.*

V.W. swallowed hard, running a fingertip around the rim of his cup. "Lucky you," he said quietly. "I bet you'd rather have found Paul Anka or someone."

I don't think I'm clever enough for trans-Atlantic thinking, I confessed.

"You will be," V.W. promised. "Keep trying, kiddo."

I felt a swell in my chest at his words. V.W. looked around his shabby room, finding a clock on the wall. It was ten to eight.

"I've got to be somewhere soon," he said, "business to conduct and all. You skedaddle for now and I'll see you at work, right? Got the first round of the talent show on Saturday night, don't forget."

I know, I said excitedly. *Jake's going to be brilliant.*

I felt V.W. break into that sharp-toothed grin of his. His brow was rising slowly. "Is that right?" he asked. "Well, I'll look forward to that. And we'll talk more, kiddo. Maybe I can help you with this deep thought thing."

I thanked him and the link broke, as though he might have closed it from his side. I didn't understand how that was possible, but the thought of getting advice from someone who was that accomplished filled me with new hope. I would improve enough to impress Miss Cartwright. I would be set free from studying by Mum. And then, if all went according to plan, I would have my time free again to…

"'chu smiling for?" Nik asked me, his brow knitted angrily.

I froze in my thoughts. *To be with Jake.* The thought was automatic in my mind that that was what I wanted to do.

"Are you singing it tonight, then?" I asked, folding my arms expectantly.

Tommy heaved his smart, black jacket over his shoulders, wriggling into it as he tried not to crease it. I could tell by the downward curve in his shoulders that the news he was about to give me wasn't what I wanted to hear. He turned his back to me, holding up a hand mirror and perfecting the slicked-back wave of his dark hair.

"It's not ready," he replied.

I made a derisive noise in the back of my throat. We were standing in V.W.'s office as the sound of the crowd grew louder outside; kids from all over Kent had packed out Halfway to see what the talent show had to offer. Whilst most of the acts were getting ready in their cars or in the backyard of the club, V.W. had once again offered Tommy the special privilege of preparing in his office. Tommy set the mirror down on the mogul's desk and turned back to me. His pale face was fraught with nerves and apologies. He wrung his hands together.

"This contest is important, Josie," Tommy urged. "I can't win with a duff song, and the lyrics for that one just aren't right yet. I'm better off sticking with the classics until it's really something special."

"If you say so," I sighed, "but Hanne's not going to wait forever."

Tommy's lip curled. "But what if she's not waiting at all?"

he asked. "We've been getting on as friends all right, but I just can't tell if she likes me or not."

I wanted to strangle him. Hanne too. It didn't matter how many times I had told either one of them that the other was madly in love; every time they got together, they never broached the subject. Like Tommy, Hanne was coming away from each encounter more and more convinced that they were doomed to be just good friends. If I hadn't been loyal to Hanne, the frustration of matchmaking would have made me give up on them totally. As it was, I held Tommy's shoulders and looked him straight in his turquoise eyes.

"What do you want her to do?" I asked. "Turn up at your door with roses? That's your job. You're the boy. Why do think people like Sedaka write love songs in the first place? It's up to you to get this romance off the ground."

Tommy let out a long sigh, his cheeks puffed up. "Let's just get this song over with first," he said with a tremble.

With his yellow Tele over one shoulder, Tommy led the way out into the club. Noah and I had worked hard at arranging the seats in theatre-style rows and now those rows were filled with eager heads, bobbing around as they looked for signals that something was about to start. V.W. was up on the stage, adjusting a microphone, and behind him was a full backing band with some of the most expensive-looking instruments I'd ever seen. Blod Bickerstaff gave me a little wave from the judge's table, her golden jewellery catching the bright spotlights.

I took Tommy over to the bar where the other acts were waiting, all wearing those same nervous grins I had seen at the audition stage. It seemed that the addition of a huge, eager crowd had heightened everyone's emotions. Some of the girls that were about to sing had flushed faces and tears glistening in their eyes. One of the other boys looked totally green, as though he would need to run for the bathroom at any moment. When I put Tommy in line with the other hopefuls, I turned and started to walk away. He caught my arm.

"Hey, whoa," he said, eyes widening. "I thought you'd stay with me until I go up?"

My eyes travelled to the closed door leading to the kitchen. "Sorry," I said with a shrug. "I've got another contestant to collect."

When I found Jake in the kitchen, at first I didn't think it was him. He was wearing much lighter colours than I'd ever seen: tan-coloured trousers and a bright white shirt open a little at his chest. He wore a flat-cap in the same hue as the trousers and shiny, brown shoes that he was polishing with a dishrag. The scent of some kind of aftershave wafted at me as I approached. When he noticed me, he stood up straight, looking down at himself and adjusting his shirt again.

"This is crazy," he said. "I'm not sure I can go out there."

"But you look so good," I said.

I was mortified at how gooey I sounded; the words came out without me having really considered how they were going to come across. Jake rubbed the back of his neck, looking at me under the brim of his cap.

"Do you think I picked the right song?" he asked.

"Of course you did, for the millionth time," I replied.

Jake looked at the kitchen door, his lips shifting as he set his jaw.

"I suppose they'll be surprised to see you out there," I mused. Jake began to nod ruefully, but I quickly added, "But once

they hear you sing, it'll be a different story. I promise."

He let out a few sharp breaths, and then took in one long, deep one. "All right then," he said with a nod.

We walked towards the kitchen door, but Jake paused in my way for just one more moment before we could pass through it into the busy club. He looked at me deeply, a look that sent a shiver through me and made a smile leap onto my face. Jake was quiet and level in expression as he spoke.

"If anything goes wrong," he began, "don't blame yourself. This is my final decision. You didn't make me do this, right?"

I wasn't sure that was entirely true, but I nodded all the same.

I saw the first reaction of the nearby crowd when Jake emerged and joined the ranks of the other singers alongside the bar. I didn't follow him all the way down to the line, but I watched as whispered conversations began and looks were cast his way. Some of the other contestants gave him dirty looks; a few seemed to be laughing. Jake was too focused on the stage ahead to notice any of it. Tommy was beside him in the line and, upon spotting him, he turned and shook his hand. I smiled at that, some of my nerves abating again.

"Are you going to serve these drinks or what?" asked one of the girls behind the bar.

"Oh," I said, turning abruptly, "Yes, I-"

I smashed into a thin torso as I spun. I recoiled in horror, looking up to a flat-haired head where the faint sign of a purple bruise was still circling a pale jaw. Every nerve in my body went into overdrive as the beady eyes of Gil Croft bore down on me.

"Out of the way, you little cow," he snapped.

I leapt away, grateful to see that his affection had shifted, but also horrified to have someone so foul be angry with me. I secluded myself in the relative safety of the bar as I stacked up some complimentary juices to pass along the rows of guests. I made sure Gil was far away on the other side of the club before I set out to distribute them. Dai was with him and the other boys who had once formed part of Gil's band. When V.W. told them they had failed at the audition, I hadn't thought they would show up at the club again, but now I was starting to think that Halfway had become a regular weekend haunt from them away from university and their little London Light social group. I didn't like that thought one bit.

V.W.'s roster saw everyone going alphabetically, and Tommy was the first to be called to the stage. Bolton was straight after Asher, so I wouldn't have long to wait before both my investments in the show had sung it out. As much as I knew that Tommy was undeniably talented, a horrible little part of me was hoping that he would make the odd mistake to make sure Jake had a proper chance to shine. It wasn't that Jake wasn't talented, but the curious looks and turned heads in the crowd were starting to get on my nerves. I couldn't imagine what that kind of attention was doing to Jake.

I'd never been that into Billy Fury, but when Tommy sung 'Jealousy', it was like I was hearing the hit for the very first time. Every time he hit the stage, he was getting more accomplished, strumming out a note-perfect accompaniment to the pianist behind him as though they had rehearsed together for years. As I shifted around the room, handing out juices, my eyes returned time and again to his presence on the stage and the way he grinned out at the crowd with a cheeky wink here and there. Tommy Asher was a star, no mistake. The more he rallied

the crowd and whipped the girls up into a cheering frenzy, the more worried I became that Jake was going to have to follow him.

When that time came, V.W. actually had to stand up at the judge's table to quiet the crowd. He held out his bejewelled hands, patting the air down and grinning like he'd just made a million pounds at a casino table.

"All right, all right," he called. "The night's just beginning, kids. Keep that energy going for Mr Jake Bolton!"

As Jake started towards the stage, I found that I was holding my breath.

CHAPTER SIXTEEN

The Eve of Winter

There was a smattering of polite applause for Jake, most of it from V.W. and Blod, but the rest of the crowd were cowed into a stunned silence as they watched the broad, dark boy cross the stage. He stepped up to the band and spoke quietly to them. They nodded in unison, and the drummer gave Jake a thumbs-up. I watched his chest rise and fall shakily along with his bright shirt, then Jake stepped up and took hold of the microphone stand. His eyes travelled over the crowd for a moment, flickering nervously until they found mine. He kept those golden circles trained on me, and I stopped everything I was doing to will him on. I wished that I could have used my psychic skills to bid him good luck without freaking him out even more.

The drummer suddenly tapped his sticks together, beating out an intro as Jake's mouth moved silently. I watched the numbers forming on his lips. One, two, a-one, two, three four-

"You ain't nothing but a Hound Dog, cryin' all the time..."

His father's favourite song came bursting from Jake in a melodious flurry, his face contorting with the lyrics as his lips mimicked the perfect Presley curve. He lunged forward with the mic stand as though he was dancing with it, flinging it to and fro between the verses and spinning it between his fingers. Now

A Place Halfway

I could see why his father had always wanted his beloved son to be on the stage. I felt a pang of sorrow that he wasn't there to witness Jake's triumph, but I started to clap along to the beat, dancing from my spot on the sidelines to support him as best I could.

Then Blod was on her feet and clapping too. V.W. pulled Frost up, and even the chubby, old club owner wiggled a little for the sake of the King. People were clapping too in the rows of seats. Not everybody was as impressed as I thought they should have been, but there were plenty of surprised and happy faces enjoying the beat. When Jake had the courage to look out at them, the relief in his face was palpable. He let rip with everything he had, singing so loudly and proudly that Heaven itself would have found him hard to ignore. I wondered if that was his intention, he kept looking up at the rafters of the club rather than out into the crowd.

When the song was over, Jake didn't receive the wild reception that Tommy had elicited, but he seemed really happy with the moderate applause that he did get. I was outraged that he hadn't gotten more out of the crowd, since it was clear that he and Tommy were both evenly matched for natural showmanship. The first chance I had, I raced over to the bar to congratulate him with a huge, enthusiastic grin.

"Didn't I tell you?" I asked, not waiting for an answer. "You were brilliant. No boos, no shotguns, just talent."

"And you were right," Jake replied, his chest still heaving with nerves. "Even if I don't make it any further, I got up there and I sang it for Dad."

"You're going to go further," I promised him with glee. "Nothing's going to stop you now."

K.C. Finn

V.W. called a short recess after all the youngsters had performed for him and the other judges to decide on the six acts that were good enough to make it to the next round of the show. I had watched the rest of them perform with a mild interest as I got on with my work, but the record mogul had been right in his estimation that most of them were old-fashioned Sinatra copycats. Some of the girls were quite good, but they were shy and didn't have the electricity that Jake and Tommy had started the night off with. Half the crowd filed out without waiting to see the results, leaving only those that were invested in the contestants to mill around the club as they waited.

To my horror, Dai and Gil had decided to stay with their little group. I had been avoiding cleaning their table at the very back of the club all night, but now I'd been barked at by Frost himself because they had racked up about a dozen glasses on their table. I approached them with careful steps, keeping my eyes fixed on Dai all the time as I levelled my tray and started hurriedly grabbing their empties.

"Oh hiya, Jo," Dai said brightly. "You look knackered."

"Thanks," I said with a huff. Gil was eyeing me over Dai's shoulder, silent but nasty looking.

"Hey, don't tell my dad that I was yur, right?" he said, oblivious to the tension happening across the space of the table. "Only he thinks I'm out and about too much. Mam doesn't mind, I spoke to her before, but Dad says that I should be cooped up at my halls studying. What an idiot, right?"

"Right," I said flatly, wishing he'd stop talking so I could

get the rest of the glasses and leave.

"Oh, it's only the beginning tonight, mate," Gil crooned, a wicked sneer on his awful lips. "We've got *so* much more fun to have later."

The way he said 'fun' made me want to be sick. I excused myself quickly from them, rushing so fast across the dance floor that one of the glasses went tumbling off my tray. I froze in shock, waiting for the smash to come, but when I looked down, a hand with a chunky, silver watch attached had caught it. V.W. straightened up, placing it back on my tray with a smile.

"Clumsy," he chuckled.

"Sorry," I said, still flustered by the memory of Gil's presence.

"You got any opinions to add to the mix?" V.W. asked. "Only them other two aren't what you'd call connoisseurs of music."

He cocked his head towards Blod and Frost, who were taking their seats. I was amazed that he cared so much about my opinion; it lifted a little of the nasty feeling I had brewing in my tummy from seeing Gil Croft.

"Tommy and Jake, obviously," I said. "That girl called Suzie wasn't too bad either."

V.W. nodded thoughtfully, a hand grazing his triangular jaw. "But who'd you like best?" he asked. "I know who the crowd loved, but I've got a different feeling."

"Me too," I admitted. "Some of them were really cold with Jake, and he was so good."

The record mogul ran a hand up through his slick, greying hair and grinned at me. He patted me on the shoulder gently. "Thanks kiddo," he said. "That helps me a lot."

Remind me to return the favour, when we get a chance.

152

V.W.'s narrow eyes only glazed over for a second as his voice reverberated in my head. Then he was walking again, out of my sight before the echo of his psychic words had even receded. So it was true; he really was like me, and with a booming, strong-minded voice to prove it. I watched him lean over the judge's table, sharing a few words with Blod and Frost. He gave a little nod now and then, his eyes starting to roll as he waited for Blod to stop talking, then he was heading off in the direction of the stage.

"All right lads and lasses," he said as he stepped up to the microphone. "We won't keep you in suspense any longer. The following six lucky acts will be back here on Saturday December 2nd to compete once again for a place in the top three. Frank Stern, Suzie Wright, The Stepp Brothers, Collette Buchanan, Tommy Asher-"

At that, I heard Tommy give a huge whoop of joy, turning my head towards the bar. From the kitchen door, I could see Jake's bright eyes peering out, one set of dark fingers clutching at the doorframe nervously.

"And Jake Bolton," V.W. finished.

The kitchen door closed. I rushed to it with my tray of glasses, bounding through to find Jake leaving via the back door. I set down my tray, but by the time I had followed him out, he was fishing behind the back of the bins for the bottle I knew he had stowed. He wasn't as joyful as I thought he'd be. In fact, he looked downright terrified as he nervously clasped the glass neck, golden liquid sloshing inside the vessel. The night sky settled in a navy-blue hue around us as he turned, realising I was there. The bottle was halfway to his lips as it paused.

"Is that necessary?" I asked.

He looked embarrassed as he lowered the bottle. "It never used to be," he said, contemplating its label. "Since Dad... It just helps me feel less upset, I guess."

"Can't you find something else to do that?" I replied.

Jake's brow came down heavy. "What does it matter to you anyway if I drink?" he questioned.

It mattered because I cared about him. It mattered because I wanted him to be happy and confident without needing the foul-smelling stuff in that bottle. It mattered because I knew about all the pain inside his body, and I wanted so desperately to be the one to take it away from him.

I shrugged. "It just does."

Jake still had the bottle in his grip, but his focus had shifted from it to me as he stepped back towards the light coming from the kitchen. "This means I've got to sing again," he said, taking in a breath and then letting it out slowly, his cheeks puffed.

"Sam Cooke next time," I answered. "Something slow. Show them your versatility."

Jake laughed a little. "You sound like that record guy," he said. There was something off about the way he phrased it, like it was a bad thing.

"You still don't like him?" I said accusingly, "He likes you. He's crazy about you."

"I don't know," Jake replied, shaking his head a little. "Something's not right about him."

I thought of V.W. and his expensive clothes, picturing him sat alone in that tiny, dingy flat I'd seen. Maybe Jake had a point, but that didn't have to mean anything bad. I stepped up to him, taking the bottle out of his hand and looking down at it myself. I took a sniff of the powerful liquid within, wincing as an idea came to me. I let the bottle rise up to my lips.

"Wait," Jake said suddenly. He lurched forward and stopped me from drinking anything. "What are you doing? That stuff's bad for you!"

I let one of my eyebrows rise. "Then why is it all right for you to drink it?" I asked teasingly.

"I won't then," he said tartly.

Jake's lips settled into a disgruntled pout. I watched the shape that they made. He was inches from my face where he had tried to reach for the bottle, one hand still outstretched and lingering over my forearm. We stayed like that a moment too long, long enough for me to let thoughts into my head that I'd been holding back since Halloween. I'd admitted to caring for him, to wanting to spend time with him and wanting to make him happy. Why was it so much harder to admit that if he kissed me right then, I wouldn't ever have stopped him?

"I should go," he said suddenly, pulling away and folding his arms in front of his broad chest. "They're gonna think we're up to something out here."

I watched him leave, rather wishing that we had been up to something.

I tossed and turned in bed that night, fraught with excitement from the show and its favourable results. I couldn't make up my mind if it was a good or a bad thing to find myself having feelings for Jake. Sometimes it seemed as though he might be interested in me, but he was so changeable in his mood that I could never be sure. And then, of course, there was that other thing, the thing I didn't want to think about. The thing he'd suggested about Mum and about people in general. *You don't know that until you try a person.* Jake had tried his presence out on the crowd at Halfway, and things had worked out just fine. Could that be true about us, if the feelings that I had wouldn't quit?

At first, I thought I'd fallen asleep, but the deep darkness of the night sky was in too sharp a focus to be dreamlike. I was lying on a hard, cold surface, the chill of the November wind biting at my face. My face was wet. My hands were gathered over my eyes, making it hard to see anything but the slivers of the night sky when I occasionally dared to peek through them. I was crying, perhaps, the icy wetness sliding all over my cheeks and my fingers, only the substance felt thicker than the salt water of tears. Everything was still.

Then there was pain.

Tremendous pain as something, maybe several somethings, impacted with my body, the sharp toes of boots smashing into my back, my legs, my sides, even my head. It was important to guard my head; I felt the impulse run through me to protect it. I wanted to scramble to my feet, to get up and run, but it was then that I realised it wasn't my body I was feeling. When the hands I could see finally came away from the head I was in, the faint moonlight illuminated them enough for me to see the truth.

Two hues. The dark coffee-brown of coloured skin. And the deep crimson stickiness of blood.

"Perhaps this will teach you a lesson," a voice crooned somewhere above. I shivered along with the body I had slipped into, recognising its awful, mocking tone.

"You tell him, Gil," said another snide, little voice. "Show the black what's what."

Another volley of kicks shot through the body, and a cry of agony rang out.

"Please," the choked voice said. "You've had your fun, just-"

"You think I take orders from the likes of you?" Gil shouted, flecks of spit flying from his horrid lips and landing on the face of his victim.

I sat bolt upright in my bed, the vision suddenly fading away. I had recognised the strangled pleas of the voice that came from the head I'd been in. Clambering out of my bed, I reached around desperately for shoes to pull on, trying to stop my brain from spinning in my skull as I processed the single most important thought circulating within it:

Jake was in trouble.

He was hurt, bleeding, crying, and being beaten by more than just one boy. Gil Croft had come back for his vengeance after Jake had beaten him down, but now he had his slimy, little friends in on the act. In my half-dreaming state, I had found his mind, found him crying out for the kind of help Mum always wanted me to use my powers for. I was the only one who knew what was happening, the only one who could help him. I needed a car to get to him fast. Jake needed a doctor.

And I knew exactly where to find both.

CHAPTER SEVENTEEN

The Nick of Time

"Are you sure they're on this lane?" Doctor Bickerstaff asked, his red-ringed eyes peering out as far as the car headlights would reach.

"Hang on," I replied hurriedly. "I'll keep checking."

We had just left Peregrine Place, and I was leaning forward in the back seat to join Blod and the doctor in the hunt for Jake and his attackers. I took a few breaths, still peering out as I tried to lean my mind towards Jake's without getting sucked back into the full force of his experience. I found him, my vision splitting in two so I could see through his eyes but also keep my own sight. I was relieved to find him still conscious and surprised when I found him on his feet. Jake's steps pounded heavily and unevenly on the path, dark grass rising on either side of him that was coated with winter frost. It had to be our lane, or one just like it nearby.

"He's running," I said, "but he's hurt."

"Josie love," Blod said from the front passenger seat, "have this overcoat. You're only in your nightclothes. You're going to freeze out yur."

"She can't see you whilst she's in the trance," Bickerstaff told his wife.

I could see Blod just fine. I took the coat from her and put it on, still watching Jake run in the other part of my vision. He looked over his shoulder and suddenly, I saw the horrifying sight of five figures chasing him in the dark. Their manic laughter and taunting cries echoed fearfully in my head.

"Oh no," I said, choked. "Those boys are still after him. They're gaining on him. I feel like he's slowing down."

"How are you doing that?" Bickerstaff asked. His face was deeply confused in the rearview mirror as he drove on. "You shouldn't be able to-"

"Wait!" I interrupted.

Jake had fallen. Everything in my other vision went blurry as he crashed to the ground, his face connecting sharply with the dirt path. He scrambled to get back up, but I felt the faintest shadow of the impact on his back as someone put a heel to his spine. Something cracked, and Jake yelped. My heart was in my throat, tears streaming from my eyes as I watched the windscreen of Bickerstaff's car. We drove on through the blackness.

"We're going to be too late!" I shrieked and sobbed. "They've got him again."

The beating had resumed, with Gil flipping Jake onto his back so he could smash his fists into his chest. Jake was too choked and exhausted to fight back, his breaths getting more stunted and laboured with every moment that passed. I remembered with horror what had happened to his father as I felt fear capture my heart. But Jake was younger, stronger too. He could survive the beating. I hoped to God that he could survive it.

And then something wonderful happened. In the corner of Jake's vision, I saw the blurry outline of a pair of headlights belonging to a shiny, white car.

"It's us!" I shouted. "We're almost on them! I was right; he's on this lane!"

"Step on it, Steven!" Blod yelled.

The engine revved and shook us all, my contact with Jake's mind breaking. As we bounded on through the darkness, the car's lights finally brought everything into focus. Bickerstaff floored the brakes with a sudden screech. We had come upon the group too fast, they were suddenly closer, the five upright figures gathered around Jake as he lay on the floor. Four of them started to run, but the one who was nearest to us hesitated, his shadowy figure obscured by the beams as he tried to get out of the way of the car.

He dove to the left at the same moment that Bickerstaff veered to the left to avoid him. The figure landed on the hood of the car with a thump, suddenly rolling off as the vehicle finally came to a halt. Bickerstaff's hand rose to his mouth in horror, a chorus of 'Oh my God, Oh my God' coming from he and his wife as they both clambered out of the car. I got out of the back just in time to see the doctor limping up to the boy he had hit, the thug who had been beating the life out of Jake and hadn't managed to escape with his friends.

Blod and Bickerstaff pulled the boy to his feet.

"Mam… Dad… what are you doing yur?"

Bickerstaff dropped Dai almost as quickly as he had grabbed him, racing instead to Jake as he coughed and spluttered on the floor. The car's lights were still on and I followed the doctor to his patient, terrified by the livid look he was now wearing.

"Dad," Dai said weakly, clutching his chest, "I can explain."

"It had better be bloody good," Blod snapped at him viciously. She took the tall, young man by the scruff of his neck and flung him away in an amazing display of authority. "Get in the car and shut up."

I crouched beside the doctor and Jake, whose eyes had fluttered closed as he struggled to breathe. Bickerstaff put his head to Jake's chest, feeling around and then suddenly leaning down to his ear.

"Listen to me, young man," he commanded. "This is vital. Breathe all the way in for me. As much as you can, even if it hurts."

Jake did as he was told with a wheeze.

"It's going to be all right, Jake," I said, reaching out to take his hand. I didn't care that it was frozen and covered in blood; I held onto him fast. I felt a surge of wild emotion inside me when he started to squeeze my fingers back.

"Breathe again for me," Bickerstaff said, his hands feeling all over Jake's chest and listening hard at his mouth. The doctor put his arms around Jake's shoulders and under his knees, shifting him a little. He looked him over; his large, blue eyes were intense and more alive than I'd ever seen them.

"No lung damage by the sounds of it," he muttered. "Lumbar region's not damaged. Head injuries are localised to the face, not the skull. We're safe to move him, but my leg's not going to hold his weight. You'll have to help, girls. Gather round and take hold."

Blod shifted to my side and we did as instructed, getting as strong a grip on the underside of Jake's body as we could. I had his shoulders and his neck, watching his tight, pained expression as I supported his head. I looked to Bickerstaff for a signal of when to move, but he was still studying Jake desperately, his mind working a million miles a minute.

"Ooh, you're wonderful, you are," Blod said suddenly. Her face was in total awe of the man by her side.

The silver-blonde doctor gave his wife a disbelieving look. "This is the hardly the time for that," he muttered. "On three, we lift. One, two, *three*."

The overcoat Blod had given me was covered in blood by the time we got back to Peregrine Place. Jake lay with his head in my lap on the backseat whilst Dai had to squash into the far corner, trying to keep himself as far away as possible from Jake's feet, which spasmed now and then as he fought against the pain to stay awake. It was important to keep him awake; Doctor Bickerstaff had told me so. I stroked his short hair despite the places where it was coated in blood and dirt, looking into his eyes whenever they opened and speaking to him, asking him to squeeze my hand. Every time he did, I felt a little brighter.

I couldn't think about Dai just yet. He had been there with Gil when this was happening, but it seemed so wrong to think that he could have caused the horrific pain that Jake was in. I wondered if perhaps he had just arrived in time to try and stop the attack, perhaps I hadn't seen or heard him trying to prevent it in my half-vision. Anger welled within me amid the sadness and the desperate hope that I was clinging to for Jake's sake. I didn't believe my own excuses for Dai, and the look in Steven Bickerstaff's steely eyes told me I shouldn't try to either.

Three of us sat on a long bench in the hospital room of Peregrine Place. I was wrapped in a red medical blanket from one of the spare beds in the ward, Blod's arm secured tightly around my shoulders. About a foot away from us sat Dai, his blonde head in his hands. He hadn't spoken a word since those first pleas he'd made to his father at the scene of the crime. Doctor Bickerstaff was in the treatment room with Jake, and had been for almost thirty minutes. Every second that ticked by on the huge black-and-white clock on the wall drove me mad.

"You heard what he said before," Blod soothed, her bright Welsh lilt comforting me a little. "They're nasty wounds, but no vital injuries. Steven's patching him up, that's all."

I nodded, sucking back yet more tears. I had cried enough already, those salty droplets falling almost constantly the whole way back. When Jake was close to me and holding my hand, I had felt involved somehow, like my presence was helping him. Now, sitting and waiting outside the treatment room, I felt lost and totally useless.

"You were brilliant," Blod told me gently. "You found him. You stopped it from getting any worse."

It was true, but in that moment, it didn't make me feel any better. Another ten minutes passed, and I was about ready to tear my hair out when the treatment room door opened. Doctor Bickerstaff stood before us, his shirt splashed and smeared with blood, removing a pair of rubber gloves from his hands. He gave me a slow nod, but he didn't smile.

"He's sleeping now," he said. "He'll be all right, with proper rest."

I leapt from my seat and threw my arms around Bickerstaff's waist. He stumbled back and I felt his legs wobble, a startled noise caught in his throat. He patted my head softly and I broke away, pushing another tear out of my eye.

"Sorry," I mumbled.

"It's quite all right," he said briskly, though his cheeks were flushed pink.

Blod gathered me up in her arms again, her bright face looking hopeful. She tried to take Bickerstaff into the hug too, but he stepped away. The flush had faded from his cheeks as quickly as it appeared, replaced by a grave pallor where his jaw became set and stiff. I watched those hands that had treated Jake with such care balling into tight, veined fists. His gaze was one of abject fury as it fell to the other end of the bench.

"I need a word with my son," he said simply.

Blod made to take me away, but the doctor held out a hand.

"Oh no," he added, "I want you to witness this. I think it's vital that Dai knows that other people will hear what I'm about to tell him."

Dai's hands came away from his face and, for the first time, I didn't see the handsome boy I usually looked upon. His eyes were ringed red and sore, his face hollow and pale as he rose to meet his father's gaze. Bickerstaff stepped up to him, matching his height. Dai seemed cowed and small before the doctor.

"To think that a son of mine could be such an idiot," Bickerstaff spat.

Dai flinched. Steven Bickerstaff didn't need physical force to frighten his son; the tone of his voice was enough to send shivers through us all. I remembered then why I was usually so uncomfortable around him; the doctor had a coldness to him that left me uneasy sometimes, and now it was directed, full force, onto Dai. I could see the boy suffering under the invisible weight of his father's judgement, his expression cracking as dampness formed around his already-aching eyes.

"I had to do it," he croaked.

"*Had* to?" Bickerstaff repeated with an icy laugh. "Why exactly, pray tell, did you *have* to beat a poor, innocent boy to a bloody pulp?"

Dai swallowed hard, his gaze directed at his father's chest rather than his face and those damning, judging eyes. "The London Light," he muttered. "That's what they do."

"The what?" Bickerstaff demanded.

"The club he joined," I added, my voice shaking. "Gil Croft's exclusive little gang at university."

"What are they?" the doctor asked.

"Nationalists," his son replied.

"Ha," Bickerstaff barked harshly. Dai leapt away from him at the volume of the sound. "*Supremacists*," the doctor concluded. "I might have known."

"You don't know though, Dad," Dai pleaded, the fear palpable in his tone. "That kid... He was sniffing around Josie. It's not right."

I felt a pang in my chest, a horrible dagger of guilt cleaving into my heart at the thought that Jake's injuries were my fault.

"Who says it's not right?" Bickerstaff asked. "*You?* What right have you to say that? There are nine years in age between your mother and me, and there are plenty of people who liked to tell me that that wasn't right, but we've been happily married for twenty-one years."

With every syllable he spoke, Doctor Bickerstaff became more and more enraged. His usually dry and placid expression was awash with rage, his brow growing crimson and more deeply lined by the minute. Blod stepped out and put a hand on his arm, but he didn't break eye contact with his son. Dai, for his part, was

retreating every moment, like he was fearful that his father was simply going to snap. A cruel little part of me wanted Bickerstaff to fly off the handle, just to make sure Dai suffered for his role in what had happened to Jake.

"I didn't fight a war that brought down a genocidal fascist to give my own son the freedom to *become one!*" Bickerstaff yelled, his words echoing throughout the hospital room, bouncing off every facet of the dark-panelled walls. "Why is it that you don't understand, even after all the times you've seen me help people, that compassion is something every self-respecting man ought to have?"

Dai had no answer. He mumbled the start of something, but it fell from his lips weakly and almost inaudibly. He was breathing in sharp, stunted bursts, his face damp with the cold sweat of terror and shame.

"I'm sure you've heard your mother tell you that I can be a very cold man when I want to be," Bickerstaff added in a lower, more rasping tone. "I suggest you mend your ways rather than test her theory. Do I make myself clear?"

Dai nodded several times, his once-booming voice reduced to a childlike whisper as he said, "Yes, Sir."

"Get out of my sight," Bickerstaff spat.

The boy began to walk away, limping a little.

"Oh," Blod said, "but his ribs… You hit him with the car."

Dai paused, looking back at his mother with a glimmer of hope in his eyes. But I looked to Bickerstaff, noting the cold, unforgiving stiffness of his face. His eyes had a harsh, silver fire burning behind them.

"He'll live," he coolly surmised.

CHAPTER EIGHTEEN

Conscious

Mum had been frantic when I rushed out of the flat to get the Bickerstaffs, but she was too heavy-headed to get up and pursue me in the middle of the night. When Blod finally relayed to her all that had happened, she insisted that I come home to change my clothes and get some sleep. I agreed only on the condition that, as soon as the sun rose, I could get up again and go back to the hospital room to visit Jake. I was amazed at how deeply I slept despite the devastation I was feeling; total exhaustion forced me into unconsciousness for a good few hours before the sunlight ripped me back from dreamland into existence.

When Mum returned me to the place where I had left Jake, we found Doctor Bickerstaff flat out on one of the beds in the main ward. He was still covered in blood and in last night's clothes, his stubbly jaw lying slack as he slept. On the next bed behind him was Jake, now transferred from the treatment room. He looked odd amid all the bright white blankets and bandages, his dark skin showing through the gaps in the pale cloth bands. His fingers were bound and splinted together, and I realised with horror that that had to mean some of them were broken. I felt awful for holding his hand all that time in the car.

I stifled a sob at the sight of him, and Mum put a hand on my shoulder. She had wanted to come with me to see the boy I had helped to save from a worse fate, telling me over and over how proud she was of me for finally putting my psychic skills to use. Looking at Jake as he lay in that bed, I didn't feel proud at all. It was my fault that he was here, because he'd been right all along about people not seeing our friendship the way I did. I didn't realise how much I was shaking until Mum soothed my shoulders with her warm arms, wrapping me up completely.

"It's all right, sweet'eart," she cooed. "'e's resting now. 'e will get better."

Her words stirred Bickerstaff, and he jostled on his own bed. A horrible thump sounded and I leapt back for a moment, shocked by the sight of his leg dropping to the ground. It was made of wood. I blinked at it several times before the doctor righted himself and reached for it sheepishly, shoving it back up under his trouser leg to reattach it. I had always known that he limped, but I'd never stopped to think about why until now. Nobody had ever told me that his leg wasn't real. I started to wonder what other horrible things the grown-ups around me might have lived through that I had no comprehension of, and what other secrets they might be keeping.

"He's slept straight through the night, I think," Bickerstaff said, rubbing the back of his head as he glanced at Jake. "He's looking better already, actually. I think a few days of rest will do the trick."

The doctor stifled a huge yawn, and Mum approached him with one of her kindest smiles. He gingerly accepted a little help to get to his feet.

"Go and get some proper rest, Steven," she said gently.

"We can keep watch over 'im for now."

"His parents will need to be notified," the doctor stated.

"Mrs Bolton," I said suddenly. "I think she lives near Bennie's Café in the village. Everyone on her street knows her. Her name is Emma."

Bickerstaff nodded. "She'll be worried sick. I'll get onto her. The father?"

I shook my head. "I don't suppose you remember the coloured man who died on Carlisle Street a couple of months ago?"

Bickerstaff gulped audibly, turning his head away with a shudder. Mum gasped, her hand racing to her mouth.

"I'll try to contact his mother," the doctor concluded grimly, limping away.

"'ow do you know all this?" Mum asked me, aghast.

"That's Jake," I said weakly, feeling teary again. "Jake from work."

Understanding dawned on her face. "This was the boy you went to see at the bonfire?"

I nodded. Mum picked up my hand, clasping it between hers for a moment as she kissed the tops of my fingers.

"You can stay with 'im today, if you like," she offered, her voice growing sad and quiet. "Forget classes for the moment."

I nodded fervently. "Please, yes," I stammered. "I want to be here when he wakes up, to tell him everything's okay now."

"Of course." Mum nodded. "I'll leave you 'ere. I 'ave to start breakfast for the others. But you call me on the telephone in Steven's office if there is any problem, all right?"

I promised her I would, and soon I was pulling up a chair beside Jake's bed, alone in the wide expanse of the ward.

A Place Halfway

When the world had fallen silent, I listened to the sound of his breathing, my heart breaking every time he wheezed with strain. His dark eyelids fluttered, but he looked oddly peaceful wrapped up in his bandages, though I could see the purple outlines of huge, swollen bruises creeping out from the places where Bickerstaff had covered him up. The idea kept returning to me that this was all my fault, no matter how hard I tried to make it go away.

It was more than an hour before Jake awakened, and I had got myself into such a deep state of sorrow that, at first, I didn't even notice. He made a croaking noise like a wounded toad and I looked up, realising that he was trying to get the blankets away from his face so that he could speak. I pulled them down, loosening them around his chest when he pushed against them, until they were settled somewhere near his stomach. His ribcage was bandaged so tightly that I could see the deep lines where his flesh was held in, lines where bruises that looked almost black were poorly concealed.

"Oh Jake…" It was all I could manage to say before the tears came again.

"Noah's going to worry," Jake whispered, "And Mom and Dad."

I froze. He shut his eyes for a moment, pursing his lips before he added.

"Not Dad. Forget I said that."

I reached out, looking for a part of him that wasn't so damaged that I could touch it. The inside of his elbow seemed to be the only place safe to rest my fingers. He smiled at my touch, turning his head to see me better. Salmon-coloured sticking plasters covered large grazes and cuts across his face, but his golden eyes were still shining, flickering like tiny candles

170

competing with the morning light.

"It's still November, right?" he asked.

I nodded. "For a couple more days. You've only slept through the night."

"Where's-?"

"Everything's taken care of," I promised him. "Doctor B's gone to get your mother."

"Who?" he croaked.

"The school doctor," I explained. "It's my school that you're in."

Jake lay back and looked around the dark-panelled room. A grand, high ceiling sat some nine foot above us, gilded with golden-leaf patterns and dark green ferns. There were eight beds including Jake's, all spaced out in the room with little, wooden dressers beside each one, and large, arched windows with their curtains drawn, where thick shafts of winter sunlight were breaking through the gaps.

"This is some place," he murmured. "Help me sit up; I might never see the inside of a private school again."

"It's not all that cool," I assured him.

I perched on his bedside table to hold him around the waist, my forehead resting near his shoulder as I helped to take on the weight of his torso. At first, he cried out and I almost let go, but he told me to keep helping, even if it hurt him. Once we had jostled him upright, I fetched him a glass of water and he patted the spot next to his wrapped-up legs on the bed. I sat with him, sinking a little into the mattress as I watched him take huge, grateful gulps of cold water. He spluttered and gasped after every one, but he looked relieved and brighter than when he'd first woken.

"All right," he said with a nod that caused him to wince. "Now I feel a bit more like me again. Got to look presentable. I don't want to frighten Mom."

"Frighten her?" I repeated. "Jake, you were beaten up by a gang of white supremacists. I don't think there's much you can do not to frighten her right now." He gave a little sigh. "What were you doing on the lane so late?" I added.

"Frost paid me extra to give the kitchens a deep clean after the show," he replied. "I didn't finish there 'til gone eleven, and I was waiting in the backyard for Noah to come pick me up. That was when that gang rolled back in, in their little London town car."

"Five against one's no way to settle things," I mused, feeling the venom bubble in my stomach at the thought of what might have happened if we'd got to Jake any later.

"How did you even find me?" he suddenly asked.

I panicked then, knowing that the obvious explanation of 'I saw you with my psychic gifts' wasn't going to play out well with the injured boy. Leighton had tried to teach me once about the art of excuse making, but I couldn't remember anything he'd told me as I racked my brains for something to say. Eventually, it was the memory of V.W.'s sharp, cheeky grin that inspired my reply.

"Never you mind about that," I said, tapping the side of my nose.

Jake quirked a dark brow at me, but he couldn't ask any more questions. We were interrupted by the sound of the hospital room doors opening and the sobs and wails of a woman not far away. Mrs Bolton's curly hair was flying in all directions as she raced to her son's bedside, her wide eyes gleaming like pools, a waterfall tumbling from each down her pale face. I made to move from Jake's bed but he reached out for me, clamping my hand between his thumb and his bound, broken fingers like an injured crab. Mrs Bolton saw him do this as she ran a hand gently over the back of his head, then she reached out and put the other one on my shoulder.

"I can't thank you enough for finding him," she sobbed, barely getting her words out. "What a stroke of luck that you and that lovely couple were driving out for medical supplies."

A little cough sounded behind us. Blod and Doctor Bickerstaff stood some way off at the door. The doctor was cleaned up, but he still looked exhausted; the way his hand rested heavily across his wife's shoulders suggested that she was holding him up a little. Blod smiled at my confusion; apparently, they had fared much better in coming up with a believable excuse than me.

"How are you feeling, young man?" Bickerstaff asked.

"Like a punch-bag," Jake replied. His mother stifled another wail.

"Don't try to walk just yet," the doctor advised. "Plenty of fluids and I'll check you over, once your guests have gone."

"Thank you," Mrs Bolton said, her watery eyes turning to Bickerstaff. "Thank you ever so much."

"He can stay yur with the doctor as long as he needs to recover," Blod explained, "and before you ask, there's no charge. No charge at all."

Mrs Bolton looked like she would burst with exposure to such kindness. I rose quickly to fetch her a chair and she took it, landing with a clumsy bump and looking back to her son.

"The foreman's only given me a half-hour to see you," she said. She bit her lip for a moment before continuing. "You don't have to tell me what happened. The Bickerstaffs have filled me in on it all. But tell me, how are you? Are you hurt badly? Should I bring you some pyjamas and things? Do you want your radio?"

"Mom…"

"Oh no, silly me. Of course you wouldn't be allowed your radio in a hospital ward. But I could bring you your music books."

"Mom…"

"And some of those cold-cut chicken sandwiches that you like. I'd need to pop to the grocer for some mayonnaise, but that's no trouble."

Jake looked up to me and rolled his eyes as his mother kept on talking. I beamed back at him, pleased to see him so chipper after what must have been one of the worst nights of his life. The more Mrs Bolton babbled, the less she cried, and soon she had run her energy down to just sitting and stroking her son's short hair, much to his dismay and embarrassment. He was too badly hurt to squirm out of her way and, try as I might, I couldn't stop the smirk I was wearing from seeing the surly, tough Jake Bolton being coddled like a poodle.

"You need to get back soon," he told her, trying to bat her hand away with his bandaged fingers. "Or else all those toothpaste tubes will have no caps."

"That is *not* what I do," Mrs Bolton said with a mocking smile. "I am the quality supervisor."

"Same thing," Jake replied, straining to grin widely.

His mother looked like she wanted to clip him playfully, but she just ran her hand down the side of his face for a moment, holding him at the chin whilst she surveyed him. Then she leaned in and planted the ghost of a kiss on his bruised cheek. "I'll bring you some things after work to make you comfortable," she concluded.

Mrs Bolton rose and straightened out her skirt, looking to me with a heavy, smiling sigh. "Look after him for me, won't you, Josie?" she said. "And thank you so much."

"Of course I will," I replied.

She pulled me in for a hug, but even as her warm arms closed around my back, that sickening sense of guilt returned to me. If the Bickerstaffs had told her who attacked Jake, then it was clear to me that they had left out part of the reason why. I caught Jake's eye over his mother's shoulder as she squeezed me; he was still beaming at the sight of us both. I closed my eyes, wishing I knew of some way to tell them both the truth without making a bad situation any worse.

When Mrs Bolton had gone, Jake and I were alone again in the little ward. He reached out for me and I took hold of his thumb, the only part of his hand that I was certain wouldn't harm him. He pulled me back towards the bed and straightened up again, leaning in towards me as I sank into the mattress. The dip where our weight was heaviest forced us closer together. Jake ran his sore fingertips down a long strand of my hair, which was darker in the winter now that sunlight was scarcer in the sky. His eyes travelled all over my face, searching me as his lips moved slowly.

"I might have been right about the rest of the world," Jake began, "but I was wrong about you, Josie, and about this place. It's like the people here know what it's like to be different from other people, even though you're not."

If only he knew how much more different we really were. We were so different that we'd have to hide our supernatural talents from everyone for the rest of our lives. Leighton sometimes joked that society would put us on the operating table and cut up our brains if they found out what we could do. Now, having seen Jake's fate for the mere colour of his skin, I was starting to wonder if there wasn't some grain of truth to Leigh's jest. It occurred to me that we were all going to have to be careful with a stranger to our ways staying at Peregrine Place.

"Everyone has things that make them different or strange," I said softly.

"You don't," Jake replied, smiling faintly. "You're perfect."

His eyes had a distant look as he moved closer still, those golden rings focusing lazily on my lips. I should have stopped him there and then, but even with all the guilt I was feeling, those butterflies were still zooming around my insides at the mere thought of what he was about to do. Jake leaned even closer, our lips grazing one another's with hesitance, as though he still wasn't quite sure whether to continue or not. When he did, I had no complaints. His kiss was soft and warm, the kind of perfect first kiss I'd seen in movies and always imagined that I would have, if you didn't count the fact that he was bandaged up like a mummy.

When we broke apart, those bandages came into better focus. I stood up from the bed, overcome with wild nerves that danced like bolts of lightning over my skin. I shook my head once, tears brimming as I found Jake's gaze again. At first, he was gleeful and grinning, but when he saw my disturbed state, his smile faded off. I folded my arms over my chest, suddenly cold and rubbing at my biceps.

"You were right about this not being a good idea." I spoke quietly, reluctant to even let the words out of my mouth, but Jake listened in the silence and I knew by his face that he'd heard every word. "Being anything more than friends is going to be dangerous," I added.

There was a long pause. Jake swallowed hard, rubbing his bound fingers over the bruises on his face. Eventually, he gave me a solemn nod. "For both of us," he agreed.

CHAPTER NINETEEN

Rest and Rehabilitation

I went back to classes the next day, though my study-prison terms had been lifted for me to spend my afternoons with Jake in the hospital room. Mum said he needed a friend and I was determined to be exactly that, and nothing more, no matter how ardently my emotions tried to persuade me otherwise. It was two days before Jake was given the all clear to walk by Doctor Bickerstaff, after the multiple fractures in his ribcage had started to heal. His hips and legs were badly bruised, but he could move well enough to start wandering around and looking out of the windows, if a little stiffly.

It seemed to me that he was starting to get restless from being cooped up in the same room all the time, so I asked Mum if it would be all right for him to walk down to our flat one evening for a change of scenery. She was more than welcoming of the idea, suggesting a multitude of dishes that she could cook for him, a thought that filled me with utter dread. Eventually, I made her settle on a simple chicken dinner and went to give Jake the good news. I found him seated on the windowsill, clutching at his ribs and looking out into the cold, frosty evening as the sun came down far too early. The hospital room was growing dim, but he hadn't put any lights on. He was a shadowy figure in his dark clothes, illuminated only by the early sunset.

"You've gotten dressed," I said as I approached.

He nodded, heaving himself off the sill to stand up straight. "I got sick of being in bed," he replied.

I told him of his invitation to dinner, and he nodded eagerly. There was a sudden rush within me at the sight of his smile, but I forced it back down and tried to stay calm. He looked at my lips for a long, noticeable moment before he blinked, like the rush had hit him too. I offered him my hand and he took it, his fingers wiggling a little under the bandages as he tried to get them moving again.

"It's a bit of a walk from here," I said sheepishly. "About ten minutes. And there are stairs."

"I'm ready," Jake promised. "If I want to be back on that stage for the second round next week, I'm going to have to start walking around sometime."

My heart fluttered like a trapped bird at the thought. "You're going to sing again?" I asked him, "Even after-?"

"Yeah," he answered. "I want to, more than ever now."

Before the attack, I would have been the first one to reward him for his bravery, but now, I was getting less keen about Jake putting himself in the public eye. He had already become a target for one lot of supremacist scum—who was to say that there weren't more of them out there ready to strike? I held Jake's hand firmly as we walked through the halls of Peregrine Place, lit for the evening by small, golden lights in sconces on the walls. Jake looked at all the portraits and fancy tapestries as we walked, but all I saw were the curious expressions of the other students as they passed us by.

It was bitter thought, but I was starting to feel like any

of them could have turned out to be the kind who'd pick a fight with Jake just because of his colour. My nerves rose rapidly when we hit the stairs, a highly populated area where students went about their social business after dinner. A few were kind enough to nod and say hello to us and I found that I appreciated those generous few so much more than I had before, especially when I noticed the others who skulked away when we came near them. Even in my own school, the home that I trusted, there was plenty of prejudice to be afraid of.

I was relieved when we reached the private staff quarters, but I still carried some trepidation for how Jake would feel about the sight of our pokey, little flat. He knew that Mum was the cook and I wasn't some rich, private-school kid, but I still wondered how he would feel about our shabby furniture and décor that was badly in need of renovation. When I opened the front door, those worries evaporated for a moment as I was greeted by the sight of a chubby-cheeked face glaring up at me.

"Whereyoubin?" Nik asked.

"Right you," I said, pointing a finger at him immediately. "No running around like a monster tonight. This is Jake, and Jake's very poorly. He doesn't need you crashing into him and breaking his bones, got it?"

Nik had stopped listening to me, his eyes focused solely on Jake. He looked up at him as if he was awestruck, his little mouth open slack with his pudgy hands gathered in front of him. Jake crouched down with a wince, his face coming level with Nik's as the little boy continued to gaze at him. Jake put out his bandaged fingers and tickled Nik's little belly gently. A fascinated smile came over Nik's face; he was as still and placid as I had ever seen him.

180

"So you're Hanne's little brother," Jake mused.

"Nik," Nik mumbled.

"How about you show me where to sit down, eh Nik?"

"Kay," he said.

The toddler wandered off as I helped Jake back upright. I beamed at him, trying to ignore the rush once again.

"He's always so much better with boys than girls," I explained with a sigh. "I could scream at him all day, but as soon as a boy starts talking, everything changes."

"Maybe I'm just charming?" Jake suggested with a grin.

I didn't agree out loud, but I was sure he could see the answer in my eyes. A clattering sounded from our little kitchen and, as we followed Nik towards the battered sofa, my mother's head popped around the kitchen door. I was genuinely surprised to see her face smoothed out with a little make-up and her usually wayward hair tucked back in a bun. She smiled at us both like we were made of solid gold.

"There you are!" she said brightly. "The roast 'as just come out of the oven. I'll be just a moment."

Mum's head receded. I shivered at the sudden feel of Jake's lips approaching my ear, his hand leaning on the middle of my back for support.

"Your impression of her was spot on, actually," he said in a voice dripping with mirth.

"Told you so," I giggled back.

I helped him into a seat at the oak dinner table, which I suddenly noticed was crowded with seats for seven. Jake's eyes were travelling over the other seats too as he counted them. A knock sounded mere moments later at the door. I rose sharply, hoping dearly that it wasn't Dai Bickerstaff that I was going to

find on the other side when I opened it up. The sandy-blonde head of hair that greeted me was a huge surprise, especially coupled with a cheeky grin and an armful of records.

"Leighton!" I squealed.

"All right, cheeky monkey?" he asked. "Your mum invited us, and you know how I miss her cooking when I'm away."

I stifled a laugh as Leighton entered the flat, followed swiftly by Hanne and Mr and Mrs Haugen. Nik made a beeline for his sister through the crowd, kicked her hard in the shin, and tried to run away again, laughing like a maniac. Mr Haugen caught him and lifted him to his chest where he couldn't cause any more trouble, smiling at us all but looking very tired. The merry group trundled towards the table, pausing for a moment when they saw one of its seats already occupied.

Jake looked at the ground awkwardly, and then up to me for help. I had one awful moment where I thought the Haugens were going to ignore him, but then Mrs Haugen came forward with her walking stick. She pushed her curls out of her face and leaned towards the table, extending a hand to Jake. He got up immediately, but I saw him jerk with pain even as he did so. Mrs Haugen quickly took hold of his shoulders and put him back in his chair.

"I'm sorry, my dear," she said quietly. "I didn't mean for you to get up, but it's very polite of you to do that. My little brother here stopped bothering long before he reached your age."

"I was saving my legs," Leighton protested.

Jake was at one end of the table, and I sat to his right. Leighton took the seat on his other side opposite me, still smiling at us both.

"All right, mate?" he asked Jake. "I'll save you my sister's inevitably long-winded introductions. That's Kit and Henri Haugen; they run this school, more or less. If you know Josie, then you probably already know Hanne. And I'm Leighton Cavendish. Please don't call me Mr Cavendish; I like to think I'm not that old yet."

"Got it," Jake answered with a nod. "Nice to meet you all."

"You take all the fun out of things, Leighton," Mr Haugen said, settling with Nik on his knee. "I thought I'd found a teenage boy to practice on."

"Practice what?" I asked him.

"Intimidation," he replied. "It's going to be an important skill, when Hanne gets a little older."

"Daddy!" she protested in a high, embarrassed squeal.

Laughter at the table broke any remnants of surprise at Jake's presence, especially when Mum served the food and we began to eat. The Haugens and Leighton carried on at the dinner table as they usually did, exchanging jokes and asking Jake about his job and his schooling. At first, he was shy to answer them, but the longer the meal went on, the more comfortable he seemed to become. He told them that he had finished school this summer and followed Noah straight into work at Halfway.

"I should have been going to work with my dad at the car garage," he explained, "but..." His face fell.

"Yes," Mrs Haugen said sadly. "Steven told us. We're very sorry for your loss, young man; it's a crime in itself that no-one spotted your father to help him."

Jake looked sad, but he nodded forcefully and thanked her.

"Was he a mechanic?" Mr Haugen asked.

Jake nodded again, looking brighter this time. "He was a

ground mechanic in the United States Army. That's how he came to Kent in the first place."

Leighton and Mrs Haugen rolled their eyes as Mr Haugen burst into a spirited conversation about the war. As much I loathed hearing about it over and over again, it was wonderful to see Jake telling tales of his father's skills and exploits. He looked proud and bright as he spoke and that rush was back in my chest as I watched him, with what seemed like a permanent smile on my lips.

Have you kissed him yet?

Hanne. I found her at the far end of the table next to my mother, her head bowed in her lap and a little grin on her lips. With a rueful glare, I let my mind reach out to hers.

We're not doing this tonight, I told her. *Jake doesn't know about psychics. Don't make him suspicious!*

You're avoiding the question, Hanne replied. *So I think that means yes.*

When dinner was through, Leighton let us loose on the bag of records he'd brought, another batch of older singles that he was finished listening to. Hanne carried them to my room as I helped Jake up and showed him the way. My room wasn't as tidy as it could have been, with schoolbooks strewn over the bedside table and new pictures and posters piled up as they waited for a space on my wall. Jake looked around, smiling all the while, until he laid eyes on the massive record player. His mouth fell open a little.

"My friend Ness gave it to me," I said proudly. "She used

to work here, but now she's a nurse at Ashford A and E. What do you think of it?"

"I think I need to hear how the King sounds on this thing," he replied.

Jake sat on the edge of my bed as Hanne and I rifled through the records to find the best of Elvis. In the new bag that Leighton had brought, I found 'I Feel So Bad', the double a-side, right at the bottom. I pulled it out and showed it to Jake. He nodded eagerly.

"We talked about that one," he said.

I couldn't help but be elated that he'd remembered that. Jake put his legs up on the bed to rest them, and Hanne and I sat on the floor near the player so we could change the vinyls as needed. We were into our third Presley track when I started to feel an empty kind of longing in my stomach. The lyrics washed over me, fading like a daydream as I looked up at Jake's smiling face, his lips moving to the melody. This was what it could be like if we were together, spending hours listening to our favourite singles, arguing over who'd have control of the radio. A life filled with music and romance.

It was what I'd always wanted, but Jake Bolton was the last guy in the world that I'd expected it to come from. He was handsome and tall, but nothing like the blonde-haired, blue-eyed boys I'd always fawned over in the past. Being attracted to someone with dark skin was never even something I'd discussed with Hanne before; the idea hadn't existed in my mind until I met him. Yet now I knew that I was going to harbour these feelings for him whether we could be together or not. The conflict in me was ruining such a perfect moment with my friends, but I couldn't find a solution that fit.

Josie, a rasping voice suddenly crooned. *Have you got a minute, kid?*

V.W.; it had to be. The voice was powerfully strong, almost deafening, and I recoiled suddenly on the floor. Jake and Hanne looked to me, but I waved a hand at them, getting onto my feet.

"Are you all right?" Jake asked.

"Fine," I mumbled. "Just clumsy. Need the bathroom. I'll be right back."

I rushed to the bathroom and shut the door behind me, pushing the bolt across until it clicked. I felt dizzy from the sheer strength of V.W.'s presence; it was like I could feel him leaning on my brain.

Perhaps you'd better come to me, he suggested.

The weight lifted. I sat on the edge of the bathtub, collecting myself for a moment before I reached out for his mind again. V.W. was at the outer door to a small block of flats, standing next to a sign that read **GROSVENOR PARK**. He fished a key out of his pocket and put it into the lock.

"Can I ask what Jake Bolton's doing in your bedroom with a bashed-up face?" V.W. asked casually. "Frost told me he was off sick."

He is, I replied. *He got beaten up really badly by this gang who hate coloured people. He's been recovering in the ward at my school.*

V.W. nodded. He had passed through the door and was walking up two flights of stairs, onto a landing labelled as the first floor. Doors with dark numbering flew by on either side as he swiftly walked the length of the long corridor ahead.

You're really powerful when you're in my head, I told him. *I felt like my brain was going to explode.*

"I *have* had fifty years to practice," V.W. answered with a chuckle. "And I'm much more interested in your powers than mine. What's the problem with them, exactly?"

He had reached a door marked **41**. I was about to start explaining the split-vision effect of my powers to V.W. when his door opened from the inside, before he'd even got his key up to its lock. Tendrils of thick cigarette smoke escaped the room, hitting V.W. in the eyes and making them water a little. When his vision cleared, I saw three stocky figures waiting for him in his lounge. The nearest one was a bald man with a long scar running down one side of his face. He cracked the knuckles of his thickset hands together, grimacing and showing off the gaps in his teeth, replaced by golden ones instead.

"We've come to collect," the bald man snarled.

And suddenly, I was back in my bathroom, the vision of V.W.'s flat nothing but a memory. I felt a force, as though he had physically pushed me away from him, and it was all I could do not to fall into the bath as I gripped the sides and kept myself steady. That awful heaviness settled in my head again.

Sorry kid, unexpected company. I'll catch you another time.

V.W.'s usually cool voice sounded speedy and alarmed. Even after the pressure of his presence had gone, I heard the panic of his tone echoing in my mind. I got to my feet, splashing my face with water as I tried to calm my nerves after the suddenness of it all. Who were those thugs that were waiting for him and what were they collecting? Was he going to be all right? A knocking at the door made me jump half out of my skin.

"Josie? Are you okay in there?" Hanne asked.

"I think so," I replied, though I had to admit, I wasn't all that sure.

CHAPTER TWENTY

Round Two

On Jake's last morning at Peregrine Place, Mr Haugen excused me from drill so that I could help him pack and say goodbye. Jake was moving around much more fluidly, his torso and legs becoming flexible again, so Doctor Bickerstaff had given him the all-clear to go back to work washing dishes, though he had advised him against getting back on stage any time soon. I knew that Jake wouldn't listen to that for a second, so I wasn't surprised when I entered the hospital room to find him holding a broom handle in place of a microphone stand. He was practising his tricks and moves with it, looking somewhat successful. When he noticed me, Jake set the broom down, putting his hands into his pockets with a small grin.

"Is that the state of your packing skills?" I asked him.

The little brown suitcase his mother had brought with his clothes was bulging and un-closable, shirtsleeves and shoelaces hanging out over its ends.

"I've never had to pack a case before," he told me.

I moved to it and emptied the contents out, setting about re-folding everything and putting it back neatly. Jake put his arm around my shoulders and gave me a squeeze. I dropped the shirt I was holding, hands suddenly limp.

"You've been really great to me," he told me, still holding me close. "I wish things were different, you know?"

I did know. I turned into his touch, looking up into his gleaming eyes. My gaze fell to his lips. "Couldn't they be?" I asked, leaning closer.

Jake let me go, shaking his head. He started to help me pack, following how I folded the shirts, his newly healed fingers moving stiffly.

"Your mum and dad were together," I reasoned.

"And now she's a widow because of it," Jake replied, his voice hollow. "I don't want that for you."

We worked in silence for a few moments more, until the sound of laughter caught my ear. Jake and I turned just in time to see the giggling, bounding form of Nik Haugen racing past the hospital room doors. I quirked a brow.

"That's not right," I said. "What's he doing up here?"

"Come on," Jake said quickly. "That huge staircase is that way. He's gonna get hurt."

We raced out into the hallway and chased after the toddler. I was mortified to find that Jake was right and Nik was heading directly for the stairs. The toddler kept on laughing and looking around him, paying no attention whatsoever to where he was going. I heard a sudden cry from behind us.

"Nik!"

It was Blod Bickerstaff, struggling to catch us up. She ran barefoot with a pair of high heels in her hands.

"Nik! Get him, will you? He's going to hurt himself!"

The stairs were getting closer, but we weren't gaining enough ground on the little boy to reach him. I heard a sudden groan from my side and Jake burst into a faster run, blasting past

189

me with a cry of pain as he let his long legs break into a proper sprint. Nik was almost at the top of Peregrine's grand staircase when Jake made a dive and scooped the youngster into his arms. I reached them not long after that, grabbing the protesting toddler to stop him from kicking at Jake. Blod arrived a few moments later, helping Jake to his feet. He held his chest, wincing.

"I don't think that did my bruises any favours," he said in a hoarse, wheezy tone.

"Thank you so much," Blod cried, wrapping her arm around him and planting one of her sticky kisses on his cheek. "The little bugger slipped out whilst I was doing my hair. Kit never told me he could open doors."

I wrestled with Nik all the way back to the hospital room. I was worried for Jake and his healing bones at first, but by the time we'd returned to the half-packed suitcase, he had his breath back and he seemed steady as ever. Doctor Bickerstaff met us at the door, his eyes brimming with concern.

"Did you catch him?" he asked his wife.

"Did I heck," Blod scoffed. "Jake nabbed him at the top of the stairs."

"Thank God," the doctor replied. He clapped Jake on the shoulder. "Good man."

Jake smiled back proudly. Bickerstaff turned to me then instead, taking the baby out of my arms and passing him to a reluctant-looking Blod. He waggled one finger, motioning me to follow him towards his office. When we were inside the whitewashed room, the doctor closed the door gently and perched on the edge of his desk. I felt the tiny hairs rising on the back of my neck as I wondered what this was all about.

"Josie," he began, "I've been talking to Miss Cartwright

about your psychic sight."

I groaned, feeling that my morning was about to be ruined by yet another adult lecturing me on the weakness of my skills.

"I'm sorry," I said automatically. "I'll try harder in the future."

"Harder?" Bickerstaff said. He ran a hand through his silver-blonde hair. "I don't think you understand me. The sight that you possess is very unique, Josie. Being able to see into the present moment and the mind of another at the same time is a highly valuable skill. Why haven't you told anyone that you can do this?"

I froze, repeating what he'd just told me in my mind. I had a valuable skill? Surely, I'd heard him wrong.

"I…" I began, shrugging as words eluded me. "When I couldn't stay in the deep thinking thing that Miss Cartwright's always banging on about, I just thought I was doing it wrong."

Bickerstaff smiled—a rare sight.

"Just because something's different, that doesn't make it wrong."

A knock sounded at the door, and Jake suddenly poked his head around it as it opened. "Sorry, Doctor," he said sheepishly, "but my mom and brother are here to take me home."

"Of course," Bickerstaff said.

He and I walked from the office to find Mrs Bolton packing the last of Jake's things into his case. I waved at Noah and the absurdly tall boy gave me a grin in return, putting an arm around his brother's shoulder when Jake approached.

"If I might have a word before you go?" Bickerstaff asked Mrs Bolton.

"Oh!" she exclaimed. "Of course, Doctor, of course. Very important. Noah, keep packing."

"Sure thing," he complied, delving into the case.

Jake and I looked at each other across the short distance between us. I wanted to hug him, to hold him close and not let him go. It had been so nice to see him every single day—now we would have no excuse to do that anymore. We'd have to go back to seeing each other for a few measly hours at work. I didn't want my life to return to that, but I could hardly say so in front of Jake's family and the Bickerstaffs. Instead, I just stood there, feeling trapped, until Jake stepped forward and took my hand. He gave it a gentle squeeze.

"I won't forget any of this," he said quietly.

"Me either," I replied.

"Hey," Noah said. Jake and I broke contact instantly. "This isn't your book, is it?"

He was holding up a small book with a hard cover. Jake took it from him, looking surprised, and then suddenly thrust it into my hands. I searched his face, finding him apologetic.

"Sorry," he stammered. "I swiped it from your room the other day. I was bored and it looked like science fiction, but it's not."

I looked down, horrified to see the words **Techniques of the Synsk** staring back at me. Mrs Bolton was suddenly upon me, her warm arms trapping mine as she gave me a hug.

"Sorry we didn't have time to chat, Josie sweetie," she said. "You'll have to come for tea sometime. Come on, boys, or I'm going to be late at the factory."

And then they were gone, and I stood with the textbook in my hands. A million questions for Jake raced in my mind, like how much of this book had he read and, even worse, how much did he believe to be true? What did he think of me for owning it, for keeping it on my bedside table? The pivotal secret that I wasn't supposed to reveal had just been left wide open for Jake to explore, but now he'd set off home and taken that secret knowledge with him. A panic spread all over me as I gripped the book hard.

The next time I saw Jake was the day of the second round of V.W.'s competition. It had been dull at work without his surly grumblings in the kitchen, so when I arrived and heard him moaning that the bar staff had reorganised everything and done it wrong, I felt calmer than I had before. He didn't seem to look at me strangely when we greeted one another, save for the blush in his cheek when I smiled. His bruises were mostly healed and hardly visible against the dark hue of his skin, and I wondered if I was just being paranoid about him getting his hands on Cartwright's book.

I looked around for something to distract my thoughts. It was perfectly possible that Jake had taken one glance at the book and just discarded it.

"Ooh, a new milkshake flavour," I said, noticing a box of flavouring on the worktop. "Do you think Frosty will let us try it?"

"How would I know?" Jake asked, a glint in his eye. "I'm not a *mind reader.*"

I could tell by the curl in his lip that he thought it was a joke, which was better than confirming that the national secrets of Peregrine Place had been revealed. I shrugged the comment off with a chuckle of my own, passing through the kitchen and out into the main room. I didn't realise how relieved I was to see V.W. until I caught sight of him poring over a sheet of paper at a table as per usual. The threat of the thugs who had been waiting for him had been hovering in the back of my mind for a few days, but now I felt a cool sense of relief fill my chest.

"Better get this place spick and span, kiddo," V.W. crooned with his sharp smile. "It's going to be electric in here tonight."

He wasn't wrong. Mr Frost stood at the doors, proudly surveying his club as it became progressively more packed. Kids were lining up along the wall to queue for the bar and get theirs orders in for shakes and ice cream, meaning that I was rushed off my feet trying to keep the dirty glasses circulating back to Jake in the kitchen. I dreaded to think what was going to happen when Noah took over soon for Jake to get ready to sing in the show; he wasn't half as well acquainted with glassware and soapsuds as his speedy brother. If this were a military operation, reinforcements would have been called in hours ago. As it stood, I was a troop ready to collapse on the firing line.

"Crikey, you look knackered," a voice told me.

"Don't say that, Leighton," another snapped. "You look lovely dear. Very grown up in your workplace."

It took me a moment to pull my focus from the busy room to see Leighton and Mrs Haugen stopping in front of me. I admired Mrs Haugen for bustling through the crowds with her walking stick; I was finding it hard enough to cope being able-bodied. Leighton tipped me a wink and looked around the club, his shoulders bouncing to the beat from the jukebox.

"Nice stage, nice tunes," he said with a nod. "Can't wait to see the acts go up."

"You came to watch the talent show?" I asked them.

Mrs Haugen nodded. "Well, now that we know two of the boys trying to make the finale, it would have been rude not to support them," she surmised.

"Plus, it was a good excuse to leave Henri at home with the baby," Leighton added.

Mrs Haugen smacked him really hard in the arm, in the way that only an infuriated older sister could. I found myself thinking of my father for a brief moment. If he'd stuck around, would I have had a little brother to be a thorn in my side too? Mrs Haugen had a playful, youthful look about her as she too spied the place out.

"We mustn't keep you from your work, dear," she said as she noticed my full tray of glasses. "If you could show me a nice place to sit, then we'll get settled and not bother you again."

I was pleased that they were bothering me; it was an excellent excuse not to wade back into the fray as I skirted around the rows of chairs in the club's centre and led the pair to a quiet table at the back of proceedings. We were near the office door where I knew Tommy was already getting ready. He would be pleased to see a familiar face in Mrs Haugen when he emerged, though I was almost certain it would once again put him off singing his song for Hanne. Not that she was here to witness it. That thought hit me as I helped Mrs Haugen into her seat.

"Is Hanne not coming?" I asked her.

Mrs Haugen shook her head. "She didn't want to," she said, sounding as surprised as I looked. "I did think it was strange.

Has there been some teenage drama that I'm not aware of?"

I was as clueless as she was, but two sad possibilities hit me at once. The first was that, due to his reluctance, Hanne might have given up on Tommy. The second, more depressing, thought was that I had been so wrapped up in my feelings for Jake that my best friend was going through something, and I had failed to notice it.

"Maybe she's a bit afraid," Leighton suggested. "I mean, that attack on your boyfriend was awful, Josie. It just goes to show that there are some nasty characters about the village right now."

The 'b' word struck me with a flush to my cheeks, but Mrs Haugen jumped in and started asking Leighton something about the stage lights, so there was no time to correct him. He didn't seem bothered by the fact that Jake and I might be together at all, nor did Mrs Haugen for that matter. Had they all just assumed it the other night at dinner? I didn't understand how they could be so unfazed by Jake when people like Dai and his awful friends had taken such violent exception to him. I found myself wishing that more people were like Leighton and his sister. When I glanced across the room to see Jake waiting at the bar, ready to perform, the gossipy expressions and occasional sneers of the onlookers told me that my wish wasn't coming true anytime soon.

"Right, right. Settle down, you lot."

Frost had assumed the stage, tapping at his microphone repeatedly, like he wasn't sure that the crowd of youngsters could hear him.

"We're almost ready to get started," the round gent began, his moustache twitching. "Just a few words from our dear Mr Walsh to introduce tonight's kids."

Glorious applause erupted from the assembled masses as V.W. got to his feet. He was sharply dressed in a dark grey suit with shiny, silver lapels, making him look like a shark as his slim, tall shape cut through the crowds. V.W. stepped up onto the stage and clapped a few times to make sure he had everyone's attention, his toothy grin adding to the final shark-like effect. He waited patiently for the murmurs to die down, patting the air with his beringed hands, the silver catching in the spotlights.

I felt a sharp tug at my sleeve.

"Josie," Leighton whispered with a snap, "who is that guy?"

"Vince Walsh," I answered hastily, trying to hear what V.W. was saying. "He's a record producer, why?"

When I finally turned to look at Leighton, I was shocked by the expression on his face. He was studying every inch of V.W. where he stood addressing the crowd. He was terribly pale, his jaw turned slack, his fingers trembling against the table edge.

As if he had seen a ghost.

CHAPTER TWENTY-ONE

Skeletons and Closets

I continued working as the six acts vying for a place in the final took their places on the stage. Tonight, V.W. had designed the show so that Jake was second to last and Tommy was at the very end, ensuring that the crowd would stay and wait for the true talent to appear. Though I was enjoying the singers and their efforts, I kept sweeping past the back of the room to see the far table where I'd seated Mrs Haugen and Leighton. His grave reaction to V.W. wasn't their only strange moment of the evening.

Since then, the pair of siblings had been in heated conversation, their voices low and their faces close to one another. They frequently looked as though they were arguing and they kept looking up toward the stage and the judging table, but their eyes weren't focused enough to be watching the acts. Had they not been far superior psychics to me, I would have already tried to access their minds to hear what was going on. In the break, when the band was setting up for Jake's song, Mrs Haugen went to the tables to try and speak to Blod, but she returned looking more frustrated than ever.

Jake sang Sam Cooke's 'Cupid', as I'd advised, and he was note perfect as his wonderful voice carried out over the crowd. He received a ton more applause than he had the last time, his chest swelling with pride even as he panted to get his breath back after the number. I was glad that he'd done a slow song whilst he was still getting his strength back, and even gladder when I saw V.W. get up to shake his hand in front of everyone else. He seemed to be congratulating him, then he applauded again and set the crowd off into a new round of cheers.

Even as I watched and wanted to be fully immersed in Jake's glory, my eyes still kept slipping back to Leighton and Mrs Haugen. He was openly pointing at V.W. now where he stood ready to bring Tommy to the stage. In all the years I'd grown up with the happy-go-lucky Leighton, I had never seen him wear so serious a look. What was it about the mogul that had set him off?

Tommy and his Tele came to the stage with a Sedaka medley that blasted from his strings as his fingers flew over them. He had arranged his own seamless transitions between the songs, giving about thirty seconds of each rock 'n' roll melody before he shifted into the next. The crowd screamed wildly, leaping to their feet to dance even in the rows directly in front of the stage. I was at the bar handing some glasses over when I saw V.W. turn in his seat to assess the frenzy. He nodded at them, looking very satisfied with himself. I wished that he might catch sight of Leighton to give me some clue as to what was going on, but all the kids on their feet were blocking his view of the back of the room. Instead, his narrow eyes found mine and he gave me a thumbs-up. I smiled back, still desperate to know what all the whispering was about.

My chance soon arrived to find out. As soon as the contest was over, V.W., Blod, and Frost retired to the office to make their decisions. When they bypassed Mrs Haugen and Leighton at their table, I saw Leighton shield his face deliberately by turning away before any of them got there. Even Blod didn't notice them as she breezed by, laughing and chatting with the two men. When the trio of judges were out of sight, Leighton and Mrs Haugen got up and went as swiftly as they could to the front door.

"I'm taking a break," I said firmly, setting my drinks tray down on the bar.

One of the servers shouted something after me, but I set off like a rocket to pursue my targets. When I left Halfway's front doors, I caught the very edge of Mrs Haugen's walking stick rounding the right side of the building. I followed slowly, peering around the corner to find that they were walking towards the backyard. I crept after them, stopping at the next corner, near the kitchen door, and crouching down beside a dustbin.

"I'll try and get Claudette," Leighton said, putting a hand to his forehead with a look of concentration on his face.

The pair were standing in the semi-darkness beside the Bolton brothers' little mint green car. Mrs Haugen put a hand on her brother's arm. "Are you sure it's him?" she asked. "We could be giving Claudette a terrible fright over nothing otherwise."

"Do you think I'd forget that face?" Leighton asked, fraught with tension. "That man…" He choked on his words, pointing back towards the club. "He beat me to within an inch of my life when I was just a kid. I still had nightmares about him five years after they'd put him in prison. I never thought I'd have to see him again."

Mrs Haugen soothed her brother's shoulder with a patient hand. In the muted light, I could see her face weighed down by worry.

"All right then," she conceded.

They were contacting my mother by the link in Leighton's

mind. I saw him focus hard with a hand to his temple, his eyes glazing over as he reached her. Silence followed. There were long, agonising moments of that silence, filled with psychic words that I couldn't hear, but desperately wanted to. After a moment, Leighton shook his head, his mouth twisting in frustration even though his eyes still had that absent look.

"Oh, you tell her, Kit," he barked suddenly. "She won't bloody believe me. I'll let her hear you; I'm opening up the link."

Mrs Haugen stepped closer to her brother. "Claudette, can you hear me?"

Leighton nodded. I was amazed by the variety of skills they had, my mind flickering for just a moment to what Doctor Bickerstaff had told me about my own talents.

"Claudette, it really is him," Mrs Haugen continued. "It's Victor Webb, going by a different name. Vince Walsh, he's called. Not very imaginative, I'm sure you'll agree. But we've seen him, Leighton's seem him, and he's certain. He's posing as a record producer."

Posing? What did they know about V.W. that I didn't? Leighton had said something about him being in prison, now Mrs Haugen was suggesting that he was living under a false name. I thought of the sharp-suited mogul and all the kindness he'd shown to Jake, Tommy and, perhaps, especially, me. I couldn't make the pieces fit in my head to be sure that what I was hearing made sense.

"She's asking what he wants," Leighton told his sister. "What do we think he's doing here?"

"I should think it's quite obvious," Mrs Haugen replied. "He must be here for Josie."

A lump as big as a cricket ball expanded in my throat.

Me? What did I have to do with any of this? If V.W. was a
criminal, then what on earth could he possibly want with me?
And what was he doing running a talent show in a music club in
the middle of nowhere?

"Claudette says Josie was talking about him a few weeks
back," Leighton explained. "He must have made quite an
impression on her."

"He made a beeline for her, I bet," Mrs Haugen added.
Then, after a long, serious pause, she added, "He knows."

"Can we be sure?" Leighton asked fearfully. "Perhaps it's
a fluke that he's here?"

"A coincidence this big would be nothing short of a
miracle," Mrs Haugen answered. She shook her head briskly,
pointing a finger like she did when she was making a point in the
classroom. "Vic's tracked her down. He was very well connected
back in the day; I bet he can get his grubby hands on all sorts of
information."

"If he knows about Peregrine Place, then we're in big
trouble," Leighton supposed. He paused, holding his head again.
"Claudette's frantic. She wants to pull Josie out of the job at the
club. She says we're to bring her home right now."

I felt a desperate resistance building within me, and I was
relieved when Mrs Haugen told him no.

"We can't do that, much as I'd like to," she replied. "If we
pull Josie out, Vic will know the game's up and he might come
after her directly. We can't take the risk of someone like him
getting into Peregrine."

I couldn't believe what I was hearing; it was as though
they were suggesting that V.W. wanted to hurt me or take me
away. He had been nothing but nice to me since the moment we

met, full of praise and jokes, sharing his opinions with me. He had even offered to help me train my gifts. None of that was a sensible accompaniment to a man who was supposed to be a danger to me. I was beginning to think that Leighton had got it wrong, that V.W. wasn't this Victor Webb fellow that sounded like so much bad news. A lot of time had passed since Leighton saw this man; it probably happened before I was even born. He had to be wrong.

"So what do we do then?" Leighton asked, his fists balling.

"We wait," Mrs Haugen decided calmly. "We find out what he's doing here, on the sly, then approach him when the time is right and get him to leave."

She took in a deep sigh, leaning more heavily than ever on her walking stick. "And in the meantime," she continued, "we hope and pray that he doesn't tell Josie that he's her father."

I spent a long time outside in the dark after that, at least twenty minutes after Leighton and Mrs Haugen had gone back inside. It was only when a bright shaft of light cut a slice across the backyard that I looked up, walking in the direction of the kitchen door. As I weaved through the parked cars, my heart caught in my chest at the silhouette emerging from the doors. It was V.W., moving sharp and fast, his head craned back through the kitchen with a watchful tension in his neck. I quickened my pace to reach him as he fumbled in his jacket pockets, searching frantically for something.

"It's you," I said, my voice barely a whisper.

He looked up. I took in his sharp features for a moment.

He had high cheekbones and so did I, but Mum's face was rounded and rosier. My hair was straight when hers was curly, and V.W.'s greying locks didn't seem to have any curl to them at all. I was built tall and slim, like him, without what my mother called her 'French curves'. And, when he saw me coming across the yard, I finally noticed his eyes.

They were so narrow that I'd never bothered to look closely at them before, but now I saw that they were dark, with a violet circle around their edges. Though my eyes were paler, leaning more towards blue, that violet circle was something I recognised with a start. I couldn't speak, but V.W. was too preoccupied by his worries to notice my hesitance. He flashed me a smile and went back to his pocket search, producing a set of car keys with a jingle.

"You're not going?" I pleaded, panicked that I wasn't going to have the conversation that I so sorely needed.

"Something urgent has just come up," he explained, eyes shifting to the kitchen door again, like he was concerned someone was about to walk through it. Had he spotted Leighton in the crowd at last? "You should get inside, kiddo; you'll catch your death out here."

He patted me on the arm, making to leave, but it was then that he paused. V.W. stooped, looking into my face and rubbing my upper arm a little with his slim, warm hand. "Hell's bells, you're frozen!" he said. "How long have you been out here? It's bloody December, Josie. Get in there now, unless you want to spend Christmas with pneumonia."

It was a sincere sentence. No gimmicks, no wink, no cheeky, sharp-toothed grin. No tap on the nose to let me know that he and I were in on the same thing, even though I knew now that we were. He clearly didn't think that I knew anything, but in that moment, I heard the parenting tone in his voice, the way he lingered at my arm with concern etched all over his face.

"We were going to talk, you and me," I said weakly.

"We will," he promised, looking back at the kitchen again, "but not tonight. I'll catch you in the week, all right?"

He tapped the side of his head to let me know what he meant. I nodded fervently.

"Are you feeling okay?" he asked, eyes roving over my face. "You look like you're going to cry."

I couldn't speak; I had no idea what to say that wouldn't give everything away in that single moment. "I'm fine," I lied. "Just cold."

"Get in then," he urged again, pushing me gently towards the kitchen door. "We'll speak soon."

"Soon," I repeated, feeling numb as I watched him walk away.

I saw his slim shape vanish into the shadows beyond the club, and the sound of an engine soon revved. Headlights flickered into existence, and I found myself watching the outline of his car as V.W. drove away.

He was my dad. I was certain of it; I didn't need to be told by Leighton or anyone else now. Everything was clear in his face and the way he'd been treating me ever since we'd met. I had been seeking his approval even before I knew how much it would mean to me to have it, and he had been proud of even the tiniest things that I had done. There was only one problem with the conclusion that I had come to.

If it was true that he was my father, then everything that Leighton had said half an hour ago was also probably true. He was a criminal, or he had been, in the past. He was violent. They were terrified of him. He was the man that laid-back Leighton had nightmares about, the man whose mere presence had turned a cool, collected thirty-two-year-old into a frightened little boy again in seconds. That was how Leighton had come to know my mother all those years ago. It all made the most terrible kind of sense and, as much as I had always wanted to know my father, now I had to face the horrible truth of who he had been, and who he *still* might be.

"Josie?"

Jake was behind me in the bright kitchen doorway. I turned and fell straight into his arms, tears exploding from my eyes, held-back sobs of shock and confusion suddenly bursting forward. He didn't ask me what was wrong at first; he simply wrapped his arms around me and let me cry. Dishes went unwashed for a long time as we stood there in a close embrace. Jake ran his fingers through my hair and I tried my best not to squeeze his battered torso too hard, though I wanted to cling to him so desperately. He was all that I had—the only person I could turn to who wasn't connected to the mixed-up past between my father and my extended family at Peregrine Place.

When I had calmed down enough to breathe at a normal rate, Jake straightened me up and handed me a dry tea towel to wipe my face.

"I came to tell you I got through to the big finale on Boxing Day," he said, "but I can see something bigger's going on."

Jake rubbed my shoulders firmly, his heat radiating through my empty, frozen body. I fell back into his arms, craving his warmth and comfort.

"If you don't want to tell me, that's fine," he said, pulling me closer. "I'll just hold you. I'll do whatever you need." I took a very deep breath, and told him everything.

CHAPTER TWENTY-TWO

Proof

On Jake's advice, I decided to act as if nothing had happened. The only part of the story I'd left out was the part where Leighton had been psychically linked to my mother, relaying the conversation as if it had only happened between him and Mrs Haugen. Jake reasoned that, if I wanted to be sure that V.W. was my dad without their interference, then I would have to pretend nothing at all had happened until I could confront the record mogul and ask him for the truth.

We didn't have as much time to talk as we needed, since the evening at Halfway was drawing to a close, so Jake told me he would take his mother up on the offer that I could go down to his house for dinner one night. Mum got a call on Monday morning from Mrs Bolton, inviting us both to their house in the village on Tuesday night, so I went to class that morning feeling placated, at least, that I would have Jake to confide in again soon. I hadn't seen Hanne since she'd neglected to come to Halfway for the second round of the show. When she met me at the door of my flat to go to class, like she always did, it was with a vague smile and a completely disinterested look in her eyes.

"Are you feeling better?" I asked her, trying to sound upbeat.

"Better?" she replied, her tone oddly snappy.

"Well," I mumbled, "you didn't come to see the singers. I thought you must have been sick."

"I wasn't sick," she answered, storming ahead of me with a few stomps. "I was banned from going out."

"What?" I demanded, catching up to her. "Why? What happened?"

"Nothing!" Hanne cried, her freckled face twisting in frustration. "That's the worst part."

I nudged her elbow as we walked. "Come on," I urged. "We only have about ten minutes before we get to Cartwright's class. Tell me what went on."

She looked reluctant, making me wonder what could possibly be so bad that she was resisting telling me. A few footsteps went by before she gave a little sigh, slowing her pace once more.

"On Friday, Tommy asked me to meet him," Hanne explained. "It was totally out of the blue, but obviously I went. We met out on the sports pitch between classes, up in that quiet spot where Dad stores all the footballs in the big shed. Tommy said he had something important to tell me."

I waited with bated breath, hoping the conversation was going where I thought it would.

"But then Dad was actually there, *in* the shed moving things around," Hanne continued, almost whining. "He burst out and told Tommy to get lost, then he marched me back to the apartment and gave me this huge lecture about boys." She gave me a bitter glance. "He said that just because you've got a boyfriend doesn't mean I need one; I'm too young to start all that, *apparently*, even though I'll be fifteen *really* soon."

"A boyfriend?" I repeated.

"Yes," Hanne snapped. "And I can't believe I have to hear it from my dad first that my best friend has a boyfriend! Why didn't you tell me that you and Jake are together?"

"Because we're not," I exclaimed. Hanne blinked at me. "All right, we did kiss once, but we decided it wasn't safe to date or anything."

"Why not?" Hanne asked.

"Because Jake got beaten up just because we're friends," I said, feeling the familiar, bitter sadness rise once again, "Can you imagine what those nutters might do to him if we were actually boyfriend-girlfriend?"

"I suppose it would be a bit unusual," Hanne mused, "but if you really like each other…"

"It's not relevant anyway," I concluded. "We're just friends. I'm going to dinner at his house with Mum tomorrow and we'll do friend things."

A pause followed. "What was it like to kiss him?" Hanne asked mercilessly.

I gave her a look. "Really? I just said we're going to be friends. I'm not thinking about things like that anymore."

She carried on, looking at me like a hopeful puppy waiting for a tennis ball to be thrown.

"It was really, really good," I said quickly, rushing on towards class before she could see how much I blushed at admitting it.

It was a bizarre sight when Miss Cartwright looked happy.

A Place Halfway

The stark December sun lit up her face and illuminated her pale golden hair to make the strands look like shafts of sunlight. She was standing in the doorway of her classroom side-on, ushering everyone in with a huge, repeated sweep of her hand.

"Come on, come on," she said, sounding frighteningly gleeful in her impatience. "We've got a very important demonstration to do today. I want to get on with it. Pick your feet up, Tommy!"

Tommy was rushing into the room a few feet in front of us, looking back over his shoulder as though Miss Cartwright's mirth was some terrible trap he was being lured into. We followed and took our seats, joined by only two other latecomers before the class was full and assembled. Miss Cartwright shut the door, striding across to the board in her usual teacherly way. I couldn't remember a time when I'd seen her *not* standing with her arms folded. Today, she leaned them on her desk as she watched us all, sea-green eyes eventually focusing in on me.

"We shan't be working from the textbook," she told us. "Today, we're doing something brand new."

Excited murmurs followed her as she prepared a single sheet of paper and a pencil. She moved to Tommy and set the page down before him as the class watched in tense fascination. From her pocket, she pulled a fresh stick of chalk. As first, I thought it was coming to me, but Miss Cartwright took a long step to her side and presented it to Hanne. My best friend took the stick and waited patiently.

"Up to the board with you, Hanne," the teacher urged. Hanne went. "The rest of you, gather around Tommy's table here, where you can see his page."

I didn't even have to get out of my seat to see it, but the

other kids stood in a semi-circle around Tommy's back. Miss Cartwright rubbed her hands together.

"In a moment, I will ask Hanne to enter Tommy's consciousness," she began to explain.

Tommy made a strange noise in his throat. "Uh, Miss," he interrupted. "What if she can read my thoughts?"

A few of the boys laughed at him. Even Miss Cartwright's stern lip curved a little.

"Hanne is not yet that advanced," she assured him. "But if she were, then I'd say more fool you for not learning proper mental discipline to keep them to yourself."

Everyone laughed nervously. Miss Cartwright didn't usually make the kind of jibes that you could laugh at, but then this whole moment was very unusual. The teacher pushed the pencil across Tommy's desk and into his grip.

"When Hanne enters your mind, you will begin writing down a succession of random numbers," Miss Cartwright replied. "You can do as many as you like for about twenty seconds. I will tell you when to stop." She turned where she stood to give Hanne a nod. "It will then be Hanne's job to remember and record as many numbers as she can on the blackboard. Is that all clear?"

Hanne nodded. Miss Cartwright stood in front of Tommy's desk so that his page of numbers would be blocked from all sides. She told them to commence, counting the seconds silently on her watch. Tommy scribbled like a madman, filling the top half of the page with numbers of all shapes and sizes. By the time Miss Cartwright told him to stop, I realised that nobody could possibly have remembered that many in one go.

The blackboard began to fill up, but after about the first seven numbers, Hanne's memory started to fail. Other kids were saying, "No" and "Close" and "You've done that one already", until she put her chalk down and looked back at Miss Cartwright, frowning deeply, as though she was thoroughly disappointed with herself. Miss Cartwright looked her over thoughtfully.

"Difficult, isn't it?" she asked the class. "Remembering everything when you come out of a trance is no easy feat. Come and sit down, dear, you've done rather well."

Hanne slumped back to her seat amid the crowd gathered near Tommy.

"Josie, clean the board," Miss Cartwright said.

I grumbled under my breath. Of course it would be me that got the clean-up job. Sidling over to the board, I ran the eraser over Hanne's attempts with a lazy hand. I almost jumped with surprise when I saw that Miss Cartwright had joined me at the front of the class. She was holding the stick of chalk, which she slowly offered me.

"Josie," she said, "I'd like you to try to recount some more numbers from Tommy." She gave me a knowing sort of glare. "By whatever means you choose," she added.

I had a feeling that I knew what she meant. Doctor Bickerstaff had been talking to her about me, after all. Keeping my eyes open and focused on the board, I let just a little of my mind slip away until it found Tommy's. I could see behind me, directly onto his desk where his pencil was poised, waiting for Miss Cartwright's signal again.

"Commence," she ordered.

No sooner than Tommy had written a number, I wrote it too. I could feel a little shadow of his frustration from my distant, but connected state. He tried to write faster, messier, and upside-down, but I could see every number and recall it. When our twenty seconds were up, I broke the connection and stepped back to look at the chalkboard full of information.

"Thank you, Josie," Miss Cartwright said, guiding me back to my seat. She ushered everyone else to return to their places too.

"How did she do that?" a girl demanded as she took her seat.

"My textbook teaches you that there are two states of consciousness," the teacher began to explain, "but it seems our Josie has discovered a third."

It was hard to believe that Miss Cartwright had built an entire lesson around me, especially one that didn't use me as a bad example like she had in the past. Her face was bright and youthful, eyes dancing over all of us as she interlocked her fingers with a wistful smile.

"Josie has discovered a state halfway between one's own consciousness and that of another," she said. "One of the greatest challenges that we psychics face in the field is having to be immobilised and trance-like when we use our gifts to gain information. Josie, can you walk when you use this power?"

"Yes," I answered. "Well, not very well, but I'm getting better the more I practice it."

"Motion, thought, and action, all at the same time as the psychic link," Miss Cartwright continued proudly. "Can you imagine what advancements we can make to field espionage with this kind of skill? Being in two places at once will revolutionise the whole way the government operates."

"But how do we learn it?" Tommy asked, glancing across at me with awe, like I had suddenly turned into Marilyn Monroe. "I'm used to the trance; I wouldn't know how to break away from it and only be half-present."

A Place Halfway

"Yes, well," Miss Cartwright said thoughtfully, "that's where we're going to need Josie's help, isn't it? All of us."

I froze in amazement. "My help?" I asked, "You want me to teach with you?"

Miss Cartwright smiled the most genuine smile I'd ever seen on her lips. "Not *with* me, dear girl," she explained, "because I'm going to need to be your student too."

The class was dismissed early, and I found that it had been arranged for me to be excused from the rest of the day's lessons. Just a few hours ago, the thought of spending an entire school day with Miss Cartwright would have been enough to see me leaping out of the window and running for freedom, but now things were vastly and rapidly different. It was like a new woman sat before me, reawakened and energised by the possibility of learning something special. Miss Cartwright had always been the most accomplished and knowledgeable psychic in the whole of Peregrine Place, but now she was asking me questions about my mood, my breathing, my thoughts when I stepped into the place halfway in my mind.

She could just about manage to mimic my halfway state by the end of the day, so we arranged to continue on Tuesday right up until Mum and I would leave to get to the Bolton household for dinner. By the time I was getting into a taxi to head down to the village, the whole school was abuzz with the story of Josie and her brand-new power. I felt like a scientist who'd discovered a new element. For once, I was clever and doing something right. Better than all of that, Mum wouldn't stop beaming and overflowing with pride-fuelled words. Even as we sat in the taxi, she wrapped her arms around my shoulders again and kissed my head.

"My daughter, the genius," she crooned.

Jake's house was a little, terraced structure about five minutes down the road from the junction to Carlisle Street. It was the same street where Mrs Bolton had gathered everyone to serve them food on the night of the bonfire, but by the fading light of the winter afternoon, it looked more grey and austere than I remembered. I was nervous as I stood beside Mum when she rang the bell, but the welcome we received soon set me at ease.

"There you are!" Mrs Bolton exclaimed. "Come in, you must be frozen! Did you walk?"

"We got a taxi," I replied.

"Oh no!" Mrs Bolton added, flapping a hand. "You should have said you didn't drive. I would have sent Noah up in Godwin's old car! Oh and you must be Josie's mother! It's Claudette, isn't it?"

"That's right," Mum said, embracing the other woman politely where they stood in the porch.

"You must call me Emma," Mrs Bolton said. "Come through, please! The boys are laying up the table now."

As we walked down the short corridor that veered off to the left, I caught sight of a sign beside the doorway. **It's not much, but it's home.** Beside the words was an old photograph depicting a young couple with their arms around one another. In the picture, Mrs Bolton had short, curly hair and she sat on a step, laughing like the man behind her had told her a really good joke. Mr Bolton was leaning his chin on her shoulder, his long, dark arms sliding around his young wife's shoulders. She clutched them as though she never wanted to let go. I looked at the contrast in their skin, a guilty lump forming in my throat. Mrs Bolton had been brave enough to marry who she wanted to, and the pair of them looked so joyous in the picture.

In the dining room, Jake was hitting Noah with a napkin rolled up into a spiral like a whip. The boys stopped laughing and stood up straight when we entered the room, but I could see Jake still suppressing a chuckle. My mother approached him and gave him a small, gentle, hug.

"'ow are your bones?" she asked. "Are you 'ealing all right?"

"Yes, thank you, ma'am," Jake answered. "I'm feeling fine."

When Mum was introduced to Noah, it left Jake and me a brief moment where we didn't really know what to do. I couldn't hug him like I wanted to, not in front of both our mothers, but it didn't seem right to try and shake his hand. Instead, we stood awkwardly, looking at one another as wordless thoughts passed between us. Once again, I found myself wishing that he knew me well enough for me to speak into his mind.

And then it hit me. Why didn't I just do it? He had been making those little jibes about me being a mind reader ever since he'd mistakenly read some of Miss Cartwright's book, so what was there to stop me from having a little fun? We were sitting down at the dinner table as I ran the thought over in my mind. He might freak out. He might never want to speak to me again if he knew I had powers that weren't natural. He might think I was too different for us to be friends.

But if I had thought that about the colour of his skin, then none of this would ever have happened. I'd taken a chance on getting to know him without even thinking about the repercussions, but I didn't regret it. Surely, he would give me that same kind of acceptance? Mrs Bolton was placing a steaming tureen of carrots on the table. Jake looked at me over the tendrils of steam between us, like he had so much that he wanted to say. Noah and my mother were talking animatedly about his father's old car as Jake and I watched one another. The tension was too much.

I know, I said. *I really want to talk to you too.*

The picture formed in my head as I spoke to him, and it was strange to see myself in his eyes. I focused instead on the other part of my vision, where through my own eyes I could see Jake start suddenly. A knife clanged against his plate on the table, and Noah gave him a funny look.

"Sorry," he said, looking startled again as his mother arrived with more vegetables and ushered everyone to help themselves to a plate-load whilst she fetched the roast.

How much of that book that you stole from me did you read? I asked him. Jake froze again, staring at me uncertainly. *If it was only a bit, pick up your fork. If it was a lot, pick up the knife first.*

Jake swallowed hard, his eyes focused suddenly on his plate. I watched his coffee-hued fingertips as they gingerly reached out for the knife.

It's all true, I told him. *Except for the part about reading your mind. Don't worry; I can't hear what you're thinking. I'm not advanced enough for that yet.*

He let out a little sigh, which I took to be relief. I didn't speak to Jake again during the dinner, except out loud when we were both asked how things were going at work. It was only later, when both our mothers were making coffee in the kitchen, that he approached me quickly, his lips grazing my ear.

"Does this mean that you could talk to me whenever you want?" he asked. "Like, when you're at home and I'm at home?"

"Yes," I replied bashfully.

He ran a hand through his short hair, still looking fairly shocked. "I guess I could get into that," he mused, "so long as you don't go snooping at bath-time."

The very idea of it, mixed with his close proximity to my face, started my skin tingling. When I met Jake's gaze again, he too was blushing, but there was a mischievous glint coming back to his golden eyes. He looked more nervous than I'd ever seen him.

"I knew there was something off about you," he insisted.

"Yeah right," I hit back. "You told me I was perfect before."

Jake looked over his shoulder, as if checking for eavesdroppers, even in his own dining room, then he took hold of my hand. "That hasn't changed," he replied.

CHAPTER TWENTY-THREE

Hearts Turned Loose

"So let me get this straight," Jake said, tossing a ball up and down as he lay back on his bed. "Your dad, V.W., is a super powerful psychic who got your mom pregnant and then went to prison before you were born?"

That's what I think, I replied. *That's what I could piece together, anyway.*

It was Friday night and I was wrestling with Nik to try and get him to put some pyjamas on. The Haugens were out late for a fancy dinner with the Bickerstaffs, so Hanne and I had to try and get Nik off to sleep at a sensible hour. We were in my bedroom, watching as Nik took hold of his little pyjama shirt and swung it over his head like a miniature Tarzan. In the other part of my mind, I could see Jake's hands as he caught and threw his faded tennis ball, looking up at the pale, cracked ceiling of his bedroom. I knew which place I would have rather been in, but having him connected to my mind was as good as I was going to get for now.

"Have you asked anyone else about this?" Jake said.

Not yet, I answered slowly.

I cast a guilty look at Hanne as she chased Nik down off my bed to try and catch him. Was it wrong of me not to trust her with the information about V.W.? I had an awful feeling that she would want to do the right thing if I did, and confess to Leighton and Mrs Haugen that I knew everything. It seemed to me that they would take me away from my job in a heartbeat if that happened, and I just couldn't take the risk yet. It felt terrible to keep the secret from my best friend, but she was still so young, really. She didn't know what it was like to have family problems; her life was always well ordered, apart from the little terrorist who wouldn't put his pyjamas on.

I'm afraid they'll coop me up here if I start asking questions, I confessed to Jake. *Mum knows that V.W.'s around, but she's been really calm about it all week. It's unnerving.*

"Yeah," Jake scoffed, "but that's now, whilst you're home safe. You wait until you're headed to work tomorrow. I bet she won't be so cool about it then. My mom's been crazy every weekend since I got attacked."

But that's different, I retorted. *You got hurt. My dad doesn't want to hurt me.*

Jake stopped throwing the ball around. "What did you say he went to prison for?" he asked.

I don't know, I answered. *I just know Leighton said he was violent. That he attacked him years ago.*

"When Leighton was young like us?"

I felt a tension overcoming my senses that might have belonged to Jake just as much as me. Hanne had chased Nik out into the hall, and she was calling for my help somewhere not far away. Thoughts of the thugs who had been waiting in V.W.'s flat came back to me with fresh perspective. What if they weren't there to threaten him? What if they were his friends? I shuddered at the idea.

"Josie," Jake said slowly, "just don't do anything unless I'm there to protect you, all right? I've got to be nearby. I can't stand the thought of something happening to you."

A calmer feeling settled into my heart. *I promise I won't,* I replied.

Jake suddenly sat up, spinning my view of his room so fast it felt like I was snapping out of a daydream. "Noah's coming," he said. "I've got to go."

See you at work tomorrow, I added quickly.

Jake only nodded, and I saw the tall, lanky form of Noah entering their shared bedroom before I let my mind slide away from his. I walked out into the hall to see Hanne holding Nik around the waist as she tried to prize his pyjama shirt from his pudgy grip. I took the little monster out of her arms and set him down on the floor again.

"What are you doing?" Hanne hissed. "It took me ages to catch him!"

"Forget it," I said calmly. "I don't care what he does anymore." I turned to Nik with the most nonchalant look I could manage. "Go on," I told him. "Do what you like."

I took Hanne's elbow and led her into the living room, where we sat down on the sofa together. She gave me a querying look, but I silenced her before she could speak. After a few moments, Nik ambled in after us, dragging his shirt behind him. He looked very confused by the sudden freedom I had given him. Our game of cat and mouse was over. He stumbled towards me, waving the shirt like a flag.

"Shirton," he asked. "Shirton."

"Come here then," I said serenely.

He stood still for me, letting me pull the creased shirt

down over his head, his dark hair flying in all directions as I tried to smooth it down. Nik clambered up onto the sofa beside me, sinking into the broken, dipped part as he curled into a ball like a kitten would. He released a little yawn, closing his eyes.

"I know Miss Cartwright said you had hidden talents," Hanne began quietly, "but what was *that*? When did you become Super Babysitter?"

"He likes winding us up," I explained, "and I realised that when you give in to it and get angry, he gets worse. So I thought I'd try the opposite for a change."

"And it worked," Hanne marvelled. "What made you think of it?"

I just shrugged, but in truth, I knew that I'd started craving things to be calmer and less dramatic ever since the attack on Jake had occurred. All that time I'd spent arguing with him before he got hurt was wasted energy; we were so good together now that I could hardly remember what his surly face looked like. I relished the thought that he had learned to be happy again in the time that I'd known him, even with the grief that was surely still swirling inside him. The peaceful path was definitely the right one to take from now on.

"Hmph."

Hanne gave a little sigh, resting her chin on her fists as she leaned forward and gazed at the carpet. The toes of her shiny shoes tapped against the frayed fibres.

"This is going to be about Tommy, isn't it?" I asked her. Hanne nodded sadly. "Didn't you find out what he wanted to tell you when your dad interrupted him?"

"No," she groaned. "And he hasn't been near me since, apart from when we were connected in Miss Cartwright's class

K.C. Finn

the other day. It's like I've got the plague or something."

I stood up slowly, not wanting to wake the now-sleeping toddler at my side. I pointed at Nik. "Put him in my bed when you're sure it's safe to move him. I'll be back soon."

"Back?" Hanne asked, eyes widening. "Oh Josie, you're not going to talk to him, are you?"

"Of course I am," I replied. "I'm sick of you two mucking about. This is getting sorted tonight, end of story."

I could see Hanne nibbling at her nails as I headed for the door. I started off down the dark staff corridor, lit dimly by the odd sconce here and there on the panelled walls. I was almost at its end, on the precipice of stepping out into the rest of the school, when the slamming of a door behind me caught my ear. I turned, expecting to see Hanne chasing after me, but took a few steps back when I saw the figure approaching. His tall, muscular frame did nothing but repel me now, those blue eyes filled with concern as he pushed his blonde locks back against his head.

"What are you doing here, Dai?" I said with a huff. "Your parents are out."

"I know," he said, breathing heavy as he reached me quickly. "I wanted to talk to you."

I turned, heading out into the foyer of the old manor house. "We've got nothing to say to each other," I told him as I walked.

"Well, I'm finished at uni for Christmas," Dai replied, matching my stride. "So you're stuck with me for the next two weeks, whether you like it or not, see?"

Christmas. I had barely even thought about Christmas. It was a week away and I'd been putting my wages aside to buy some presents, but I hadn't actually gotten around to it yet.

A Place Halfway

Hanne and I were supposed to go gift shopping in the village on Sunday. Soon Peregrine Place would be an empty chasm again, void of all but staff members and their families as all the boarders went home until after New Year. A horrible thought hit me as I walked, my pace quickening. Tommy was a boarder. And soon he'd be gone.

I burst into a run as I reached the stairs, the soles of my shoes casting loud echoes out into the huge reception hall as I bolted towards the students' living quarters.

"Josie, don't run off!" Dai shouted. "I've got something important to tell you!"

"Later!" I yelled back. "I've got stuff to do!"

He didn't follow me, for which I was grateful. The last thing I needed was Dai poking his nose into why I was wandering through the boys' corridor at night. It was my good fortune that Mrs Cavendish always put her students' names on the front of their dormitory doors, so I found the plaque with Thomas Asher written on it swiftly. He shared with two other boys who I vaguely knew. When I reached his door, there were muffled laughs coming from inside. I gave it a knock.

"Oh," said a boy with sandy hair as he peeped out, "we thought you were a teacher."

"Is Tommy there?" I asked.

The door widened, revealing the small room. Tommy's bed was unmistakeable by the plethora of music posters dotted everywhere, but I was horrified to see his suitcase sitting there, already packed up. A tube of Brylcreem sat atop it, waiting to be added to the contents.

"He's not here," the boy replied. "He's rehearsing."

I nodded and thanked him, taking off again for the

far-off room where I knew he would be. The muffled strains of his guitar reached me no sooner than I had set foot in the long corridor where the disused classroom lay; I bounded along in the dark until I reached the door, my footsteps slowing when I reached its edge. From that closeness, I could hear not only the notes coming from his guitar, but also Tommy's own voice as he practised his lyrics. I was already opening the door before I realised what it was that I was listening to.

"'Cause I can't help it if I'm in love with the girl who's Teacher's pet..."

Tommy leapt out of his skin when he saw me, his guitar hanging limp suddenly as his eyes went wide. "Josie! What are you doing here?"

"Is that Hanne's song?" I asked him, starting to smile excitedly. "You're still practising it. Thank God." I reached him, fixing a firm hand on his shoulder. "You have to sing it for her soon, Tommy. She's giving up on you."

Tommy's shoulders slumped. "Maybe she should," he said forlornly, "after the yellow-belly I've been."

"What are you on about?" I asked him. "That song sounded brilliant. She'll love you forever if you sing her that song."

"But what about her parents?" Tommy retorted, turning off his amplifier and setting down his Tele against a chair. "I assume she told you about her dad accusing us of all sorts of things behind that shed the other day? He scares the life out of me, Josie."

"He's her dad," I replied. "It's his job to protect her." A flash of V.W.'s concerned gaze ran past my mind. "But if you show him you're going to treat her right, he'll have to come around sooner or later. And that starts with being honest about how you feel."

Tommy shook his head. "But her Mum doesn't like me either," he insisted.

"Now you're just being ridiculous," I scoffed. "Mrs Haugen never dislikes anyone."

"Well, all this week in class, she's been really weird with us," Tommy explained, "snappy and bossy and distracted. I thought it must have been because I was there."

"That's not to do with you," I told him, V.W.'s face in my mind once again.

"Can you be sure?" Tommy asked.

I nodded. "You'll just have to trust me on that," I said, "and on the fact that you absolutely must sing that song for Hanne."

I watched him swallow hard before he nodded. "All right," he replied, "I suppose I can give it a try. But I'm going home for Christmas, first thing tomorrow."

I grimaced. "I can hardly drag her out here in the middle of the night for a secret meeting with you," I whined. "Mr Haugen really would brain you then."

Tommy winced at the thought. He took in a sharp breath, and then puffed out his chest. "Right then," he concluded, "It'll have to be at the finale. Mum and Dad are driving me back up on Boxing Day for the last round of the show. I'll do it then. All or nothing."

I put my hands on my hips. "Do you promise?" I urged him. "No chickening out this time?"

He looked scared, but sure. "I swear."

He still wouldn't let me hear all of the song, pushing me out of his rehearsal room and promising over and over again that his yellow belly wasn't going to be on show come Boxing Day. I was immensely pleased with myself as I strode back through the dark halls of my home, skipping down the huge staircase in the semi-dark, eager to get back and tell Hanne not to give up hope. It was only when I reached the edge of the staff corridor at the back of the manor that I remembered what had happened before I found Tommy.

Dai Bickerstaff was outside the door to my flat. He was curled up with his long arms wrapped around his knees, sitting in the dark and staring at the floor. Had he been waiting for me in the cold and the darkness all this time? I approached slowly, wondering what it was he could possibly want and marvelling at how young and small he seemed where he shrank against the doorframe. When I was close enough for him to hear me coming, he lifted his blonde head and gave me that sad look once more.

"You're still here," I said, trying not to give him even an inch of sympathy.

"It's really important that I tell you something," he said, his Welsh boom reduced to a throaty whisper.

"If it's 'Sorry', then it's about bloody time," I hissed.

"I am sorry," Dai said, failing to meet my gaze. He got to his feet. "But that's not all. I'm hoping what I have to say might make you feel a bit less angry with me. I saw Gil on the platform this morning before I got on the train to come yur."

"And?" I asked, revolted by the image of the slimy young man as he came into my head.

"And they're planning another attack," Dai revealed, his whole face looking grave. "They're coming to Halfway tomorrow night, and there's going to be serious trouble."

CHAPTER TWENTY-FOUR

Spoiling

"We should have called the police," I said for what felt like the fiftieth time.

I was drying the last of the glasses in the kitchen at Halfway, standing shoulder to shoulder with Jake as a cold wind crept in through the gap in the door. Jake shook his head, glancing at his wristwatch. Ten to nine. It was nearly time for us all to go home, but there hadn't been a single sign of Gil Croft or his band of thugs all night. To my eternal disappointment, there was no sign of V.W. either; Mr Frost had told me that the record mogul had had to go into London on some urgent business and that he wouldn't be back in the area until much later that night. I wasn't exactly in the mood to hang around and wait in case he showed up.

"The police aren't as helpful as you might think," Noah reasoned. He looked as worried as I felt, his skin abnormally pale. "When they see a bunch of boys fighting and some of them are coloured, you can guess which ones they think started it all."

"I hate this world sometimes," I griped, piling up the glasses.

Jake bumped me gently in the shoulder. He had hardly said a word all night, not since I'd told him of Dai's premonition.

I'm worried about you, I said into his head.

He dried his hands and drained the water, turning to me with a determined look in his eyes. Putting his arms around me, he pulled me in for a squeeze. "I'm prepared this time," he whispered. "We have a plan, remember?"

It was my plan, a cowardly plan, with a very physical back-up plan suggested by Jake immediately after I'd said it.

"And I'll be there with you," Noah asserted. Jake gave his older brother a nod.

"And me," I replied.

"Josie, no," Jake said firmly. "I don't want you anywhere near this mess. You should have gone home already; they could be here any minute."

I could be useful to you, I thought, folding my arms.

"He's right," Noah agreed. "We'd better get your bike and see you off before-"

The back door burst open and the three of us spun instantly, ready to tackle whoever was entering. I breathed a relieved sigh when I saw that it was Dai, looking dishevelled and heaving out his breaths. His face was flushed bright pink as he puffed, leaning on the sink for support.

"They're yur," he said. "About five minutes away. I've been watching down the road, waiting for Gil's car."

When Dai's breath calmed, I could see that he was shivering. His fingertips were blue where they poked out of the sleeves of his thick overcoat.

"How long were you out on the road?" I asked.

"About two hours," he replied.

I wanted to stay angry with him, but Dai's contrition was there in every guilty move he made. He was too ashamed to look

Jake in the eye as he stood guard at the kitchen door, peering out every now and then to see if Gil's car had pulled up.

"Put the lights off quick," I said, racing to the switch.

The plan I had suggested was simple enough. If they thought we had already gone home, then they might just go away. I plunged the kitchen into darkness and Dai continued to wait at the door, keeping it open just a notch with his frozen fingers. Jake held onto me in the darkness and, despite all his brave words, I could feel him shaking. He was still terribly weak from the first time those thugs had got hold of him, and flashes of what had happened to his father continued to plague my mind. If I was thinking about Jake's dad so often, then I could only imagine how much worse those thoughts were in the Bolton brothers' minds.

Soon I heard an engine not so far off in the distance. When it came nearer, it suddenly stopped and the sound of footfalls and conversation emerged in its place. I couldn't tell how many voices there were exactly, but it sounded like more than there had been before. Six? Seven? How big was Gil's car? How many extra people could he have crammed into it to give himself extra back up tonight? I was ready at any moment to use my powers to call for help, knowing that Peregrine Place was only a short drive away if I needed to alert the Bickerstaffs at the manor. I hoped that my wait-it-out plan was going to work and that we wouldn't need to involve anyone else in this messy affair.

A clang sounded outside, and then another. Jake shifted out of my arms and went to Dai at the door.

"What are they doing?" he snapped.

"They're smacking your car with something," Dai said. "Looks like a cricket bat to me."

K.C. Finn

"They've got weapons?" I asked, horrified, my nerves rising like an electric current all over my body. I had forgotten about the car.

Even through the sound of their occasional thumps and clangs, I heard Jake's knuckles crack in the darkness. "That's my father's car," he growled.

"Keep calm," I said, reaching out to hold his hand. "It's only a car, even if it is special to you. It's not worth your safety."

He squeezed my hand tightly. Then there was the smash of a window caving in, followed by the merriest, most awful laughter I had ever heard.

"It's not just a car."

Those last words had not come from Jake. Everything happened so quickly that I hardly knew what was going on, but Jake and I were being shoved to one side as Dai went flying to the other. Noah came blasting out of the kitchen right past us, his tall, lanky frame streaking out into the night as he approached the shadows surrounding the peppermint car.

"Noah, no!" Jake cried, racing out after him just as swiftly.

"They're going to get themselves battered!" Dai shouted and then he too was gone.

I was alone in the darkness for one short, shocked moment, before my own call to action kicked in. As the three boys ran across the backyard towards the car, I reached again for the lights and flicked them on, opening the kitchen door wide to bathe the scene in a shaft of yellow electric light. It cut a slice towards the Volkswagen Beetle, now dented and covered in broken glass, where seven tall figures were turning to the sight of Noah's shouts. The flat-haired figure of Gil Croft was evident amongst the others, for he was the skinniest of the bunch, but he was not the one holding the cricket bat.

That honour belonged to an even taller young man with short, black hair, who started running towards Noah, shouting every obscenity he knew. I watched in horror as the motion between the two unfolded when they met. Though it happened quickly, in my mind, the world seemed to slow as the bat-bearing boy slid down onto his knees on the concrete, sweeping the bat across Noah's lower legs. There was a sickening crack as everything fell silent. Noah dropped to the ground with a cry that made me feel as though my heart was being plucked out of my chest.

There was no more time to dither; I had wasted enough seconds in shock. The boy with the bat had to be stopped. I reached out my mind to its full extent, way beyond the halfway state that I was used to, and suddenly, I could see myself in his body as he got to his feet. He looked down at Noah, who was clutching his shin and wailing. The boy lifted the bat high into the air and I felt a wild rush of rage and elation in his awful, messed-up body.

And I screamed.

I thought of the loudest scream that any girl could ever make, greater than that of any horror movie, and screamed it right into the boy's head. He dropped the bat instantly, grabbing at his ears and crying just as loud as Noah was. It was then that Jake was upon him, and I felt him jab the boy sharply in the ribs. I experienced every moment of the boy's sharp agony as he fell back onto his knees, now woozy and aching from my continued scream. Before he shut his eyes to the world, I saw Dai Bickerstaff's frozen fingers taking away his cricket bat.

When Jake kicked the boy hard in the side, I flew out of his mind, flustered and terrified to suddenly be back at the far edge of the scene. The fighters were too busy to have seen me, and now the whole crowd was rushing in on Jake and Dai where they stood flanking Noah, doing everything they could to protect him. Thanks to calm, patient Noah suddenly finding an outlet for his held-in grief, our plan had gone horribly wrong. I let my mind reach out again, this time only partway into the darkness.

HELP! I called. *There's an attack! It's happening again! We're at Halfway, and I don't know what to do! Help us, please!*

An image blinked into my mind as Doctor Bickerstaff dropped the book he was reading. He leapt up, ambling haphazardly on his leg and shouting something suddenly to his wife, who was deep into a magazine by the fireside.

"Get Henri and Leighton!" Bickerstaff cried. "We're going to Halfway right now. There's trouble."

I couldn't afford to stay with them; they were draining my focus from the scene ahead. When I assessed the situation in the half-lit yard, I was horrified to see Gil Croft had managed to get Jake onto the floor. Dai was swinging the cricket bat wildly as he tried to reach Jake, but two large boys were keeping him at bay for Gil to hone in on his real target. The other four boys were all occupied with dragging Jake up again and holding him still, his arms and legs stretched like a punch-bag ready to be laid into. Noah was still crying on the floor, trying to scramble towards his brother. It earned him a kick in the face from Gil, who balled his hands into fists.

"You had this coming to you, you filthy black bastard!" Gil shouted.

"No!" I cried.

There was a moment's pause from the boys. I was right; they hadn't noticed me at all until the moment when I came flying across the yard, racing into Gil with all the strength I could muster. The sheer force of my speed combined with his total surprise meant that I instantly smashed him down onto the floor. I had no idea what I was doing, only that a wild rage had grown within me at the sight of Jake's brave face as he struggled against his bonds. I smacked and scratched at Gil's face as my weight pinned him down, getting in a few good blows before he realised what had even hit him.

But when he did realise what was happening, I knew it. He flung out a hand and grabbed my wrists, wrestling me off him until he could get into a crouching position. Jake was crying out my name as Gil Croft stood up and put his foot right against my chest. He booted me so hard that I lost all my breath, panting with sudden tears as I fell back onto the hard yard floor. The sound of a cricket bat clattering to the ground followed, and then I was being hauled up by the tall boy who had once owned it. I looked across in despair to see that Dai too was now restrained.

Noah lay fearfully still on the ground, either knocked out or passed out from the impact of his wounds. It was no use. We were completely outnumbered and restrained, and now I had a front-row seat to Jake's beating. I was too breathless and dizzy to even access Gil's mind to try and delay him, hoping against hope that Doctor Bickerstaff was already on his way with Leighton and Mr Haugen. If I just had a few more seconds to think, perhaps there was something I could do.

"What's going on here then?" said a voice in the darkness.

I recognised its throaty rasp, my heart leaping for joy as a pair of shiny shoes stepped into the faint light cast from Halfway. V.W. was dressed in his sharpest suit trousers, but missing his jacket, a white shirt and a bright orange cravat covering his upper half. His silver rings glinted in the half-light as he shucked his heavy watch a little higher up his wrist. His triangular face was sharp in the shadows, high cheekbones and narrow eyes giving him a serpentine kind of menace. For the first time, I genuinely believed that he might have been a criminal years ago.

"This isn't your business, old man," Gil said, stepping up to V.W. with an unhinged sort of confidence. He was spoiling for his fight and picking on everyone who stood in his way now.

"Is that right?" V.W. snarled. "You reckon you're just going to beat up a couple of kids and I'm going to walk away all la-di-dah, do you?"

Gil looked him up and down with a sneer. "A couple of blacks, a coward, and a little tart," he surmised. "Nothing for you to worry about, Grandpa."

The smack came at Gil so fast that I missed it in a blink. All I saw was Gil falling sideways to the ground as V.W.'s beringed hand cast the arc of a shadow through the air, those silver rings glistening suddenly with something wet and red. Gil landed with his eyes closed and didn't move, the only motion was the trickle of blood starting to pool where V.W.'s ring had slashed into the side of his head.

"Oi Gramps," said the boy holding me. "Watch yourself, right? Or this girl's going to get hurt."

He suddenly reached around and grabbed hold of one of my fingers, bending it backwards so far that I knew immediately what he was threatening. I looked into V.W.'s eyes, my father's eyes, pleading desperately, hoping that he would know a way to stop this situation from getting any worse. He tipped me a wink, that sharky smile unleashed with a sudden, vengeful look. V.W.'s eyes glazed over, his mind eerily absent from his grinning face.

A Place Halfway

One by one, the boys dropped to the ground. The one holding me went first and I clutched at my hand to get it away from him, wriggling out of his grip. Each one started to wince as though they were experiencing a terrible headache, but before they could even cry out, they were all unconscious on the cold surface of the yard. Jake and Dai clambered straight to Noah, lifting his limp head and listening to his chest. I just stared at my father, awestruck by his devastating skills. As his eyes refocused on the present moment, they rested on me with a solid, unwavering look.

"You all right, kiddo?" he asked.

I raced forward, wrapping my arms around his middle. V.W. stumbled a little, apparently shocked, but eventually, he put one hand on my head gently. When I pulled away, his eyes were filled with concern.

"How did you do all that?" I questioned in awe.

A guilty sort of curl crept into his thin lip. "It takes a thug to beat a thug," he admitted.

"Josie," Jake said sharply, "Noah's unconscious. I'm worried about him."

"Help's on its way," I promised. "Doctor Bickerstaff's coming down now with the others."

V.W. stepped sharply away from me, the guilt in his gaze replaced instantly by fear. "I've got to go," he said quickly.

"Don't," I pleaded desperately. "I need to speak to you!"

"Another time," he answered, already turning away in the darkness.

I watched him as he started to jog into the shadows, determined that he wasn't going to get away again.

"DAD!"

V.W. froze on the spot. I raced up to catch him as he rotated on one heel, staring at me like I'd said the most awful curse word you could ever imagine. I took hold of his hand, not caring that Gil's blood was slick under my finger where I touched his jewellery.

"I'll be in the village tomorrow," I told him, my voice quaking. "Find me there in the afternoon. Please."

He said nothing; he just kept staring at me like he couldn't believe any of this was happening. I squeezed his hand.

"Please," I repeated.

The sound of a car engine in the distance caught our attention. V.W. raised my fingers to his lips and kissed them, his eyes starting to gleam with what couldn't possibly be tears. He wouldn't be crying; it had to be the light, I reasoned. He nodded noiselessly, letting me go and racing out into the dark. Moments later, Doctor Bickerstaff's white car pulled into the yard with a jerky squeal of the brakes, but I was too frozen in place to hear what any of them were saying about Noah and the help he needed.

My father had just saved us all.

CHAPTER TWENTY-FIVE

Father Figures

"How was Noah this morning?" Hanne asked.

We were stepping out of the gates of Peregrine Place after Sunday lunch, our ears, noses, and mouths wrapped up in thick scarves as the nip of winter tickled any exposed skin. I gave a little sigh, condensation soaking my nose.

"His leg is broken," I explained, "but Doctor B's set it in plaster. Do you know something? Mrs Bolton said she would rather bring Noah here again than take him to the hospital in Ashford. Isn't that strange?"

"I don't know how he does it," Hanne said, eyebrows drooping. "He's a miserable old thing, but everyone always goes on about how wonderful he is."

The memory of Bickerstaff fast asleep in the hospital bed came to me then. The way he had guarded Jake like a watchful dog that night, in spite of his own needs, was something I wasn't likely to forget.

"I suppose it's not about the outward stuff," I mused. "I mean, Jake was so rotten when we first met him and now he's... well, he's wonderful."

"Oh, is he?" Hanne giggled, poking me in the arm.

My coat was so thick that I hardly felt her do it. I gave

her a push in return and she stumbled forward, still laughing at me.

"It sure was lucky that V.W. was there to sock it to those boys," she added brightly. "I wonder what made him do it; surely, he could have got battered if there were, what six of them?"

"Seven," I correctly proudly. "He's tough as nails, V.W. is."

I looked at Hanne as she skipped along, the guilt of secret-keeping weighing down on me once more. I had never liked secrets—I used to be livid when I found out people were keeping things from me—but now I'd come to realise that secrets were one of those things you couldn't avoid in life, especially when you grew up and things got complicated. What I'd also learned, however, was that secrets left buried for too long brought a lot of upset with them when they were finally set free. I took a deep breath into the woolly warmth of my scarf and made a decision.

It was time to tell Hanne the truth. I knew that Dai would have to tell his father that V.W. had come to our rescue, but I made him promise that the 'd' word he had heard me shout would not enter the conversation. Nobody could know that I knew what was going on, not until Sunday afternoon was out of the way, but Hanne could surely keep things quiet for that long at least. We began to walk the winding lane that led down into the village, wrestling with the tightness of our best winter coats and thickest stockings. As we trudged down the road, I recounted to Hanne everything that had happened from the moment Leighton recognised my father at Halfway.

When she had heard it all, she blinked her bright eyes several times before she spoke to me. "Well," she surmised, "It sounds as though he doesn't want to hurt you."

"That's a good start," I said, relieved that she wasn't angry that I hadn't told her sooner. "But what about the criminal thing?" I pressed. "How am I supposed to feel that he used to be, or might still be, involved in that sort of thing?"

"Nobody has a perfect set of parents," Hanne answered. "My mum can't run or skip or play hopscotch with me because of her muscles. And your mum, sorry about this, is a terrible cook."

"True," I said. "But your dad, Hanne, he's perfect. He does everything for you and for Nik."

Hanne turned quiet suddenly, looking away into the bright field filled with frost. "But he was in the war," she answered, "and that probably means that he killed people."

I absorbed that fact slowly in the silence that followed. Mr Roth often went on about the bodies piling up and how men were fighting violently for their lives in the war, but I had never really considered the idea that most of the older men I knew had done those sorts of things for real. It was no wonder Doctor Bickerstaff didn't mind sleeping rough in his clothes on a hospital bed. It was no wonder that Tommy was so afraid of the kind, laughing figure of Mr Haugen, if he'd taken the time to think about what being a solider in that war really meant.

"I don't usually think about it," Hanne said after the pause had faded, "but he must have had to do some bad things sometimes, to survive and come home to Mum."

I put my arm around her shoulders and gave her a squeeze. We walked like that for a few minutes, the village slowly coming into view in the distance. Halfway was getting nearer and nearer to our left.

"I'm going to meet my dad today whilst we're out shopping," I explained to her, "to set things straight between us. You can keep that secret for me for a while, right?"

"So long as you tell me everything that happens," Hanne said with a nod. "And I want to be near, just in case he does turn out to want to kidnap you."

"Deal," I replied, finding I was a little relieved to hear her say that she would stay close.

I spotted V.W. walking into Bennie's Café about an hour after we'd hit the village shops. We were across the road in the record shop, deciding on the perfect new single for Jake's present, when I glanced up through the shop window and spotted the tall, slim frame. He was wearing a trilby hat in the same dark grey shade as his suit and when he entered the café, he sat in the window, reading the papers. I smacked Hanne in the shoulder repeatedly until I had her full attention.

"What is it? I'm trying to find Fats Domino for Mum... Oh."

We stared out through the shop window for a few long moments.

"He came," I whispered. "He actually came to find me."

As if more proof was needed, the waitress soon arrived with a cup of steaming coffee for him and a tall, pink milkshake that could only be for me. He put a coaster over the top of it so the froth wouldn't spoil, then took a silver flask from his jacket pocket and added a drop of something to his coffee. Hanne took the records I was holding out of my hands.

"I'll buy these for Jake," she offered, "and then I'll get a bag of chips and sit on a bench out there, somewhere where I can see the café."

"Thanks, Han," I replied, giving her a quick hug before I raced out onto the street.

He saw me coming before I'd even crossed the road, those narrow eyes lifting over the newspaper to watch me approach. He set down the pages as I entered, taking the coaster off the top of my drink. I took my place opposite him as nerves coursed through my upper half, unsure of what to say.

"Hope you like strawberries," V.W. began.

I nodded slowly. "How did you know you could order it so soon?" I asked.

He tapped his nose twice. My mouth fell open as I realised what he meant.

"You spied on me?" I accused.

"Only for a second," he said pleadingly. "Father's prerogative."

He said it like he wasn't too sure about the words. I sipped at my straw, taking in a gulp of freezing cold strawberry milk that stung my back teeth a little.

"How long have you known?" V.W. continued.

"Since the last round of the talent show," I answered, "but you haven't been around much since then, not until last night."

"How are your friends?" he asked. "Noah looked pretty battered."

"Broken leg and a concussion," I informed him, "but they're taking care of him up at the school now."

My father nodded slowly. He leaned forward, resting his elbows on the table and interlocking his fingers, silver rings clashing against one another. He leant on the frame he had made with his hands, his face turning more solemn and sorrowful with every moment that passed.

"I'm sorry I didn't try to find you sooner, Josie," he admitted. "I had another kid, years ago. A boy named Sid. He turned his back on me and…" He pursed his lips like someone had dropped lemon juice on them. "Well, I didn't think I was cut out to be a dad again after how badly that went down."

"What changed your mind?" I asked, consumed by nervous fascination.

"It's daft," he said, waving a hand.

V.W. sat back and downed his coffee, snapping his fingers at the waitress until he could signal for another. I waited patiently, watching him with expectant eyes as I continued to sip at my shake.

"I presume someone in the family's told you about my colourful history?" he supposed.

"Nobody's told me anything," I answered. A dark brow rose on V.W.'s forehead. "I eavesdropped on some of them talking. They don't even know that I know who you are."

He grinned widely at that. "You're sneaky," he assessed, nodding at me. "That's definitely not from your mother. She was a very open-hearted girl."

"She still is," I said, more proud of her than I'd realised. "But you're my business now, not hers, or anyone else's. I want to know the truth. Why did you come here?"

V.W.'s second coffee arrived, but he didn't add anything extra to it this time from the flask. "All right," he sighed. "I was banged up about three years ago for some petty theft. You don't usually stay in prison long for that stuff, but I'm a repeat offender, so I had about eight months inside. I was with a bunch of other blokes my age who were tried for similar things, but above their beds, they had these pictures of their wives and their kids. Even

grandkids, some of them. And then I realised that there was nobody waiting for me on the freedom side when I got released."

"So you started looking for me," I concluded.

He nodded. "You were tricky to find. Anything to do with that school of yours is under some pretty heavy locks and keys. I broke a whole new set of laws getting your name out of their files."

"And are you really a music producer now?" I asked, fearing the worst.

"More of an agent," he reasoned. "They like smooth-talkers in that business, and a lot of them are crooks anyway so they don't mind me having a record, provided I keep my hands out of their bank vaults."

"So you're on the straight and narrow then?" I said, feeling an uncontrollable grin sweep my features. "No more crimes?"

My heart sank as I saw V.W. curl one side of his mouth into an apologetic sort of grimace.

"There is one tiny problem," he admitted. I tried not to let my hopeful feeling fade away as he began to explain. "Do you remember those blokes you saw in my flat? The scarred slaphead and his two mates?"

"Yes," I replied, the image of V.W.'s thuggish associates flooding my mind.

"I owe them quite a lot of money," he confessed. "With a past like mine, you can't always make a completely clean break, even if you want to."

"What did you borrow the money for?" I asked him.

He smiled again. "To fund the break-in for the information on you."

V.W. must have seen my face drop, because he reached

out and put one hand over mine at the base of the milkshake glass.

"Don't go blaming yourself for that. It was my decision," he told me, "and I'm going to take care of it straight after Christmas, no worries."

"What about after the talent show?" I said, swallowing hard. "Are you going to stick around?"

"I want to," he replied, "but it might not be as simple as that."

His hand was warm on mine, except for the part where his thick watch lay against my fingertips. It reminded me of my satchel and the purchases I'd already made that afternoon. I reached down quickly, rummaging for a slim, black box that I knew was there somewhere.

"I don't expect I'll see you 'til Boxing Day," I explained, "so you'd better have this now."

I slid the box across the table. My father took it in both hands, examining its outer case, before he slipped off the lid and peered inside. I peeped in too, even though I had already seen the bottle of fluid and the brushes and small cloths inside. I was about to tell him what the present was exactly when he gave a little laugh.

"Jewellery cleaner," he said, grinning.

"I thought…" I began sheepishly. "You know, because you keep your rings and watch so shiny."

"I love it," he answered. Relief hit me once again. "You can tell a lot about a man from the way he presents himself to the world. You ought to tell your Jake that."

My Jake. The thought warmed me. "You don't mind him?" I asked tentatively.

V.W. pointed a finger at the air between us, his face filled with meaning. "I saw the look in his eyes when that little creep kicked you down last night," he told me. "That boy looked like he would have torn the thug to shreds if he'd been loose. I can respect a man who has that much love for my daughter."

I sucked up the heat around my eyes, not wanting to cry, even though the sentiment felt like someone had given my heart a good shaking.

"And if you're worried about him being black, I've got no issues," V.W. added. "Most of my mates when I was inside were black. You can trust them better, because half of them are wrongly imprisoned."

I laughed at that, more out of relief than anything else. My father was the first person to address Jake's colour out loud, and he didn't care a bit about it.

"Having said that," he continued merrily, "I do happen to know a particularly handy group of dark lads in London. If you could give me the name of that little band of idiots who tried to hurt you last night, I might be able to frighten them into submission for a good long while."

"They call themselves the London Light," I told him gleefully. "The one who kicked me is called Gil Croft."

V.W. nodded with a devilish glint in his gaze. "I'll make sure my friends frighten him *especially*," he said, tapping his nose once again.

My father promised me a present on Boxing Day, after the finale of the talent show, and we talked a while longer about all sorts of things, mostly about my life and my psychic skills. When I told him what Miss Cartwright had discovered about my powers, he seemed unusually pleased that I had gotten the better of her, but I didn't press the subject. He was proud of me, that much was clear, and it was enough in that moment to make me feel like I finally had all the pieces of my life together.

Except for one.

When I returned to my flat for dinner that night, I was once again greeted by the familiar sight of Dai Bickerstaff waiting at my door. This time he was standing, kicking at the wall with the toe of his boot. He was sporting a nasty purple bruise under one of his eyes, which were bloodshot and tired looking at this late hour of the day. By the sconces on the walls, he looked thinner and less healthy than he had just a few weeks ago.

"Josie," he said as I approached, "are we all right now, you and me?"

"I suppose so," I answered with a shrug. "So long as your days as a white supremacist are done."

"I don't think I was ever a proper one," Dai countered sheepishly. "It was just what all the other law students were doing."

"That's a scary thought," I mused aloud.

"Most of them have stopped now," he explained. "It shouldn't be too bad when I go back after the holidays, so long as I steer clear of Gil."

A little smile crept into the corners of my mouth. "You might find him starting to mend his ways too by then," I promised.

I made to leave, satisfied that we had made some sort of truce, but Dai got in my way and took hold of one of my hands, my palm flat on his with his other hand sandwiched on top. I turned to face him, looking at his handsome smile as he beamed

247

at me in relief. His perfect sweep of blonde hair was loose in style, a single strand falling down into his face.

"You're brilliant, you know," he said in a low, Welsh whisper. "I can't believe I've known you for so long and not realised how strong and smart you could be."

I realised where his words were going all too late. As I tried to pull my hand away, Dai continued in an almost pleading tone.

"I know you used to like me," he said, "and I'm sorry for what I did. If you wanted to, I could take you out on weekends. I'd come back every Sunday for you; we could have a lot of laughs together."

He was the boy I'd wanted so badly for almost four years, ever since I'd really started thinking about boys and their handsomeness. My first crush, the one who made my heart almost explode with joy when he turned up unexpectedly and flashed his perfect smile my way. And now he was right there before me, practically begging me to go along with him.

"Sorry Dai," I murmured gently. "There's someone else."

He let my hand go. "You know you're going to get a lot of flak if you go out with Jake, don't you?" he asked sadly. "The world's not used to seeing people of different colours coming together."

"They'll never get used to it, if people don't start trying," I replied.

CHAPTER TWENTY-SIX

Mistletoe and Wine

I was waiting until I saw Jake in person to tell him of the decision I'd made, which meant that I spent the whole of Christmas Week lost in a daydream of how that conversation was going to play out. He had been up to the manor with his mother to visit Noah a couple of times, but the only time we could get to be alone was when I snuck into his head after dinner in the evenings. Now that his brother was not at home to share his room, Jake and I could steal a few hours to chat each night before my mother demanded that I get some sleep. On Christmas Eve, I found him knee-deep in brown paper as he tried to wrap presents.

If there's anything for me, hide it quick! I warned him.

"I thought you didn't like surprises?" he challenged.

I trust you to get me something good, I answered.

"I wrapped yours this morning," he said. Jake turned his head to show me a small pile of badly wrapped gifts in the corner of his room.

Pity I won't get them 'til Boxing Day, I whined.

I felt Jake grin even before he made a wicked, little chuckling sound.

"You want some great news?" he asked.

Always, I replied.

"When we came up this morning to see Noah, Doctor Bickerstaff said he couldn't come home for Christmas," Jake revealed. "He's clumsy as a mule now that he's learning to walk again, so he needs more time in the hospital room to learn."

How is this good news? I queried.

"It means that your mom invited us all to your big family Christmas dinner tomorrow," he said with evident glee. "We get to spend all of Christmas afternoon in your big, fancy manor house."

You're not going to love the cooking, I mused with a giggle.

"Believe it or not, the cooking is not what's attracting me," Jake admitted.

I could feel the reddening of cheeks, but I couldn't work out if they were his or mine. Jake gave up on his wrapping, shifting awkwardly to sit on his bed. I could see him twiddling his dark thumbs as he awaited my reply.

It's going to be a brilliant Christmas, I promised him.

"You got some surprises for me?" he asked hopefully.

I smiled to myself where I lay on my own bed. If only he knew.

Christmas was always a busy affair at Peregrine Place, even though the huge dining hall was only occupied by staff and immediate family. We sat around a long table in the hall's centre with a varied selection of Christmas food before us that, mercifully, Blod and Mrs Haugen had helped my mother to create. The sight of family around the table warmed me, a sense of calm in my heart that I hadn't had for months. With everyone gathered, I felt like things were finally going to be all right again.

There was Nik climbing onto the table itself, mashed potato all around his little mouth, whilst Mr Haugen tried to simultaneously pull a cracker with Hanne and keep control of his wayward son. Mrs Haugen clinked a glass of deep red wine with Doctor Bickerstaff, who was smiling so brightly I couldn't quite be sure that he hadn't been replaced with an identical twin. Blod and my mother were laughing at Dai, who had spilt gravy down the front of his white, woolly jumper, and Mr Roth and Mr Cavendish sat in a heated debate, whilst our headmistress Mrs Cavendish rolled her eyes at every other thing that they said. Even Miss Cartwright was giggling as Leighton whispered something close to her ear.

And then there was Jake. He sat beside me, with his mother and Noah opposite us at the table, but all through dinner, his knee kept knocking against mine deliberately under the table. He was dressed in his absolute best clothes; a crisp blue shirt the colour of the sea and smart black trousers with shiny matching shoes. A shimmering golden wristwatch hung from his left hand, a Christmas gift that his father had been saving for him long before he passed away. Mrs Bolton had joyful tears in her eyes as she cut up Noah's turkey for him, much to his animated complaints.

Merry Christmas, kiddo.

Dad's presence was only there for a moment in my head, but it was enough to make me feel that the day was complete.

Leighton had hefted a television into the dining hall for us all to gather and watch the Queen's Christmas Message. The adults sat nearest the set with great interest, whilst Jake and I hung back a little from the small, brown set. I let my fingers slip

into Jake's grip whilst everyone's attention was turned. He stifled a grin. On the flickering screen, the Queen was giving thanks for the birth of Jesus Christ.

"For that child," she said, looking perfect and strong, "was to show that there is nothing in heaven and earth that cannot be achieved by faith and by love and service to one's neighbour."

I felt Jake squeeze my hand tightly at that. The speech went on, talking about the varied peoples of the world and how they made up the Commonwealth family that our queen ruled over. I found myself feeling prouder at every moment, listening harder to her message that the nation should accept anyone with good values, regardless of their race or religion. If she could do it, then why couldn't the rest of this country? Perhaps her call for tolerance would make a difference once the New Year rolled in.

Soon the families were scattering into groups to do their own thing. An exhausted Mrs Haugen left to lie down after dinner, whilst Blod, Mrs Bolton, and my mother fussed over who should attend to the dishes. Mr Haugen was dutiful as ever whilst he entertained his two children, trying to teach Nik the rules of Snakes and Ladders. Noah sat in a comfortable chair, his broken leg propped carefully on a pillow stack, talking animatedly to Doctor Bickerstaff as they dealt out a pack of cards, ready to play.

"Are you two having a game with us?" Noah asked.

Jake opened his mouth to speak, but I gave him a sideways glance and he closed it again promptly.

"Later," I replied. "I want to walk off my dinner."

I tried my best to ignore Doctor Bickerstaff's knowing

look as I quickly pulled Jake out of the hall's double doors. We stayed linked at the fingers as I led him up the stairs, walking slowly along the long corridor that led to Tommy's disused classroom. It looked strange and silent without him and his Tele filling it with rehearsal sound, save for the one patch on the floor that I had prepared earlier on.

"What did you do?" Jake asked with a grin.

A striped picnic blanket lay over the carpeted floor, upon which I had placed two small cakes and a pot of clotted cream. In front of the snacks were the records I had purchased for Jake, splayed out for him to drink in their colourful jackets. His Latest Flame by Elvis Presley caught his eye immediately and he lifted it, eyes roving over the smiling face of the King on the cover. He reached out blindly to find me, pulling me in at the waist and holding me close.

"I almost bought this one for you," he chuckled.

"I'm glad you went with Pat Boone instead," I replied. "I've been meaning to get him for ages."

I had made Jake wait for his gifts even though he'd thrust mine into my arms the moment I saw him before lunch. We sat down on the picnic cloth and Jake set his records down after careful inspection, looking at me greedily as I slopped a great spoonful of delicious cream onto the top of a cake. I handed it to him, the familiar rush hitting my chest again. He was grinning ear to ear, cream all over his top lip as he ate.

"Guess what else?" I said.

Jake shrugged, his eyes eager for me to tell him. I reached under one corner of the picnic blanket and produced a jam jar half-filled with a deep red liquid. I sloshed it a little before him.

"Mulled wine," I explained. "Sorry it's not hot, but it

should still be good. Actually, I'm not sure; I've never had a drink before."

"And you don't need to," Jake said.

He took the jar from my hands and set it behind him, out of our way. He took hold of my hand, his face suddenly more forlorn as his tongue snaked out to lick the cream from his top lip.

"I thought you'd like it," I mused with a frown.

"I've stopped the drinking," he revealed. "When Noah got attacked, I realised that the whiskey was slowing me down. I wasn't as sharp as I could have been to protect him. It was damaging me, and it didn't help the pain go away after Dad. He'd be ashamed if he saw how many bottles I wasted my money on."

Jake's head hung low until I used my other hand to lift his chin. "But think how proud he'd be to know that you've learned your lesson?" I asked.

He nodded sadly, leaning into my touch as my hand lingered at the base of his jaw. I traced a line up his cheek, remembering the bruises he had worn there for my sake. He looked smart and proud in his best clothes, and he was honest and brave. If there was ever a moment that would help me make the hardest decision of my life, then this was it.

"I got something else too," I said. "Look up."

Jake lifted his head with a perplexed look, craning to see the tiny clump of something green that was pinned to the high ceiling. "What is that?" he asked.

"That is the smallest sprig of mistletoe known to man," I explained. "I could only cut a tiny bit off the one in Leighton's car, else he would have noticed."

"He keeps mistletoe in his car?" Jake asked, eyes still focused upwards.

"It's better if you don't ask." I giggled.

"You could have broken your neck putting that up there," he mused, eyes finally back on me.

I gave him an expectant, irritated look. "You're spoiling my moment with all this chattering, you know," I told him.

Jake smiled an awkward, lopsided smile. He looked down at himself for a moment before he would meet my gaze again. He didn't look sad anymore, but there was still something off in his expression.

"You really want to do this?" he asked. "Because there's a whole world of stupid people out there that we have to fight if we want to be together."

I let my hands slide up his biceps, circling around to meet at the nape of his neck. I felt him shiver a little under my touch, shifting himself closer to me on the blanket. "You're worth fighting for," I assured him.

I had barely finished the words before his lips were on mine. We fell backwards onto the floor in surprise, lying side by side and kissing until my lips felt raw. Jake's warm hands wrapped me up tightly against the cold winter chill creeping in around us, and I felt a kind of elation I had never before known. It was happening, for real this time. No regrets and no looking back. He was going to be mine for good.

"Josephine Fontaine! Where on earth 'ave you got to?"

My mother's voice echoed so loudly that I jumped, terrified that she might have been about to walk into the room.

"Jacob!" Mrs Bolton called alongside the first voice. "If you've ruined that new shirt of yours, I'm going to lock you up until next Christmas!"

Jake scrambled to his feet and pulled me up after him,

looking down at his blue shirt in a panic. It was badly creased from where my hands had held him close, but otherwise unharmed. He grinned at me, flustered and giggling, reaching out to help flatten my hair down where he had been running his fingers through it only moments before. I gave him one more quick kiss before I turned towards the door.

"Sorry, Mum!" I shouted. "I was giving Jake the tour!"

Mrs Bolton was the one to reply. "If you think you're the only generation to use that excuse, you've got another thing coming. Jacob, down here *now*."

"Just when we'd decided the world couldn't stand in our way," Jake said in a low, merry tone.

I let out a contented sigh as we exited the classroom, starting back down the long corridor where I could see our mothers waiting at the top of the staircase.

"You sound happy," Jake said quietly.

"Of course I am," I answered in the same half-whisper. "I've got my job, school's great, I found my dad, and I have you. Everything's as it should be now."

I saw the uncertain look pass across his features before he could hide it.

"Why?" I asked him. "Aren't you happy?"

"Sure," he answered, eyes flickering to the ever-approaching shapes of our mothers, "But I've got a funny feeling about tomorrow."

The finale of the show would take place on Boxing Day afternoon. I waved a hand at Jake. "It's just nerves," I assured him. "You'll do fine on the day."

"Yeah," Jake replied, rubbing his palms together. "I'm sure that's all it is."

CHAPTER TWENTY-SEVEN

The Big Finish

In my excitement at seeing my father again, there was one huge thing that hadn't occurred to me about the finale of the talent show. My whole family wanted to come and see it. When Mum revealed that she would be among the tribe of ten trekking down from Peregrine Place to Halfway on that afternoon, I didn't have a leg to stand on in persuading her not to come. I could tell by the look on Leighton's face at breakfast that he was behind the scheme; there was something steely in his usually bright eyes that told me they had chosen this, of all days, to try and confront my father.

I thought about telling them that I had already beaten them to it, but if I did, then I was certain that I wouldn't be allowed to go down to Halfway for the show, and I couldn't let Jake down after everything he'd been through for me. I wondered if it would have been prudent to warn Dad that they were coming but, judging by the way he'd scarpered the last few times he'd smelled company, I didn't want to run the risk of him not showing up at all. That left me with no option but to play along with the ignorance they all presumed I had, so I found myself sitting in Doctor Bickerstaff's overcrowded car as we all trundled down the lane towards the music bar.

"Do you think I'm all right to do this?" Dai asked nervously, "I mean, will Jake want me there?"

"It's the least you can do to apologise to the poor boy," Blod chided. "It takes a proper man to admit his mistakes, isn't that right, Steven?"

The doctor said nothing, but I saw him eyeing up his son in the rearview mirror. Even at Christmas, they hadn't spoken much, despite Dai's obvious and very public attempts to befriend Jake all day long. I had a feeling Bickerstaff was going to take a very long time to forgive Dai; it wasn't necessarily a bad thing at all.

"We're here," the doctor said after a moment. The car came to a jerky halt. "Everyone out and don't go running off yet. We're meeting Mr and Mrs Asher outside."

I got out of the car, shielding my face immediately from the frosty wind whipping up around my face. Hanne followed me out and clung to my side; she was so small and skinny that I felt as though the winter gale might just pick her up and take her away.

"I've got you," said a voice I knew. "It's all right."

Tommy had reached out for Hanne, wrapping a caring arm around her shoulders. The Ashers' deep burgundy car had pulled up mere moments after us, and Tommy stood firm, holding onto Hanne as his mother, father, and two little brothers clambered out of the vehicle. They were a dark-haired family, but only Tommy and his mother had the striking blue eyes that made them stand out from the crowd. She was a kind-looking woman with a round face who made an immediate beeline for Mrs Haugen across the front yard.

"Let's get you over to the doorway, eh?" Tommy said.

He was grinning down at Hanne, who leant into the crook of his shoulder and nodded in amazement. I walked with them over to Halfway's entrance, careful to keep a few paces away and let them have their languid steps. When we reached our destination and were sheltered from the wind, Tommy was suddenly called away again by his father, a short fellow who was pointing to his little brothers. They had started fighting over Tommy's Tele, which was halfway out of its case as they scuffled. Tommy ran to them in an angry panic, leaving Hanne to watch him march away.

"How about that?" I said, arching an eyebrow. "Very gentlemanly behaviour. And romantic, I might add."

Hanne narrowed her eyes. "What's he up to?" she asked.

"Oh Han," I groaned, extra loudly for effect. "Just go with it. Keep your mouth shut and let the boy do his thing today. I think you'll be pleased with the results."

She turned her suspicion on me then instead, but I waved a hand and opened the door to the club, drowning out her questions with noise from inside. Halfway was abuzz with people of all ages, looking the most crowded I had ever seen it. I was grateful for the collective warmth of the throng inside, weaving through the masses with Hanne close in tow. We took our coats and winter warmers off at the bar and I gathered them into a bundle, retreating to the calm of the kitchen for a moment to store them somewhere safe.

Jake was getting changed for the show, a brilliant bottle-green shirt completely undone as he combed his hair. I got a good look at the muscles and lines of his chocolate-brown chest and stomach before he caught me, eyes wide and embarrassed. He dropped his comb, the yellow plastic thing clattering to

259

the ground as he quickly ran his hands up his buttons. He was tucking the shirt in as I approached, the scent of spicy aftershave tickling my nose when I moved towards him for a kiss.

"Spy," he accused me grumpily, though I felt him smiling as we kissed again. "I wouldn't walk in on you half naked."

"I wouldn't be getting changed in a kitchen," I reminded him, dropping the coats by the sink. "What are you singing? It'd better be good."

"It's for you," he said, his words punctuated by several more kisses. "It's a surprise."

"Oi," said a sudden, rasping voice from nearby, "you're supposed to be warming up the crowd, not the waitress."

Jake froze as V.W. stepped in from the back door, carrying a box wrapped in bright red paper and string. He let go of me quickly and stood, head bowed and shoulders dropped. "Sorry, Sir," he muttered.

V.W. looked him over with his narrow eyes, and then looked to me. He pointed at Jake with a merry grin. "He knows who I am, doesn't he?" he asked.

"Yes, Dad, I'm afraid so," I replied, stifling a grin.

V.W. thrust the bright box into my hands and stepped up to Jake, straightening the collar of his shirt for him. I didn't know if it was meant to be a helpful gesture or not, because Jake seemed to be all the more tense when it was over.

"Well," V.W. began, clucking his tongue thoughtfully, "I suppose there's nothing wrong with getting a kiss from your best girl for good luck. Not that you need it, kiddo."

He held out his hand, rings shining extra bright. Jake took it and gave it a shake, smiling at last when V.W. tipped him a wink.

"Get out there and tell the band what your music is," he ordered. "We've got to get started soon."

"Yes, Sir," Jake said quickly, bounding away at a jog.

"Do you reckon I did that fatherly intimidation thing right?" he asked me with a grin.

"I'm not sure if you were supposed to give me permission to kiss him or not," I said with a giggle.

My father shrugged. "You love him; you're going to do it whatever I say."

Love. It was the first time the word had come around, yet it fit with Jake and me so well. I found it hard to imagine any part of my future without him and, win or lose in the talent show, we had already found our reward with one another. V.W. poked at the big box I was holding.

"Open it then," he urged, checking his watch. "I've only got a minute."

"Oh," I exclaimed, remembering his promise of a present. I set the box on one of the counters and pulled at the string. The topmost part of the paper came away easily to reveal a lid, which I flipped off and threw aside as my anticipation grew. Inside the box, folded neatly and packaged with care, were six of the most beautiful dresses I had ever seen.

"You're always wearing the same thing when I see you," V.W. mused, "so I guessed you didn't have much worth showing off."

"They're so beautiful," I said, my eyes still taking in the bright patterns and colours. "But they must have been expensive. What happened to paying your debts?"

V.W. shrugged, a worried twinge pulling at the corner of his mouth.

"I reckon I'll find another way around that," he said. "Keep them waiting for a bit longer."

"Thank you," I said, wrapping my arms around his middle. "Thank you so much, Dad."

I felt him breathe in sharply when I called him Dad, his arms resting at my shoulders. He planted a gentle kiss on my head, his whole sharp-limbed frame feeling relaxed and gentle. Until the moment when it suddenly wasn't—the moment when everything in his body turned solid again.

"Take your filthy 'ands off *my* daughter."

I leapt back, shocked to see Mum at the other door to the kitchen. She thundered into the cramped space, looking beautiful and terrifying in her best clothes as she put herself between V.W. and me, pushing me back against the countertops with a fierce sweep of her arm.

"She's *our* daughter," Dad answered, "but I expect you didn't know that she'd figured it out."

Mum turned then, staring into my eyes with a searching, accusing look. I could do nothing but nod, feeling desperately guilty that I had hidden something so vital from her. She shook her finger at me, her eyes gleaming.

"'e's never what 'e seems, Josephine," she warned me. "I am your family. I'm the one who's looked after you for all this time."

"Yeah," V.W. said bitterly, "you're the one who vanished and took my little girl away, before I ever got to see her born."

"You were in a police cell when she was born, where you belonged," Mum retorted sharply. "I'm not afraid of you anymore, Victor; I'll fight you tooth and nail before you tear my Josie away from me!"

Dad paused, his mouth open a little as he studied my

mother's face with curiosity. He looked as though he was seeing her for the first time; there was a lightness in his brow as he surveyed her fierce expression. For her part, Mum didn't falter in her desire to protect me. She even had one hand balled into a fist, half-raised like she was ready to batter V.W. if he came too close. I wanted to tell her there was no need, that Dad and I had already worked things out, but I knew she was too upset to listen.

"I just want to see her," Dad said, his voice low and cool. "I'm not here to tread on your toes, Claudette. I just need to know who my daughter is."

Mum's eyes narrowed at him. "She's a smart young woman who 'as done just fine without you for sixteen years," she told him. "And she will continue to do so. Come Josie, back out there, now."

She took my wrist as if to lead me, but I tried to resist. She turned, horrified by my reluctance, looking between the two of us like we had delivered some devastating bombshell of news to her.

"Couldn't you just give him a chance?" I asked in a tiny voice that didn't even sound like my own.

"'e used up all 'is chances with me a long time ago, sweet'eart," she told me. Her whole face was breaking from the damned-up sobs she was trying to hold in. "I'm sorry, darling, but you can't trust 'im. I don't want you to 'ave to find that out the 'ard way."

This time I let her lead me, because I couldn't stand the thought that my resistance would make her cry. We were all supposed to be outside in the main room anyway, so I went first towards the door, looking back only when I realised she hadn't followed me. Mum was face to face with V.W., looking up at

his pained and irritated expression. He was foreboding with his sharp eyes and downturned mouth, but Mum didn't seem to care.

"If you did your research well on Peregrine Place," she began, "then you know who they are and what they do. You know what life will be like for you if you try to contact my daughter again."

My heart sank as I saw the sadness well in my father's eyes. He sniffed in a sharp breath, straightening his jacket. "I've got no time for this," he said all-too-proudly. "There's a show to run out there."

When he passed me in the doorway, I focused on his mind for a moment, sending him my silent words. *Dad, we can fix this,* I promised. *We'll find a way around it when Mum's calmed down.*

He sent me no reply.

By the time the acts were ready to perform, I had thought of a hundred different things that I would say to Mum to convince her. I needed my father in my life, but I would never forget everything she did for me just because he was there. He didn't ever have to set foot in Peregrine Place if they were worried about security; I would always take Jake with me to meet him if they feared that he was still going to try and take me away. I assured myself that I wouldn't give up on Dad; that everything would be better once the joyous music of the talent show had lifted all of our hearts.

My father was every inch the showman up on stage; you wouldn't have even known the scale of the argument he had just had from the way he revved up the crowd. Aside from the tightness in his jaw when he smiled, he seemed excited by the prospect of the show and the only two remaining acts that were competing for the winning title and the promised signing at the record label up in Manchester. Of he and Tommy, Jake would take the stage first, the band poised with his music and ready to count him in. He beamed at the crowd with the most promising smile I'd ever seen him wear, taking the microphone and nodding to the pianist. Drumsticks clicked, and the music began.

It was the Drifters: 'Save The Last Dance For Me'. The bounce of the melody suited Jake's voice and, through every moment of the song, he kept his golden eyes shining straight at me. Several people turned to see who he was singing to, to see the girl that could make a boy with a golden voice croon with so much passion and praise. I was proud that it was me he wanted to sing to, and I sang along when the chorus came around:

"Baby, don't you know I love you so? Can't you feel it when we touch? I will never ever let you go. I love you oh so much…"

When Jake was exiting the stage, Hanne was suddenly beside me, knocking me with her elbow. "He loves you!" she squealed in delight, "and he picked out that song just for you. You are officially the luckiest girl in the world."

"You might want to hold that thought for a moment," I told her with a grin.

Guitar slung over his shoulder, Tommy Asher was taking the stage.

CHAPTER TWENTY-EIGHT

Smash and Grab

Tommy was the most confident I had ever seen him, slicking his hair back as he stepped up to the microphone. Girls at the front of the crowd were already clapping and screaming, even though he had yet to so much as open his mouth. Tommy flexed his Tele with a practised grace, sliding his fingers over the strings as he prepared to play. He looked as though he had come to Halfway to win not just the title, but also everything he could ever have wanted in his life.

"This song is for my best girl," he said with a cheeky grin. "A-one, two, three, four-"

It was obvious the moment we met,
You were a good girl, a regular Teacher's pet.
You left me in the dust, right from the start,
Always playing catch-up as you ran away with my
Heart...
Can't change the way that my mind is set,
'Cause I can't help it if I'm in love
With the girl who's Teacher's pet.
I love your freckles and the shine in your eyes
So if I say I'm your boy, don't look surprised.

K.C. Finn

I know you're special; you're a cut above,
But I'm a-gonna keep trying to win you with my
Love…
Can't change the way that my mind is set,
'Cause I can't help it if I'm in love
With the girl who's Teacher's pet.
It's been a secret ever since we met,
But now I'll tell the world that I'm love
With the girl…
Who's Teacher's pet.

I felt as though the roof would collapse from the sheer volume of applause when Tommy was done. The melody was strong and Tommy's lyrics flowed as though they had been poured straight from his heart, a kind of infectious romanticism that captured everyone in the whole crowd. Hanne stood beside me, her face a picture of shock. She turned slowly, blinking at me with a questioning look.

"Yes, it's about you!" I urged. "Do you see any other freckled goody-goodys in here? Go to him!"

Hanne Haugen's hesitance had finally come to an end. She ran through the crowds as Tommy descended the stage, jostling and elbowing her way in a very unladylike fashion. When Tommy spotted her, he dropped his precious guitar like it was nothing but an old jacket he was throwing off, still standing halfway down the stairs of the stage as she threw herself into his arms. I could see Mr Haugen standing up suddenly, but he was at the back of the crowd and far too late to intervene. Tommy and Hanne kissed on the steps just the once, embarrassed and startled by the huge eruption of cheers from the watching crowd when they did so.

"Settle down, settle down," came a voice on the microphone. Nobody had even noticed the rotund figure of Mr Frost as he clambered onto the stage. "A valiant effort from both of our singers. Please excuse the judges as we retire to make our decision."

It struck me as odd that Frost was doing the closing remarks with the microphone. Where was V.W.? I walked along the side of the bar, searching for him, but he had vanished from the crowd; his tall, slim figure was nowhere to be seen. As the rest of the throng continued to celebrate, begging Tommy for an encore, I slipped back into the kitchen in search of my father. Jake wasn't there; I presumed he was still in the main room, caught somewhere in the crowd, so I pressed on through the kitchen and out into the backyard.

The early winter sun was starting to set on the crisp afternoon as the harsh breeze knocked me sideways. I struggled to stand, eyes stinging as I looked out into the car park for a sign of life. He was there: my father was standing at the boot of his car. I ran towards him, the whistling of the wind masking my heavy footfalls until I was close enough to see what he was doing. V.W. had dispensed with his sharp suit jacket, his usually slick hair flying in the wind as he stuffed some paper bundles into a bag in the car boot. It took me a moment to realise that they were stacks of money that he was shielding against the wind.

"Dad?" I cried as I reached him. "What are you doing?"

He looked up, a horrified shock overcoming his face.

"Josie," was all he could say.

"Where did all this money come from?" I asked.

He cast a guilty look back at Halfway, and then cleared

K.C. Finn

his throat. "I'm sorry, kiddo." He sighed.

"No!" I shouted against the wind. "You can't rob Mr Frost! They'll catch you! And you'll go back inside and I'll... I'll never see you again!"

V.W. slammed down the boot of the car and put his hands on my shoulders, holding me tight in the blustering breeze. "You heard what your mother said, Josie," he told me, eyes watering against the wind. "If I don't go, she'll have the whole bloody government on my tail to make sure I can't ever see you again. There's enough cash here to pay my debts and disappear. I'm sorry, darling, there's no other way."

"There must be!" I said, grabbing his arms as he tried to let me go.

He had short sleeves on, and it was the first time I'd ever seen the prison-rendered tattoos that ran across his arms. **MUM** and **DAD** were inscribed on his wrists. I held onto them both, looking at the words with a panic and realising how badly I needed him to stay.

"Please, Dad!" I cried. "Talk to Mum again. Return the cash now before they notice! We can fix this."

He shook his hands out of my grip, cupping my face with them and moving close. "Some things aren't fixable, kiddo," he said sadly. "But I'm glad I got to meet you, all the same."

He let me go. I cried again and shook my head, chasing him as he swiftly rounded the car and climbed in. I wanted to get in with him, but I was terrified that he might just carry on driving to make his escape if I did. I wanted him to see reason, and I wanted more than anything for Mum to be wrong about him. I didn't want him to let me down the way she'd said he would, the way he'd used up all his chances with her so long ago.

269

A Place Halfway

There was a screech of tyres and a snap as the car roared into the slipstream of the wind. It was as though nature itself was happy to carry my father away.

If there was anyone who was even more inconsolable than I was, it was Tommy. Following the disastrous disappearance of the record mogul and his promising prize, the Asher family had come to stay at Peregrine Place with Tommy for the rest of the holidays. His big shot at musical fame was gone, snuffed out in a heartbeat when it was announced to the crowd that a winner could not be declared. Worse than that, Halfway was now closed until further notice, because Mr Frost had no money left to pay anyone's wages, including my own.

I spent most of the next day in tears, too numb to think sensibly about what would happen next in my life. My mother apologised to me over and over again, thinking it was her words that had driven V.W. to his crime, but I forgave her every time she asked me to. I knew that it was my father's decision to do what he did. He could have been strong and fought against the idea that we couldn't see one another, but he'd taken the easy way out and left me behind in the process. The box of dresses he had bought for me lay in the base of my wardrobe, the doors tightly closed so that I didn't have to look at them from where I lay on my bed in despair.

There came a knock at the door in the late afternoon. I didn't invite the knocker to enter, but a moment later, the door opened anyway and I watched Jake slowly walk in. Buddy Holly was blasting from the record player, but Jake crossed the room and turned its volume down a little.

"It Doesn't Matter Any More," he said, looking at the record covers strewn all over my floor. "Appropriate."

"If you're here to tell me that you were right about him being shifty..." I began, but Jake was having none of my attitude.

He crossed the room and sat down beside where I lay, pulling me up so I had to face him. He kissed me fiercely, breathing new life into my tear-stained face as it flushed with the sudden rush of delight. I felt his torso against mine, my heart thumping stronger with every moment that he held me close.

"I *was* right," he said breathlessly, "but it doesn't matter."

"Because he's gone," I added with a sob.

"No," Jake replied. "My dad's gone, Josie," he said, forcing me to lock eyes with him. "My dad is really gone, and he can't come back. But yours, well, he's just stupid, scared, and running. Maybe that's all he's ever done before. But if there's anyone who has the skills to bring their dad back, then it's you."

I shook my head, tears of anger welling alongside those that came from sorrow. "He doesn't want to come back," I cried. "If he comes back, he'll be arrested, and he'll go back to prison again."

"But you could see him," Jake urged. "If he was locked up for a while, you'd still be able to visit."

"This is pointless!" I shouted at Jake, pushing him away as I got to my feet. "He's not going to go to prison for me!"

"My dad would have done anything for Noah and me," Jake shot back. "He worked late nights at the garage so customers didn't have to see his dark face. He walked back in the middle of the night because of that. He ran into those thugs who got him killed because of that!"

"Well maybe my dad isn't a hero like yours, or Hanne's, or Dai's," I retorted, sobbing again. "Maybe he's just a shifty loser who doesn't care about anyone but himself."

"It's a father's duty to do everything he can for his kids," Jake said, his surly face back in full force. "Your dad's running scared, but he came all this way in the first place just to find you! How many laws did he break just to get your name?"

"He's a criminal!" I spat out the words. "He breaks laws for a living. A few more for the sake of my name was probably no big deal."

I knew that that wasn't true from the moment the words left my lips. V.W. had been dogged by the debt collectors for what it had cost him to find me and, even when he should have paid them back, he'd spent the money on dresses just to see me smile. The thugs had never looked like the kind who were willing to wait patiently for a payment, but my dad had always tapped his nose and told me not to worry, that he would take care of things eventually.

"Josie, please listen to me," Jake sighed. "I can't stand that you're losing your father when he's out there, probably still nearby."

He approached me, tentatively reaching out, but I had already found a calm spot in my soul. I could remember V.W. putting his keys into the lock at Grosvenor Park, going up to that dingy flat he'd been living in, and finding those ugly thugs waiting for him. It was no wonder he topped up his coffee with alcohol sometimes; perhaps it had steadied his nerves the same way that Jake used to lean on it for support in his grief. When he paid them back, his worries would be over. He was probably on his way to somewhere new right now—finally free of the debt I had caused him.

I let my mind wander, feeling utterly pathetic as I let it reach out towards the father who was leaving my life. I could feel Jake holding me and I sank into his chest as I tried to search for V.W., looking for the familiar sight of his silver rings or the sound of the low rasp in his voice. What I saw when my mind arrived at his was something else entirely.

The road was tarmac, not the kind of road we had around our village, so he had definitely fled town as soon as he got the chance. But Dad wasn't moving, not even shuffling, just staring out of what had to be one eye, for everything in his vision was skewed out of order. The world was sideways, like he was lying flat on the ground, silent and apparently alone in the darkness. A cold shiver of dread passed through me. What had happened to him? Was he drunk? Or something much more unpleasant?

Headlights blinded the section of my vision that was with him, severing the connection for the briefest of moments as Dad blinked against them. The lights illuminated a road sign in the bushes on the other side of the wide road. He was at the junction that joined the M20 motorway, the quickest way to Ashford, but there was no sign of his car, and no other traffic was stopping or noticing him in the darkness. Why was he so still?

And then I felt it. He moved suddenly and my halfway vision vanished, sending me zooming straight into his head, where I felt the full force of his crippling pain. I was with him then, inside his body, feeling the ice-cold road surface under his bruised and battered face. Dad scrambled weakly, making a noise like a strangled kitten as he struggled to breathe and move at the same time. The pain in his chest was unreal. When he reached up with his hand to rub at his aching, dry eyes, I noticed that his rings and his watch were gone. His arm was tinged blue from the frost.

With a huge, horrified sigh, I shook myself out of the connection and found that Jake was holding me up, pulling me over to the bed to set me down. When I came to, he studied my eyes carefully as I gripped at him in a panic.

"I thought you'd fainted," he said, sounding relieved.

"It's Dad," I said. "He's cold, Jake. He's cold, and he can't breathe. He's out on the road, and nobody's going to help him."

In the last words, something frightful and fierce captured Jake's golden gaze. He grabbed my hand firmly in his, dragging me up again suddenly in the direction of my wardrobe. Jake threw a pair of shoes and an overcoat at me, waiting as I hastily put them on.

"Where are we going?" I asked him, my head spinning.

"To steal a car," he replied.

CHAPTER TWENTY-NINE

The Flying Visit

Jake really was an awful driver; he wasn't safe to be in a car with, and I was starting to wonder whether either of us would survive the trip out of town in search of my father. When I checked on his mind now, V.W. had closed his eyes, succumbing to unconsciousness. Nevertheless, I was relieved every time I found the blackness in my vision, because the subtle feel of his ragged breathing told me that he was still alive. If I reached out for his mind and couldn't get through, then I wasn't sure how I would react. Jake was certain that that was not going to happen.

"This won't be like my dad," he promised, teeth gritted as he gripped the wheel of the peppermint Beetle hard. "We'll find him in time."

He was a young man possessed, consumed by the kind of angry fire I had seen in him when we first met, but now it had been redirected from pointless rage into fierce action. His eyes were scanning the road ahead in the afternoon darkness, looking for a figure slumped on the side of the road. The junction for the motorway was a long way from our simple village, and we had been driving for near to an hour by the time Jake had careered onto the right road. From a distance, I was sure that I could see the same road sign up ahead that I had spotted when Dad's eyes

were still open. I checked on him again, finding that faint, dark connection to a mind at rest.

"There!" Jake shouted, one hand leaping from the wheel as we both saw his headlights catch on a dark lump in the grass.

He screeched the car to a halt a few feet away, pulling in to the side of the road as I opened the passenger door. I was scrambling out of the car before it had even fully stopped, racing in the frozen wind to drop to my knees at my father's side. The sight of him was enough to turn my stomach over. His once-charming face had been beaten black and blue; a trail of frozen blood led from the corner of his lip to the ground. I touched his bare forearm, finding it so cold that I had to snatch my hand away again immediately. He was frozen like a slab of meat in a butcher's cold store.

In front of him was the cloth bag that he had been stuffing Frost's money into just over a day ago, but now it was ripped open and empty. It seemed that the debt collectors had taken their fee, and thanked my father in their own special way for his late payment. Jake knelt on the bag as he shifted himself close to Dad's curled form, putting his hand out to feel his chest inside his shirt. I shook his shoulder a little, peering into his face, hoping he would wake.

"Dad?" I shouted, close to his face. "Dad, come on! It's us! We're here to help you!"

"Josie," Jake said with a shudder, "I can't feel him breathing. At all."

"No," I said sharply. I took my father's face in my hands, gently using one thumb to push open his frozen eyelid. The violet circle around his eyes stared back at me, unresponsive. I slapped his bruised cheek.

"DAD!" I cried.

"Josie," Jake began again, "we didn't make it. Look at him. He's gone."

I let his head down gently, looking over the poor, frozen form of the man before me. Everything in front of me told me that Jake was right, but there was one thing left that gave me hope. I tried his mind again. Even now, there was a blackness in my vision, a connection that simply could not exist without the presence of a living mind. If studying Cartwright's book had done me any favours, then this was the greatest one. I knew, for certain, no matter how his inert body looked, that my father was still alive.

"Get him into the car," I ordered. "Help me lift him, Jake. He's not dead. I'm certain of it."

Jake took hold of the heaviest section around Dad's torso, leaning the older man's battered head against his chest as he heaved him up. I took hold at his knees and strained every sinew in my body as we lugged the frozen figure towards the Beetle's backseat.

"If he's not dead, then what is he?" Jake asked.

"That's for the hospital to decide," I said.

"We're not taking him to Bickerstaff?" Jake replied.

I shook my head. Between us, we managed to get him lying in the same curved position in the back of the car, which was considerably warmer than the biting roadside. Jake and I took off our overcoats and put them over my father's body, wrapping him snugly to fight the chill that had turned his skin that awful pale blue colour. After that, we raced into the front seats of the car, slamming the doors behind us. Jake put his hands back on the wheel, looking to me for guidance.

"Where are we going then?"

"Ashford Accident and Emergency," I said. "Get onto the motorway and let this thing fly."

The furious weather was keeping a lot of cars off the road, so we made the trip well clear of an hour. All the while, I kept checking on Dad, my mind connecting to his to ensure he had not slipped away whilst the car was in motion. When I reached back to hold his limp hand, I was thrilled to find he was a little warmer than when we had found him. I craned my arm around to rub his shoulder and his side, trying to give him some more heat. The A and E department was clearly signposted when we neared the end of the motorway, and it felt like no time at all had passed when Jake was pulling sharply into the emergency bay at the hospital's rear entrance.

"You'd better go in and fetch someone," Jake said with a quiver in his voice. "I'm not sure I'm the kind of face they'll want to see."

I didn't have time to be sad that he was right; I just bolted from the car and pushed my way into the room. All around me there was activity as people on trolleys were pushed to and fro, whilst others milled around with pained faces and sat in long rows as they waited their turn for help. Dad was not in a position to queue. My head spun as I turned, taking in the whole room, looking for someone to help me.

And then I saw her.

The one person I had been hoping for, the person from whom I had first learned that Ashford was our nearest emergency hospital.

"Ness!" I called.

She looked different in her working clothes, a simple

white uniform with thick tights and a smart hat perched atop her bob of blonde hair. At first, it was as though she didn't know it was me—she stared for a long moment before she suddenly rushed to my side. I grabbed her arms, frantically leading her towards the exit.

"Please Ness, it's my dad!" I cried, fighting the tears of panic so I could get my words out. "He looks dead, but he's not. I know he's not dead, but he's hardly breathing. We found him on the roadside. Oh please, you've got to help!"

She was calling for assistance even as I carried on babbling, and then there was a whole team of people following me outside to where Jake waved at them with the car. An empty trolley was wheeled across the short distance, and Jake held my hand as I watched a swarm of white coats and assistants descend on his frozen, battered form. There was a well-organised heave, and then suddenly they were wheeling him away, talking all the while. Ness hung back a moment, a kind but alert smile on her lips.

"We're going to do everything we can," she promised. "Come in and wait. Don't panic. It'll be all right."

"Nurse Price, I need you!" called a voice from the retreating crowd.

"Coming, Doctor Blake!" she replied.

Ness squeezed my arm and then took off across the emergency bay. We shifted Jake's car out of the way, and I used my psychic skills to tell my mother what had happened and exactly where we were. And then there was nothing to do but sit in the emergency room and wait for something to happen. We took up a space in the corner and Jake held my hand tightly, much to the dismay of some other people who had made it their business to give us dirty looks. I didn't care anymore. With my father half-dead somewhere in that building, I knew that there were far more important things in the world to worry about than a snide remark or a murky glare.

Mum arrived with Leighton and Doctor Bickerstaff, the three of them clamouring towards us with endless questions and admonishments. We were fools for taking that battered car, they said, but we were heroes for what we had done with it. Mum refused to let go of me, holding me tight to her side in an embrace that was painful, but felt so necessary. Jake was calmer than I was, and able to tell Leighton and the doctor roughly what had happened and how I had used my powers to discern that V.W. was definitely still alive. Doctor Bickerstaff rubbed his chin thoughtfully.

"Sounds like a coma," he mused. "Hypothermia from exposure on the roadside. Did you say he was beaten?"

Jake nodded. "We think the guys he owed his debts to must have done it."

"Fatigue and trauma plus inertia on the frozen road," the doctor surmised. "I wonder if he had heart trouble."

I heard a strange noise as something caught in Jake's throat. He coughed so hard that tears came to his eyes. I realised sadly that the memories of his father's tragedy must have been flooding back as Bickerstaff spoke.

" 'e never liked to be startled; 'e said it 'urt 'is chest," Mum confessed, her tone choked. "Do you remember 'ow it was with Leighton and the ghost?"

Leighton and Bickerstaff nodded in unison.

"This coma," Leighton said, looking grave, "is it curable?"

My heart felt like it had stopped beating, until Bickerstaff suddenly nodded with a thoughtful look. "It depends on the body temperature when he came in," he replied, looking to me. "Josie, how cold was he when you got him here? Did you touch him?"

I nodded ferociously. "We put overcoats on him. I rubbed his shoulder and his arm. He was warmer coming in than when we found him on the road."

Bickerstaff beamed proudly, pulling me out of my mother's arms to hold my shoulders. "Good girl," he said with a squeeze. "Exactly the thing. You may just have saved his life, you know."

I hoped to God that the enthusiastic doctor was right.

"Why on earth did you not contact us?" Mum asked me. "We could 'ave 'elped you. It's dangerous for Jake to drive all this way. I bet you 'ave no licence, do you?"

Jake looked at the floor. "No, ma'am, I'm too young," he replied.

"I couldn't risk it," I answered, looking to Mum with tears brimming once more. "You were so... Things weren't good between you two yesterday. I didn't want you to stop me from going after him."

"Oh Josie," Mum said with a forlorn slump in her shoulders, "I would never stop you from saving a man's life, least of all your father's. It's what people like you are put on this earth to do, after all."

"She was amazing," Jake said, rubbing my arm with pride.

"Steven?" said a voice behind our gathering. "Oh, you're here for Josie, of course."

It was Ness. We turned just as the young nurse reached Bickerstaff, leaning into his arm as he gave her a gentle hug around the shoulders. She pulled back with a smile, sucking in a breath before she focused on me.

"Your father's doing well," she told me. "We have him stable and taking in fluids and oxygen. He's not awake yet, but his breathing is better and his body temperature is returning to normal."

For a moment, I didn't understand what had happened, until Jake and Leighton were picking me up off the floor. It appeared that relief had swept over me in such a wild concourse that my legs had given way for a moment. Ness was offering me water, and I was seated in one of the waiting room chairs before I really understood what was going on. Dad was safe and he was getting better. Bickerstaff was right; Jake and I had managed to get him help in time to save his life.

"Come on, Josie love, drink this," Ness urged, the Welsh melody evident even in her gentle whisper.

I supped at the cold water as she felt my head. She placed her hands on my knees, leaning on them as she crouched in front of me with a smile. "You know, when I said you could pop over at Christmas, this isn't what I had in mind," she confessed with a light laugh.

"Me either," I replied, my voice weak and croaky from sobbing. I wondered how it was possible to even have tears left after all I had been through in the last twenty-four hours, yet I felt them flowing out of my control all the same.

"So he's your dad?" she asked. "You found him at last."

"Can I see him?" I pleaded.

"Once he's had a bit more rest," Ness assured me, "That is, if your mum's happy for you to stay and wait?"

We both looked up at her. Mum had one hand over her mouth, eyes wide and hair frazzled as she took in the situation.

She smiled, a mixture of sadness and relief in her expression.

"Whatever you want, sweet'eart," she told me. "From now on, it's whatever you want to do."

"I'll wait," I told Ness. "I want to wait here until he's definitely better."

The blonde nurse nodded, squeezing my knees.

"That's good," she said. "It's important for a girl to have her father by her side."

A hand reached out in front of Ness, and she looked up into Bickerstaff's oval eyes.

"I think you're needed," he said. "That curly-headed doctor is waving at you."

Ness took his hand and let him help her to her feet. The doctor who had rushed out to help my father was signalling her from the other side of the emergency room.

"He looks about twelve," Bickerstaff said with a sneer, "Honestly, do they just let any old toddler practice medicine these days?"

Ness just rolled her eyes and walked away.

CHAPTER THIRTY

A Happy New Year

"This is not how I imagined I'd be starting 1962," said Victor Webb as he hauled himself upright in the hospital bed.

"Dad!" I cried with elation. "You're awake. I'm so glad!"

He had been in and out of consciousness for several days, but now I could see the glimmer was back in my father's narrow eyes. The humour in his dry rasp only confirmed the healthy sight of a scarlet flush in his still-bruised cheeks, plus the fact that he was fidgeting with his hospital gown and trying to get it away from choking his neck. He looked me over with a smile.

"Well now," he mused. "That's a pretty dress. I wonder who bought you that?"

I wasn't sure if I was allowed to hug him—Doctor Bickerstaff had warned me that there might be damage to his lungs—but when I was close enough, Dad pulled me in and held me fast.

"That little Welsh nurse told me everything that's happened," he said, his face against my hair for a moment before I pulled back to let him breathe. "Where's that boyfriend of yours? I need to shake his hand."

"All in good time," I promised. "They're going to move you to the Cottage in Tonbridge first, to recover. You'll be a lot nearer for me to visit."

"Really?" Dad crooned. "And when will they be moving me on to H.M.P. Maidstone for thieving a couple of grand from old Frosty?"

I bit my lip, relishing the news that I had to give him. "They won't," I explained. "The benefactors of Peregrine Place have very kindly compensated Mr Frost for his losses, on the special condition that he forgets everything about the theft."

Dad's mouth dropped open, his sharky smile lost to a surprised stupor. "A pardon?" he half-choked. "You're kidding me, Josie."

"I'm not," I promised. "There are some conditions for you, like you can't ever set foot in my school, and you're not to go prying into Government business. And obviously, if you commit any more crimes, they'll lock you up for about a million years."

My father considered all this with pursed lips, starting to nod. "I'd better not do any of that then," he resolved.

"It means we can see each other," I told him proudly. "So long as you stay out of trouble, then we get to do the proper father-daughter thing."

He reached out and took my hand between both of his, a meaningful look gleaming in his eyes. "After everything you've done for me," he began, his voice cracking a little, "I reckon that's a promise I ought to keep for the rest of my days."

When I arrived back at the old manor house from the hospital visit, I found that my extended family had prepared a great big New Year's Day dinner. The table was set in the dining

hall as it had been for Christmas Day, except now we had not only the Boltons seated at it, but the Ashers too. Tommy and Hanne were holding hands under the table as I passed them, taking a seat next to Jake.

"You'll never guess what's happened!" Hanne told me, her eyes shining brightly.

"Oh tell me," I urged. "You know I hate secrets."

Tommy and Hanne looked at one another with mutual glee, then Tommy leaned forward. He looked the most joyful I had seen him for days. "A letter arrived here this morning from Sunshine Records in Manchester," he explained with a grin. "Come June, they want me to go up and record some demo tracks in their studios!"

"It turns out a certain shifty businessman had made a few phone calls before he tried to skip town," Leighton chimed in with a knowing look.

Dad had come through for Tommy after all, even though he'd been about to run away. I congratulated Tommy on his success, watching with pride as Hanne planted a joyful kiss on the boy's cheek.

"Oi," said Mr Haugen from the other end of the table. "Cut that out, you two. I told you: hand-holding is the limit until you get married."

The whole table erupted into giggles, though Mr Haugen didn't seem to be in on the joke. I turned to my mother, who was sat on my other side, and brought Jake's hand up to show her our fingers interlocked.

"What about us, Mum?" I laughed, "Is this too much? Should I only hold his thumb instead?"

My mother chuckled back. "Love is what it is," she

said with a sigh. "Sometimes it's good, sometimes it's bad." She reached forward and put her hands over mine and Jake's, pushing them even closer together. "But this love," she continued, "this is very, very good. Treasure this."

"We will," Jake replied.

I turned to see him beaming at me, all the love in the world shining in the gold of his eyes. The clinking of a spoon against a glass made me look away from his bright smile. Dai was getting to his feet at the far end of the long table, his parents seated either side of him and watching him with uncertainty.

"I just wanted to say something," he began, his Welsh boom firmly back in place as he smiled gloriously. "I've been a right idiot these last few months."

"Here, here," Bickerstaff jibed. Blod kicked him under the table, causing the whole thing to rattle.

"But," Dai went on, "if I hadn't been such a fool, I wouldn't have been able to learn my lesson about how important other people are in your life."

"And yet, this whole speech is about you," Bickerstaff added with a bitter smirk. This time the doctor managed to dodge his wife's kick before she could reach him.

"No," Dai corrected firmly, "this is about Josie."

I started, eyebrows rising as I watched Dai's eyes meet mine across the room. He raised his glass to me.

"Josie knows about love, and helping others, and giving second chances, and not caring about what the world says is right or wrong." He took in a little breath, his broad chest expanding. "And if we were all a bit more like her, then the world would be a much better place to live."

"To Josie," Bickerstaff added, taking his glass and rising

with a wobble.

The whole table rose, clinking glasses in the air above me, and I felt the flush of embarrassment invade my cheeks. Even Noah got to his feet, though the thick cast on his shin made it a little more difficult. He leaned on Mrs Bolton for support as every one of them smiled at me.

Enjoy it, kiddo, a rasping voice chuckled in my head. *You'll be back to being confined to your room and making teenage mistakes in no time. Trust me.*

"Thanks Dad," I murmured dryly in reply.

When we were all settled again, I suddenly jumped as something under the table tapped my knee. At first, I thought it was Jake, but his hands were above the table, holding a knife and fork as he cut into his food and conversed with Tommy. I leaned back in my seat and peered down at the gap between my feet, surprised to see a little face peeking out at me from the darkness. Bright blue eyes surveyed me under a mop of unruly dark hair, with little pudgy hands reaching out towards me.

"Up Josie, up," Nik demanded.

"What are you doing down there?" I asked, pulling him up from under the table and setting him on my knee.

Mrs Haugen looked down the table at us, rolling her eyes. "That son of mine is going to be a master escape artist someday," she said with a sigh.

"Not when I finish installing the bars and padlocks in his bedroom," Mr Haugen added with a grin.

"I wish I'd thought of that," Bickerstaff replied.

"You're tremendous dads, you two," Leighton interjected with a laugh.

I looked down at the troublesome toddler, watching as

he wriggled and tried to reach the bright orange carrots hanging off the edge of my plate. I turned him around, beeping his nose with a fingertip as Tommy had done when they had first met. Nik giggled at me and clapped. He was oblivious to everything that had gone on around him, all the drama, pain, and injury was nothing to this little bundle of trouble. I considered his innocence and how blissful it must have been to just sit back and watch the rest of us struggle. When he grew up, the world would be a very different place to what it was in that moment at the start of 1962.

"You're going to have a great life, you know," I told Nik, putting my face close to the baby's own. He held my cheeks in his pudgy hands. "You'll know a world where everything's a little bit easier."

The toddler pulled back, his little smile falling away as he became restless in my arms.

"You can love who you want to, and there'll be no pain and no drama," I continued brightly. "I promise you that."

Nik didn't look as though he agreed.

THE END.

CPSIA information can be obtained at www.ICGtesting.com
Printed in the USA
LVOW10s1920121014

408403LV00003B/3/P